P9-CRK-275

Acclaim for John Burnham Schwartz's

THE COMMONER

"Schwartz is a keen observer of Japan. . . . You can sternly remind yourself every few pages that this is fiction, or you can relax and enjoy the fantasy that you are privy to two of the most private public lives in the world."   —*Los Angeles Times*

"Fascinating and moving. . . . *The Commoner* is a rare novel, wonderfully researched and beautifully written."

—Peter Matthiessen

"[*The Commoner*] paints a carefully researched, evocative picture of a country that emerged from World War II with everything blown apart but its moat-protected heart. . . . Schwartz opens a gilded window into a seldom-seen world and the traditions that have sustained a monarchy through centuries, only to threaten the young lives needed to carry it into the future."

—*USA Today*

"A unique literary adventure, intimate, exotic; wonderfully imagined and achieved. The narrative impels the reader from first to last immersing us in its flow of ancient acceptances and new demands. Splendid."   —Shirley Hazzard

"Instead of overwhelming a reader with the amount of research he must have done, Schwartz instead selects evocative details to paint finely wrought miniatures of the past."

—*The Christian Science Monitor*

"[Schwartz] finds the heartbreak, the wistfulness and the poignancy within this world, demonstrating how easy it is to be trapped." —*The Philadelphia Inquirer*

"As an author who has aimed for a clean, transparent style throughout his career, Schwartz finds his perfect subject in this tale of Japanese royalty. Fans of *Memoirs of a Geisha* and royal gossip will savor it." —*Daily News*

"*The Commoner* is a lovely book, quiet, rich, fascinating in character and details, beautifully written." —Anne Lamott

"*The Commoner* is a story about conservative Japan's begrudging evolution. You'll find humanity's struggle in there, too. The research on post-war Japan rewards readers with fascinating scenes . . . and the writing bristles with a calculated swing." —*The Plain Dealer*

"This story is as ethereal and sensual as a Japanese watercolor, as magical and dark as a fairy tale." —*Booklist*

"Brave is the novelist who casts a narrative in a voice that traverses gender and a cultural divide. Schwartz makes the gambit pay off, impressively, in *The Commoner*. . . . [He] does a superb job of conveying the painful sense of isolation that comes from living in a cloistered world." —*St. Louis Post-Dispatch*

"Schwartz is a master novelist." —*Milwaukee Journal Sentinel*

"A subtle, finely wrought fiction that evokes Jane Austen. . . . A tour de force; the creation of a wholly convincing Japanese heroine by a male American writer reflects the triumph of imagination over experience."   —*San Jose Mercury News*

"It is very difficult for a twenty-first-century reader to comfortably enter the restrictive tradition that seems, even now, to be the Imperial Court. . . . While the external details of life in the palace remain stunning, it's Schwartz's grasp of the internal struggle that resonates after the last page is turned."
—*The Denver Post*

"The beauty of the story, besides the meticulous research, is the human dimension. . . . Schwartz has written a powerful, instructive book."   —*The Tampa Tribune*

"A riveting narrative, smoothly written and often heartbreaking. . . . *The Commoner* offers a fascinating, in-depth look at an ancient world of courtly institutions, formal performance and individual negation."   —*The Providence Journal*

"[An] impressively imagined and often exquisite act of ventriloquism. . . . [Burnham Schwartz is] unusually sensitive to the Japanese habits of reticence and indirection. . . . What is singular and most striking about *The Commoner* is how deeply and authoritatively it inhabits the mind and the sensibility of a young Japanese woman."
—Pico Iyer, *The New York Review of Books*

John Burnham Schwartz

THE COMMONER

John Burnham Schwartz is the author of the novels *Claire Marvel*, *Bicycle Days*, and *Reservation Road*, which was made into a motion picture (based on his screenplay) starring Joaquin Phoenix, Mark Ruffalo, and Jennifer Connelly. His books have been translated into more than twenty languages, and his writing has appeared in many publications, including *The New York Times* and *The New Yorker*. He lives with his wife and their son in Brooklyn, New York.

www.johnburnhamschwartz.com

ALSO BY JOHN BURNHAM SCHWARTZ

Claire Marvel
Reservation Road
Bicycle Days

THE COMMONER

THE COMMONER

A NOVEL

John Burnham Schwartz

VINTAGE CONTEMPORARIES

Vintage Books

A Division of Random House, Inc.

New York

FIRST VINTAGE CONTEMPORARIES EDITION, JANUARY 2009

Copyright © 2008 by John Burnham Schwartz

All rights reserved. Published in the United States by Vintage Books, a division of Random House, Inc., New York, and in Canada by Random House of Canada Limited, Toronto. Originally published in hardcover in the United States by Nan A. Talese, an imprint of The Doubleday Publishing Group, a division of Random House, Inc., New York, in 2008.

Vintage and colophon are registered trademarks and Vintage Contemporaries is a trademark of Random House, Inc.

This is a work of fiction. Names, characters, places, and incidents either are the product of the author's imagination or are used fictitiously. Any resemblance to actual persons, living or dead, events, or locales is entirely coincidental.

The Library of Congress has cataloged the Nan A. Talese edition as follows:
Schwartz, John Burnham.
The commoner : a novel / John Burnham Schwartz—1st ed.
p. cm.
1. Nobility—Japan—Fiction. 2. Women—Japan—Fiction.
3. Japan—History—Fiction. I. Title.
PS3569.C5658C66 2007
813'.54—dc22 2007015391

Vintage ISBN: 978-1-4000-9605-3

www.vintagebooks.com

Printed in the United States of America
10 9 8 7 6 5 4 3

For Aleksandra & Garrick
and in memory of David Halberstam

THE COMMONER

AUTHOR'S NOTE

While the histories of certain members of the
Japanese Imperial Family were an inspiration for
the story of this novel, the characters, incidents,
and conversations described here are the product
of my imagination. This narrative is, from first to
last, a work of fiction.

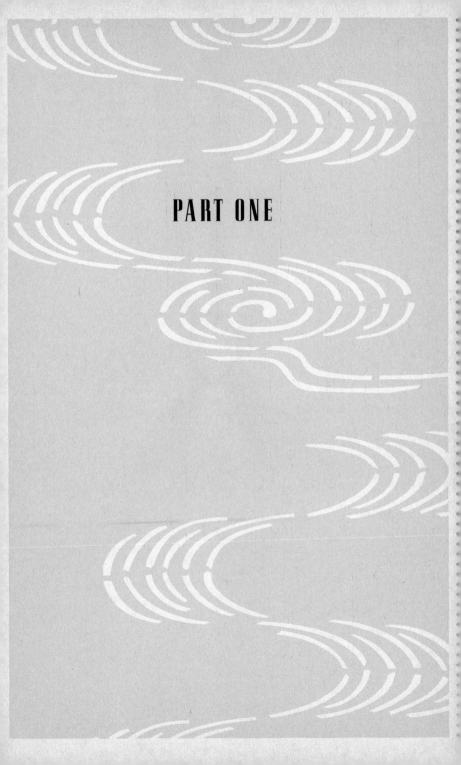

PART ONE

PROLOGUE

WHEN I WAS A GIRL, my father told me the story of two cranes who set out to fly across the world together to fulfill their destinies. Over the middle of the largest ocean, they ran into a terrible storm whose high winds battered and separated them. Blinded and disoriented, they lost their way and flew off again, this time in different directions. One headed west, the other east. Both of them eventually found land, though it was not the same land from which they had departed.

Many years passed. On different continents, the two cranes grew to old age; each was the last of her kind. The space around them, where the wide, comforting wings of a friend had once been, was empty. There was no one to understand what it was like to fly off as one thing in the morning and return as another at night, to grow old without a soul to tell one's memories to.

Then, one day, the crane in the West decided to go looking for the crane in the East. There was not much time left.

Meanwhile, on the other side of the world, the crane in the East decided that she, too, would go in search of her old friend.

The two cranes wisely told no one of their plans and received no opinions. They lived mostly in silence, as it was. The night before they were to depart, they said prayers asking for direction, and made offerings of rice.

They left on their final journeys in the same minute. Both of them flew toward the sun, which they remembered perfectly from long ago. In the West it was dawn, in the East it was dusk.

No one ever saw them land.

1

IN THE YEARS BEFORE THE WAR, my family lived in
Shibuya Ward, in a large house with a walled garden.
The sake brewing company that my father, Tsuneyasu
Endo, had inherited from his father grew and prospered
under his guidance, making him a respected figure in
the business community. My mother's family was older
and more distinguished than my father's, a fact that she
neither promoted nor attempted to hide. As for me,
born in 1934, the Year of the Dog, I was an only child
and wore the proper skirts that my mother laid out
for me each morning. I was fond of tennis, history, and
calligraphy. There was, I suppose, nothing remarkable
about me as a child, save for my father's love, for it was
to me that he always told his favorite stories.

Of the world beyond our garden walls, I had little
awareness. I could not yet read the newspapers, and it
was only in my teens that I grew to love the radio. Good
girls like me, who spent hours each day following pre-
scriptives meant to establish their unimpeachable cre-
dentials, were even more inward than they are today.
One might say that my childhood insularity was a form
of hereditary protection in whose shade, like a pale, deli-

cate mushroom, I grew. The economic depression, omnipresent anxiety, and rising nationalism that had infected our nation and others weren't things I spent time worrying about. The military was aligned under the Emperor, believing him to be a god worth dying and killing for—in his name a coup was staged and, in China, a massacre seen to its bloody end—while in his walled-and-moated palace in the center of our great capital, His Majesty remained augustly silent. On these matters, as on so many others of terrible importance, I held no opinions that I can recall, and, of course, no one ever asked me to speak my mind.

In the first days of spring, plum blossoms appeared in our garden, perfuming the air, and camellias as red as the *furoshiki* in which we wrapped our holiday gifts. There were birds, I remember: one in particular, small and yellow with gray-and-black wings, used to sit and sing on the stone lantern outside my window.

WHEN WAR CAME IN EARNEST from the far side of the world, the first major food staple to be rationed in Tokyo was rice. After that miso and shoyu went on the list, then fish, eggs, tofu, grains of all kinds. Soon everything was rationed, and whatever the size of one's house or the district one happened to be living in, the only way to feed one's family was to enter the black market and see what could be bought there for five or ten times the prewar price. This was my mother's job, as of course it was for all the women in Tokyo. Men had suddenly become a scarce commodity, if not quite as sought after as rice. It was not uncommon to see a nearly bald soldier on a street corner begging women he didn't know to add to his thousand-stitch belt. Each new stitch, it was believed, would help prevent him from being hit by a bullet.

Monzen Nakacho, in Fukagawa District, was the most reliable source for black-market supplies. My mother and I went there twice a month. The street was always congested with lines of women waiting to buy this or that. They chatted and picked their teeth; some nursed their babies. The surface distinctions of birth, which only a year or two earlier would have been impenetrable, had by then been all but wiped away by the shortages. My mother, for example, had always been an elegant dresser, but with the war it would have been unthinkable to continue wearing formal skirts, or even traditional kimonos. *Monpe,* those wide-legged pants, were what women wore, and my mother was no exception. And color? There was only one: national-defense color, the color of uniforms.

Along Monzen Nakacho was a bakery famous for its *kasutera*. When the ovens were going at full strength, the entire neighborhood smelled like warm sponge cake. Outside the shop, the line of customers would start forming early and keep growing until day's end. Family reunions took place in that line, and political discussions, and sometimes probably love affairs. To much of this drama, at my age, I was quite oblivious, absorbed in my dreams of kasutera, and of the buttered peanuts and deep-fried green peas that the bakery also sold. I wasn't the only one:

the old women around me, too, seemed lost in thoughts of food, not love or politics or war, raising their walking sticks and shuffling forward and planting their sticks in the ground again, all day long, like herons fishing in a river of silt.

Then there came the sad day when the bakery could no longer procure even powdered Shanghai eggs, and there was nothing with which to make the kasutera rise or to give it its deliciously soft but airy texture. The sponge cake loaves that everyone coveted were replaced by whale-ham sandwiches. And it is hardly an exaggeration to say that the sound of air-raid sirens, and even the roar of approaching enemy planes, caused but minor distress compared with the fishy, metallic taste of whale ham on the tongue. The smell of freshly baked kasutera, which had sustained us as a people, was suddenly gone from Monzen Nakacho, and from that moment forward the street gave off the faint putrid whiff of a marine graveyard. And still the lines outside the bakery did not shrink. So perhaps it wasn't the kasutera after all that had held us together in the street, morning after morning, but the solidarity of the line. Perhaps we had come to depend on one another in ways invisible and outside anything we'd imagined or wished for.

I remember a dog in particular, a very foreign and beautiful animal, a borzoi I believe it was. We would be standing in line outside the bakeshop and sooner or later we'd see him being walked by his owner, the son of a local doctor. The dog was so handsome that seeing him was like seeing a Western movie star, Cary Grant or Clark Gable. By comparison, the doctor's son was short and his eyes were set too close together. He was considerably less glamorous than his pet and he seemed to know it, which was rather charming. Everyone who waited in line in Monzen Nakacho was acquainted with the dog and looked forward to catching a glimpse of him.

There was something about him, something other than his well-bred good looks. I remember one day standing in line with my mother and seeing the doctor's son and his beautiful dog walking not ten meters distant, when suddenly, and for no apparent reason, the animal began to howl and moan. The crying was so plaintive it silenced everyone who heard it. It made some of the women standing in line embarrassed, they knew not why, while others became instantly afraid, and others were struck as though by the death of a loved one. Briefly we forgot about the smell of fresh-baked kasutera, and also about the stench of whale ham. We forgot about deprivation, forgot about the war, forgot to grow up or grow older.

It was a few minutes after the dog first started moaning and howling that we heard the deeper, more frightening sound that seemed to emerge from the very earth around us. We ducked and cried out. The air-raid siren was so loud it obliterated the self; it sent us running from where we stood with such terror that our pasts were momentarily left behind.

This was what the dog had sensed minutes before us, and what his howling was meant to alert us to.

And then, one day, we saw the doctor's son walking without his dog. My mother politely asked him where the dog was, and he seemed on the verge of tears. He'd been keeping the dog in a crawl space under the floor of his house, he told her, because of the howling and the moaning. But, cooped up like that, the dog barked continuously day and night. One evening an officer came by the house and complained about the noise, saying it was disrupting official military communications in the area. He ordered the doctor's son to put an end to the noise or risk punishment. As the officer was leaving, he suggested a type of poison that he knew from experience with his own animals was most efficacious. This was the poison that the doctor's son had given to his dog.

A week later, my family was evacuated to Gunma Prefecture for the remainder of the war. I left my friends in Tokyo and entered a new school. The day we departed, as we were driving away from our large house with its plum blossoms and red camellias, my mother suddenly burst into tears. I stroked her hand and told her not to worry, we would come back. She said it wasn't leaving the house that made her so sad, it was the dog, the memory of that dog in Monzen Nakacho; she couldn't get him out of her mind.

"Don't be silly," my father told her sharply. "We're losing the war. The country's being destroyed. Who cares about a stupid dog?"

It was one of the few times I ever knew him to be cruel.

ON THE WALL OF MY NEW CLASSROOM was a huge map of the Greater East Asia Co-Prosperity Sphere. Little rising suns marked those areas where Japan had won great victories, or where momentous battles were then being fought. At the beginning of 1945, when I was ten, another flag went up somewhere near Taiwan. It was the last flag that would ever be pinned to that map, but we didn't know that at the time. Our teacher put it there herself, standing on a chair, after leading the class in singing the national anthem.

The classroom was always freezing, the hard stone floor sending a constant, bone-aching cold up through our thin shoes. Many students suffered from chilblains. All day long we hugged ourselves, sneaking glances out the window at the groups of sixth-grade boys in short-sleeved shirts digging "octopus holes" in the lawn—to dive into if enemy tanks ever appeared and began firing at us. The rest of the boys were off harvesting grass for the military's horses to eat. We had all seen photographs in the newspaper of His Majesty sitting astride his tall white horse, inspecting the troops. He was a god, and you were not allowed to gaze on him directly or from above; nor could you show disrespect to his image in any way. As some old people still liked to say, "You can gaze upon the lords, but looking at the shogun will make you blind; and the Emperor cannot be seen at all." One of our classmates had recently been punished for having her lunch wrapped in newsprint containing such a photograph.

And then, in the first week of March, the air raids began to come like clockwork, about an hour after sunrise, and the soldiers we passed on the road on the way home from school began looking like unkempt stragglers. And still we continued to practice our piano pieces and run races for the track team. As if those innocent pursuits would be enough to see us from one side of history to the other.

It was later reported by some surviving eyewitnesses of the Tokyo firebombings that at the outset of the incendiary attack on the night of March 9, 1945, with countless American warplanes still droning in the night sky and a cloud of fire already ascendant over the Sumida River, cries of polite admiration were heard from citizens standing in their gardens, watching the spectacle as if it were a holiday fireworks display. A few hours later, the same people would perish in the shelter holes they'd dug in the once-cool earth beneath their small wooden houses—for every family would have loyally obeyed the government's order to defend their home against invasion and attack. The thick padded hoods claimed as correct air-raid clothing by the government, and religiously worn by the trusting populace, turned out, that night, to be highly flammable. Babies bundled in this material and strapped to their mothers' backs were incinerated, often before their mothers even noticed they were on fire. The day following the bombing, the wind continued to blow, scattering perfectly formed corpses of ash, mothers and babies alike, into unrecognizable shapes, and finally into dust. In all, more than a hundred thousand men, women, and children were burned, boiled, baked, or asphyxiated.

Aerial photographs of Tokyo at that time show, through dense clouds of steam and smoke still rising from the ruins expanding outward from the bay, a blackened, leveled husk of a city, with odd unburned patches—tall stone buildings and stark towers, stubborn edifices, here and there an iron bridge, and, directly center, like an all-seeing eye, the large, walled, moated, still mostly green expanse of the Imperial Palace—His Majesty's abode, the place from which he looked out upon his people with the care, benevolence, and wisdom that were his sacred duty.

MY COUSIN YUMI lost her father, my uncle. In May, as the rainy season was beginning, my aunt went into Tokyo to search for his body among the hills of corpses that had risen all over the city.

My mother and I were waiting with Yumi on the veranda of their house when my aunt returned. Her wooden sandals had been charred from walking through the hot ashes, and the hems of her trousers were ruined. Thumbprints of soot darkened her cheek and one of her wrists. She stopped and bowed to us, silently asking our forgiveness for her failure to find her husband's body. She touched her daughter's hair, and then she entered the house. From the *tokonoma* she took down a pair of ceramic tea bowls made by her husband's great-grandfather during the time of Emperor Meiji, and these she took with her into the back room and closed the screen behind her.

A YEAR LATER, I was allowed to accompany my father into Tokyo for the first time since the end of the war. In the intervening months, two atomic bombs had been dropped on our southern cities, killing and maiming generations of our people, and the Emperor had declared himself human. The War Crimes Tribunals had begun, with our now-human Emperor spared the ignominy of being put on trial and, if convicted, hanged until dead. Our new god, the American general Douglas MacArthur, thought it useful to keep the old god around. The general was so very tall, much taller than our emperor, as everyone soon discovered when the newspapers, at the American's directive, published the famous photograph of the two men meeting for the first time. His Majesty, tiny beside the looming giant from the West, was dressed in morning clothes like a miniature King George, while the general had not even bothered to button the collar of his uniform.

My father and I rode into the city that day in the back of his chauffeur-driven car. He was still a wealthy man. His breweries had been situated outside the five largest cities, and so had been spared the worst of the devastation. This was a fact that he accepted soberly, as a responsibility bestowed on him by fate. He'd taken to carrying scraps of cardboard in his suit pockets, on which he would scribble observations and ideas, perhaps eulogies. During the car ride that day, I watched him pull a piece of cardboard from his pocket, feel in another pocket for a stump of pencil, and make a note to himself. He caught me staring, touched his nose, and gave me a wink, which made me smile. We were entering the outskirts of the city then, and my smile did not last long.

It wasn't the same city I'd known. On plot after plot of land on which houses had once stood, there were little heaps of broken stone and warped metal. Shantytowns of tin and wood shacks had sprung up in burned-out, vine-choked gardens, and everywhere one looked one saw ground-hole dwellings covered with tarpaulins. Women as thin as furled parasols walked slowly, carrying refuse of all kinds on their backs and earthenware jars of water in their arms. It was the rainy season, the air dripping with heat and moisture, the sky dark and the earth darker still with mud and ash. Wooden sandals sank into the mud. An iron safe stood alone on a cement platform in the middle of oblivion, as if waiting for someone who could crack it. Nearby were scattered patches of some growing crop. "Wheat," my father explained, following my confused gaze as our car went by. It was harvest time, and people who'd been growing grain wherever they could—in weedy corners of dead gardens and in standing ash heaps and in the splintered spines of ruined sidewalks—were bent over their meager output all across the city, drying, threshing, winnowing. We passed a group of old women squatting by the side of the road, rubbing handfuls of wheat between their hands to make sure that not a gram was lost. They looked like Gypsy fortune-tellers.

"The rice ration is a month late," my father said grimly, before instructing the driver to take the less-traveled streets and avoid the main road. He had an important meeting with someone from the occupation forces and he didn't want to be late. There was business to conduct. Americans drank sake, too, though what they really liked was beer.

2

ALMOST TWO YEARS AFTER the end of the war, my family returned to Tokyo. Where our old house had stood was a brand-new structure of roughly the same size and proportions, which my father had ordered built to replace the previous one, destroyed by fire. The new house was Western in style, with Japanese touches. The freshly treated yellow wood reflected light, the crisp opaque rice paper of the old-style shoji crackled faintly, and in some of the rooms new tatami gave off the scent of cut hay left to dry in the fields.

On the day of our return, my mother was the first to step across the threshold. We all waited while she said nothing. Taka, our last remaining servant, was still bowing at the entrance, and my father, normally the most refined of men, gave a coarse grunt of impatience.

"You don't like it?"

My mother remained silent. She slid open the screen so that she might look out at the garden. The plum blossoms and the red camellias were gone.

"You can plant whatever you like," he said, trying to placate her. "Just like before."

She turned her gaze from the garden. She was a beautiful woman, with an oval face, a small, perfectly formed mouth, and wide-set eyes. She laid her hand on the frame of the screen and began to rub the wood as if testing it for something. Behind her, half bent, Taka waited. My mother's fingers were like the worrying tongues of foxes, searching for a language in which she might speak of the past without invoking its name.

"Dust," she murmured sadly, shaking her head and staring at her fingertips, which appeared spotless to me. "It's all dust."

THE GARDEN WAS PLANTED AGAIN, and grew. One would have noticed nothing amiss except on those days when a breeze rose up from the distant harbor and what we thought was purely soil and gravel and flowers behind our house turned out to hold ash as well. It entered our noses and our hair. Tokyo had burned and for a long time it would stay burned, and in my sleep even now sometimes it is burned. Back then, though, the smell was something to which one simply grew accustomed.

We hadn't been home long when one day my mother took me with her on a shopping excursion. My parents had forbidden me to explore the devastated city on my own, believing it to be dangerous. But on this day my mother was looking for a certain pattern of cloth for seat cushions and other household items that had been impossible to find during the past few years, and she asked me to come along.

We rode a streetcar packed with soiled hungry people

across the center of Tokyo, my mother whispering in my ear not to let any of the men press their bodies against me. The wheels clattered over the poorly maintained rails. We passed two empty occupation buses making their usual rounds; and pairs of white-helmeted, white-gloved American MPs standing stiff and tall and always silent, like human torii, in front of stone buildings bearing Japanese names—Dai Ichi, Meiji, Taisho, Yusen—but flying, now, American flags. Everywhere, two Japans. There were separate trains for the occupiers and separate streetcars, too, and these, like the occupation buses, were almost always empty. In the filthy, crowded Japanese cars, meanwhile, the cloth had been stripped from the seats; around town one would see people wearing pants and coats patched with that worn plush-green material formerly sat upon by commuters and housewives. Windows had no glass in them, and in winter the cars were freezing.

But it was spring then, not winter, and just to be going shopping in the Ginza filled me with excitement. I held my mother's elbow and looked through the bare windows at gray ruins enlivened here and there by glints of yellow new wood, as though lemon trees were growing out of the ashes. At Yurakucho, a few tall office buildings were still standing; I glimpsed them from the moving streetcar, through arms, between heads, and in their strange isolation they appeared like giants from another age. The Tokyo Takarazuka Theater had a new name on its edifice, in English and katakana: "Ernie Pyle."

"What kind of name is that?" I asked my mother.

"A famous American."

"But it's not their building now, is it?"

"Shh, don't talk so loud," my mother hushed me.

My young voice stood out briefly, then evaporated. The streetcar clattered onward. The Hattori Building's clock tower was intact. Heads in our car turned in unison to observe it—merely because, for no particular reason, it had survived. Then we came to the Ginza crossing and before us was the Mitsukoshi Department Store, completely gutted by fire, the warped empty window frames like so many melted eyes. No doubt it was a common sight to many by then, and yet the voices in our streetcar fell silent in horrified reverence. I stared, too, and it wasn't the humiliation of national defeat or the horror of burned corpses that gripped my imagination but a mental image of the famous department store as it had been before the war, its floors and aisles lined with beautiful clothes to wear and delicious foods to eat. One doesn't stop wanting certain things simply because they've been taken away; one simply wants them more. That's what it is to be young. And later in life it is those youthful desires, sharpened by denial, that are the first of the dreams one is coerced into smothering. The trick is to appear to kill desire while actually storing it away in a place so private that no greater authority will ever know of its existence. A kind of bunker, as in a war.

Our streetcar passed out of the Ginza, heading toward

Asakusa. My mother had been told of a small shop where she might buy the patterned cloth for her seat cushions. We found it, finally, in a narrow clamoring street, and a few other goods as well, including a boxwood comb for my hair, a gift from my mother.

THE DAY WAS GRAY, with infusions of yellow. At a food stall near Asakusa Station, my mother purchased two buns filled with sweet bean paste. The seller's teeth were made of brown-stained wood, not nearly as bright as my new comb. He wrapped the sweet buns in newspaper and my mother slipped them into her cloth bag. "For later," she told me, glancing warily at those passersby who'd stopped to watch us, their eyes hungrily following the food into the bottom of her bag. She took my arm and led me into the subway terminal. Alone, we climbed the concrete stairs to the tower. I was simply following her and the buns she carried like promises, already tasting their sweetness. We emerged onto the roof and stood blinking in the wide open light, downtown Tokyo spread beneath us.

What does one learn from such a view? Destruction has a pattern, the same as growth. More than two years had passed since the war's end. We'd all seen photographs of the devastation in Hiroshima and Nagasaki, and it was even worse than what had happened to us in Tokyo; but this was our nation's capital, and my home. Its physical rebirth seemed almost as inconceivable as its sudden death on the night of the bombing. And yet, slowly, it had begun. The Sumida River, a ribbon of cool silver in the distance, appeared to have stopped flowing, though I knew this was not possible. Farther out, where the chemical plants used to be, some of the canals glinted a phosphorescent green. Only the Imperial Palace stood entire, unreconstructed. The moat and the high stone walls drew a steel-colored rectangle around buildings and grounds, green within gray, an oasis in the middle of our desert of ruin. Beyond those unbreachable ramparts, throughout the enormous orphaned city, burned temples had left behind charred cavities, as if spirits had walked upon them, the soles of their feet in flames.

"His Majesty," whispered my mother, pointing over the roof's edge.

I followed her elegant, commanding finger across the half-dead landscape and over the imperial moat, just able to discern three black specks slowly moving along a pale thread of white gravel. Silently we watched, squinting and hardly breathing, as the specks gained the moat, crossed a sliver of bridge, and turned onto a main thoroughfare the width of my mother's finger. Only then did she bow and turn her face to the side, so as not to look down on the Emperor in his car.

"Haruko, you mustn't look."

"How do you know it's him?"

"That gate is only for His Majesty. Now turn your face away."

IN THE AUTUMN, I began school at Seishin, the convent school of the Sacred Heart. This was my mother's idea, and she would not be dissuaded. Her ancestors, unlike my father's, were educators and civic administrators, and one or two had become Jesuits.

The school had not escaped the fires that had engulfed so much of the rest of the city. Only one of its buildings remained intact. Past the miraculously surviving pine trees that still spread their green branches along the driveway, the charred door frames and cracked front steps of the ruined structures were a constant reminder of the war's human cost. Seeing the campus's present state, it was hard to recall that when the school opened in Tokyo just after the turn of the century it had been considered a most elegant institution. Each morning girls from prominent families wearing brilliantly colored kimonos would arrive in rickshaws, their lacquered hair gleaming like helmets of polished ebony. Forty years later, however, I arrived by car wearing a plain navy-blue uniform, my hair in a simple braid.

The hair of our Reverend Mother, Mother Clapp, like that of all the nuns who instructed us, was kept primly hidden beneath her habit. Every so often, though, depending on the angle of her head and the fierceness of her attention, we were able to steal glimpses of what appeared to be raw silk growing under the fluted white cotton. And now and then a blue-veined wrist would pop out of its protective cuff, revealing a woman some years older than the round, vigilant, virtually unlined face otherwise suggested—a face that always put me in mind of one of the school's favorite mottos: "A man's head and a woman's heart."

At *Primes*—the weekly assembly—Mother Clapp handed out blue *Très Bien* cards, brown *Bien* cards, or gray *Assez Bien* cards. Prayers and inspirational songs were in French. "*Oui, Je Crois*" was a daily staple. Unfortunately, with our strong accents it came out of our mouths in a manner that seemed to defy, rather than encourage, belief. My best friend, Miko Kuroda, and I were careful to avoid making eye contact with each other during renditions of that particular devotional, or risk being scolded for laughing. If scolded, the only acceptable response was a quick, solemn "Thank you, Mother."

Of course, we weren't allowed to speak in the hallways between classes. Amid the distribution of color-coded cards and the bouts of not quite saintly singing, we were marshaled to and fro by the insistent ringing of bells, whose echoing peals, reaching deep into our most private sleep at night, were intended to remain always with us—a practice of indoctrination, I believe, also followed by certain prisons.

And yet I find that those years at Seishin, which once felt so heavy to me, now float upon my heart with a surprising lightness. Though perhaps this is just a relative relief, keenly felt in retrospect: the sense that the strictly ordered environment of the Sacred Heart was a kind of test, or audition, for what lay ahead. The silence was so pervasive that it came to seem like a language of its own, with grammar, vocabulary, even slang. Between classes and in the hallways, on the way to and from morning Mass. When talking was allowed, a nun would always be in the vicinity, her hearing remarkably unhampered by the starched white cloth that covered her ears. Even the oral exams that we took twice a year in the school gymnasium were conducted within a veil of enforced silence— the nuns on chairs facing the students, we girls quiet and solemn in our white gloves and polished shoes.

A class mistress passed around a black lacquer tray, from which each student picked a strip of paper. On the paper was a numbered question. Once the tray was empty, the girl with the first question stood and bowed deeply to the nuns: "Reverend Mother, I have question number one." The question would fly forth like an acrobatic black bird, impossible to catch. If you missed it, you would find yourself still standing, holding in your hands nothing but silence. And where an instant ago the question had been, now came the Reverend Mother's voice: "You may sit down, Haruko."

I was a dedicated student, of course. A very serious student, if I may say so myself. But at Seishin the black bird is what I remember, and the silence, and the voice ringing through the silence, asking the question and then taking it away.

There were no loose words or easy gestures, nothing that had not been written in stone in another country, another century. Freedom of choice or speech was simply out of the question, as was any sign of native instinct.

Back in France, the Mother General of the Society of the Sacred Heart had written: "Self-control is so vital to the conduct of life that no price is too great to pay for the acquiring of the habit."

3

IN THE SUMMER OF 1950, my father took a house for
us in Karuizawa. One hot July morning we piled into
a black company sedan, my father's driver behind the
wheel, the trunk filled with our luggage. To leave Tokyo
for the countryside in those days was a revelation. For
half an hour we followed wide gray streets past still-
blackened memorials to the burned past and the bright
new-wood roofs of an as yet unimaginable future; and
then, abruptly, the road narrowed and the roofs became
thatch, some with lilies sprouting out of them. The low-
lying valley lay under a blanket of fog. In the floating
whiteness one could see ghostly fields of mulberry trees
and tea, and rice paddies in which herons stood like
spirit-guards.

Between the fields and paddies, half obscured by fog,
were compact villages. Through them our car crawled,
our driver careful of the people and the ox-drawn wag-
ons and thick-wheeled bicycles that crowded the road
to stare at us. In winter, little girls in the country wore
padded kimonos the color of trampled persimmon, the
puffed fabric making them look like flocks of curious,
full-breasted cardinals. In summer, despite the damp,

they wore nothing but shirts of the lightest cotton. In every season, the mothers dressed in those wide-legged peasant trousers that my own mother had sworn she would never put on again. Shopkeepers stood watching us from open doorways, squat round kettles hanging from the ceilings behind them.

Then suddenly, past Yokokawa, the road began to climb and curve as though to shrug us off. The fog lifted. My parents fell silent, our driver hunched over the wheel, steering the car with both hands. As we ascended, the views in all directions grew in splendor until they seemed hardly commensurate with the devastated country we knew ourselves to live in. The steep roadside was profligate with wildflowers, the air at that altitude a deep clear breath from the North.

Our driver approached a hairpin turn a bit too fast, and Taka began mumbling to herself.

"Taka, I do wish you'd stop that muttering," my mother complained.

Taka fell silent. She had been with my parents from the time before I was born. From the sleeve of her cotton jacket she pulled out a well-worn toothpick and, with one yellow-nailed hand angled like a shield in front of her mouth, began loudly to suck on it for comfort.

"Taka," I said rudely, "do you have to make so much noise?"

"Everybody be quiet," my father commanded, the car rocking and coughing as our driver shifted gears.

The climb was over. We passed a stone monument and

a sign declaring our entry into Nagano Prefecture. Ahead of us was spread a broad plateau, the reddish tin rooftops of Karuizawa appearing earth-brown in the lengthening afternoon shadows. Well beyond the village were more mountains, including Mount Asama, its peak shrouded in mist.

My father sighed with satisfaction. My mother re-arranged her skirts and ran one finger around the ink-black rim of her carefully coiffed hair.

"I hear His Highness is to visit Karuizawa this summer," she said.

THE HOUSE MY FATHER HAD FOUND for us rested on a hill above the village. It was large and comfortable, with two stories and a veranda shaded by the eaves of a red-painted tin roof. Screens opened off each room, framing every view, creating apertures. Through the pine trees in the distance, one saw mountains on a clear day. The area was famous for birds. There were warblers and cuckoos, and tiny black-and-white flycatchers with streaks of brilliant orange, which darted through the pines and under the hanging eaves and now and then passed through an open screen, becoming hopelessly trapped in the cool, shadowy rooms of our house.

The first time this happened, I called for my father to come and rescue the poor little bird. He appeared at once, hearing my panicked cry, and, using his sturdy body as an unspoken suggestion, guided the frightened, fluttering creature bit by bit toward the opening. As the bird flew away, he bowed after it. His bow was a private gesture and not for my benefit. I watched his actions carefully that day, with respect, and when, during our next visit, another bird mistook our house for freedom, I didn't call my father. I knew what to do, and I did it; and then, alone in the empty room, I bowed after her as he had done.

IN AUGUST, as my mother had correctly been informed, His Highness the Crown Prince came to Karuizawa for three days. His American tutor, a handsome Quaker woman by the name of Mrs. Pine, was renting a cottage above the village, high on the hill opposite ours. Every so often we'd catch a glimpse of her strolling in town, a straw handbasket hooked over one arm. Usually she dressed in a khaki linen suit with short lapels and a skirt that fell to her calves, and wore her hair in a neat brown bun. She was as tall as any man I'd ever seen except General MacArthur, though needless to say she was infinitely more humble. His Highness was said to be quite fond of his tutor, and so it seemed only natural that he should come to spend a few days at her house, along with his retinue of chamberlains, bodyguards, and chauffeurs. He was eighteen and just beginning to show himself in public more often, stepping—more than a little reluctantly, or so it always appeared in photographs—into the inevitable glare of recognition.

This was a time when the Emperor himself was making tours of the country that were intended to present him as a "manifest human" rather than a "manifest deity." These unprecedented trips had begun in 1946 and would continue for eight years; in all, His Majesty would cover thirty-three thousand kilometers, visiting every prefecture except Okinawa. As before the war the newspapers had published pictures of him in uniform on his magnificent white horse, so now did they publish pictures of him in his new Western clothes—dark felt hat and dark three-piece suit and tie—standing next to, or perhaps even conversing with, common subjects of the realm.

It is hard for people today to imagine the shock of those carefully orchestrated encounters, both for the people and for His Majesty. A diminutive, physically unprepossessing, intensely shy man, he had spent most of his life speaking the convoluted formal language of the Court. Out in the wide open, his eyes would blink constantly through the distorting lenses of his horn-rimmed spectacles. A profusion of moles spotted his face. His shoulders were rounded to the point of being stooped, and, when he was moving, his coordination was so uncertain that at times he appeared like a bewildered marionette pulled by unseen strings. When he was forced to stop and speak to people in his rather high-pitched voice, it became painfully clear that he had no talent for what in the outside world would be considered normal conversation. He didn't know the names for most ordinary things, and if by chance he happened to be familiar with the names, he had no firsthand knowledge of the things themselves. His hobby and particular obsession was the study of marine life, the more obscure the better. With waders on his legs or a microscope to his eye, he might finally feel at ease, awake and whole in the study of an element that was everywhere, and yet was contained.

None of it mattered. He was the Emperor and people came by the thousands. They bowed and stared—one of the new freedoms—and sometimes they wept. They collected his bathwater before it could run down the drain and sold it by the bottle, along with the pebbles over which he'd strolled. At times his subjects were so overcome in his presence that they went temporarily blind, unable to see him at all. I once saw a photograph of an old woman in a rustic kimono: she was holding a walking stick and shading her eyes from the sun with one frail hand, openly searching for the Emperor, who was right beside her. His Majesty, one couldn't help remarking, appeared equally lost.

And yet, despite the widespread attempts to present him as human, manifest or otherwise, his most awestruck subjects continued to praise him for those qualities which they felt proved him exceptional. In one English-language newspaper, for instance, it was claimed that while swimming His Majesty could "hold a fan between his toes and fan himself," and also "swim in the rain holding an open umbrella in one hand."

Thus was the father—despite the lost war and millions of dead—reported to be. If the son was anything like him, it was widely believed, even a pale shadow of the original, then he, too, must be quite remarkable, a true prince.

FOR DAYS BEFORE THE CROWN PRINCE'S ARRIVAL, there had been rumors of the festivities being planned. These came not from Mrs. Pine, who had already proved herself, to the satisfaction of the Imperial Household Agency and the Imperial Family, a safe deposit of imperial secrets; they came from those local dignitaries who were invited to meet His Highness during his visit. My father knew the governor of Nagano Prefecture through a brewery he'd once built in the region, and my mother, whose interest in imperial matters far exceeded anyone else's in our family, used this connection to gather what gossip she could.

There was to be a picnic on a cliff above Nunobiki, the ancient Buddhist temple that looks out over the Chikuma River and across the wide misty valley to Mount Asama. There would be a trip to Onioshidashi, the lava beds at the base of Mount Asama. And there would be tennis, for it was well known that His Highness was an ardent player. Mrs. Pine was putting together a four-some of appropriate, like-aged boys and the two courts— screened from the road by trees—at Hotel Mikasa were being readied.

This was as much as any normal person could hope to know.

And of course there was to be a small parade of sorts, a public occasion for the people of Karuizawa to view the Crown Prince as he passed by, to bow to him, and perhaps to see him wave in return. All of which must sound un-speakably dull and insignificant; at this point in history it is difficult, if not pointless, to attempt to describe the measure and fullness of the slow-moving pageantry on which the members of my generation were reared, and to which we still instinctively pay homage.

He came on a Tuesday, I remember. His Highness the Crown Prince. Yes, I was there, too, waiting for him by the side of the main street in my best skirt and blouse, along with my overly animated mother. My father had flatly refused to have anything to do with a "viewing parade" and stayed home with the newspapers. My mother had dressed with her usual elegance, though her mannerisms on that day, exaggerated for the occasion, were so as to evoke any number of forgotten Kabuki actors.

For more than an hour we stood waiting among a throng of mostly women and children. The weather was oppressively warm and damp. It wasn't raining, but the sky to the east, out of which His Highness was expected to emerge at any moment in a maroon Lincoln, was the color of tarnished silver. The dust on the street had turned into a thin varnish of mud that by day's end would decorate the hem of every skirt in town. The street could not have been more than seven or eight meters wide, flanked by the little wooden two-story houses typical of our villages. Truncated telephone poles bristling with ominous wires stood across from trees of equal height, as if signaling to those trees what they must one day become. Behind us was the post office, its sign written in both kanji and English. Across from us was a photography shop. The only person I saw taking pictures that day was a foreigner. He was tall and broad in the chest, dressed in a white shirt and light-blue trousers, and he held the camera in that loose, easy way of Western men, his feet wide apart and his weight on his heels, as though he had all the time in the world. His camera was omnivorous, moving and clicking. I noticed it freeze for a moment on me, and I, too, froze, not knowing how I ought to act.

A blond boy of about ten—he must have been the photographer's son—in a striped T-shirt and blue jeans was roaming the crowd, seemingly unaware of his difference. With his pale unworried face, I imagined he must be from the American Middle West. And I remember thinking to myself that no prince could be so free.

Just then a woman's voice called out in a hushed whisper, silencing the crowd: "His Highness!" The clip-clop of hoofbeats echoed faintly on the macadam. Up the street, out of the eerie sky, he appeared, dressed in a pure white blazer, a dark tie, and dark trousers, sitting very straight on a horse that, one could see even at a distance, was neither as tall nor as white as his father's had been before the war. Behind him one could just make out an impromptu train of suited men on bicycles and two impressive cars—one a maroon Lincoln.

My mother's hand was on my back, pushing me forward. "Haruko, move closer."

"If I get any closer, Mother, he'll run me over with his horse."

"Be quiet." Suddenly she broke into a rapturous smile. "Oh my, there he is!"

It was the horse's eye I saw first: dark and glistening

like a precious black stone set in ivory. Behind it was a
mane of brushed silk spun as though by the imperial silkworms; and, just behind that little bed of softness, a pair
of perfectly shaped hands, browned by the summer sun,
each holding one side of the leather reins, English style.

"Look how nobly he rides," my mother whispered.

He did ride well, very straight in the saddle yet relaxed,
as though he could have ridden with his eyes closed had
he wished. One noticed nothing militaristic in his bearing, and so as the seconds passed and the clopping of his
horse rang loudly in our ears like two giant pairs of
wooden sandals, the image of his father the Emperor on
his magnificent white horse—that image which had inspired and mystified us throughout the war, until the in-
glorious end—finally began to recede into another era.
Here was a young man not in uniform, riding a horse. He
seemed very serious and very quiet. He dipped his head at
people as he slowly passed, each dip a bow in miniature.
In return, they bowed deeply to him, the weight of history
on their backs.

I bowed deeply.

And then he was past.

"I HEAR HE'S GROWN THREE CENTIMETERS this summer alone," my mother remarked. She was sitting at the
low table arranging the flowers she'd just bought in
the Machi, Karuizawa's main shopping street. Flower
arrangement was one of her most accomplished arts,

though she wasn't doing her best at the moment, distracted as she was by the idea of the Prince's summer growth spurt.

"You mean there's more to him than meets the eye?" my father said. He was sitting on the tatami, his back to the wall, perusing some business papers through a pair of reading spectacles. It had been raining for days, and the air in the house felt like miso paste lathered on the skin.

My mother glared at him as though personally insulted. "You mustn't speak that way about His Highness."

"Then you mean there's less to him?" My father winked at me.

"I don't find that amusing." She clipped an iris stem by a third. "It's disrespectful."

"Not at all. By almost every account he's a fine young man. I'm simply trying to figure out why I should care that he's three centimeters taller than he was in May."

"I'm saying it for Haruko's benefit."

"Haruko, eh? Well, that's different. Why didn't you say so in the first place?"

"You're just as impossible as she is!" My mother spiked a last flower into the bowl of polished black pebbles, gathered a handful of clipped stems, and walked out of the room.

"Better to be impossible than measured in centimeters!" my father called after her, grinning at me now. There was no answer from the other end of the house. Amused, he grunted contentedly, removed his spectacles, and rubbed his eyes. Without the bracing frames of steel and glass, his face looked suddenly old and vulnerable to me, and my smile disappeared.

"Haruko-chan, are you all right?" He hadn't called me by that childish endearment in many years.

"I thought I heard a bird in the other room," I lied. "But there's nothing there now."

"Well, that's good—I'm getting too old to rescue birds. Soon they'll have to start rescuing me." He folded his glasses and put them in his pocket. "I wonder if this rain will ever stop." He got to his feet, straightening his papers, one of his knees making a sound like a rice cracker snapped in two. He moved and stood near me. Through the open shoji were the trees dripping with rain, but because of the mist no mountains were visible.

"So," he said, "do you really care?"

"Do I care about what?"

"The three centimeters."

I wheeled around and pinched his stomach.

"Eh! Sharp fingers."

"See how sharp if you keep saying silly things."

"That's my daughter for you."

He was smiling. He would have allowed no one else to speak to him this way. And he took my ear tenderly between his thumb and forefinger as he used to when I was small.

4

WAR BROKE OUT THAT SUMMER in Korea, and by autumn there were signs that General MacArthur and our American occupiers were purging left-wing groups of Communists while nudging our country, so newly and uncertainly pacified, toward some form of controlled remilitarization.

Kept inside the thick walls of Sacred Heart so many hours a day, we young women of Seishin were not equipped to be barometers of our times. People might have been slaughtering one another across the Sea of Japan, or dancing ecstatically to the big-band music the American GIs had left behind, but we alone grasped the crushing level of failure associated with an *Assez Bien* card, or how Mother Clapp stared pointedly at one's shoes when handing them out. We alone found ourselves humming *"Oui, Je Crois"* through clouds of steam during our morning baths. In its strictly timed periods of activity and contemplation—run, like today's Shinkansen, down to the last second—our existence at school was meant to prepare us not for human carnage (or, for that matter, dance hall fun) but for the eternal rituals of faith, education, and, above all, marriage to a man of good family.

In pursuit of this institutional goal I could claim no special prize. In those days my interests were more earthly: I was quite good at track. My nickname, in fact, was Gazelle. I ran the eight hundred meters, the fifteen hundred, and anchor on our relay team.

Between classes Miko Kuroda, who ran third leg on the relay, and I would practice our handoffs with a bolt of tightly rolled sacking tied with a piece of string. The bells would ring, the hallways filling with silent, hurrying girls in uniform, when suddenly from behind me a baton of rough cloth would appear as though by magic in my right fist—I carried my books in my left for just that possibility—and I would feel Miko's hand on my back giving me a soft push, her warm breath in my ear whispering, "Go!" I would not go, of course—the nuns were all-seeing, and running inside the school was expressly forbidden— but still, for a fleeting moment my muscles would constrict with readiness, my weight tip onto the balls of my feet, and my thoughts flatten into a single dreamlike horizon. A minute later, I'd find myself seated in English class—or arithmetic, or in the music room at the upright piano. The cloth baton still clenched in my fist. My sight fixed, as in prayer—*Thank you, Mother*—on some point just beyond where the walls met and closed. My right leg tapping and tapping, impatient to run ahead without me.

Miko was a tall angular girl with a wide face and small but lustrous eyes; always quick to make a joke at her own expense, she once described herself as "grilled squid on a stick." Fearless is what she was. She was good at track not so much because she was fast (though her legs were longer than anyone else's) as because she hated to be held back in anything. At Seishin, in Japan, for a girl such an attitude amounted to dangerous heresy, so of course there was something thrilling about it. Miko made you aware, like a butterfly, of the slightest breeze on your skin. Practicing relay handoffs in the hallways was her idea, not mine, her little gift to me because she knew I'd never think it up on my own. If I was the routine blue sky, Miko was the twilight whose darkening colors never appeared in the same shade twice. One waited for her, never knowing which girl would appear.

It was she who designed our ideogram, the symbol that we signed at the end of every letter to each other and every note exchanged in class or on the bus. It stood both for what we believed we were together and what we longed to become: a pair of wings. Not angels' wings—too foreign and incredible—but cranes'. A crane in flight. The drawing not a literal rendering but merely suggestive, a private hieroglyph difficult for the uninformed eye to interpret. Aloft on our wings of disguise, we were above it all, and plainly invisible.

MIKO'S YOUNGER BROTHER KENJI, who was twelve at the time, was different from other boys. He didn't go to school. In fact, he almost never left the Kurodas' house. I can't remember a time when I did not, somewhere in the room next to Miko's, hear his soft tentative footfall and know that he was listening to us, or if not listening—our comments were rarely comprehensible to others—then simply wishing to be close to our shared laughter and our secrets. His tenderness was like a wound that could be bandaged but never entirely protected—like his body, so badly burned in the fire of 1945 that he appeared more wound than boy. All except his spirit, which leaked out, as through a dark curtain pocked with rips and tears, in silent, unexpected slants of light that if looked at directly would have dazzled the eyes.

After the first incendiary bombings of 1944, the Kurodas, like many parents, had decided that their neighborhood was no longer safe for their children. Mrs. Kuroda had a sister who lived on the other side of the city, and it was to her house that Miko and Kenji were sent to live. Mr. Kuroda held an important position at Mitsubishi Heavy Industries, and for the "good of the country," and to avoid extending his commute, he decided to stay in his own house. Mrs. Kuroda chose to remain with him to make sure that he was properly looked after.

Miko was in Kamakura visiting friends on that morning of March 10, 1945, when flames leaped across an alleyway from a neighboring structure and engulfed her uncle and aunt's house. Fire has wings, too.

A neighbor, who would later die from his injuries, heard the boy's screams. He pulled Kenji out of the collapsing house and somehow managed to carry him through the burning streets to the concrete shelter of the nearest subway station, where an emergency medical post had been established. Dozens of burn victims already lay strewn about on every surface, even the turnstiles, the air thick with the acrid reek of scorched flesh.

Kenji lost his left ear, and two fingers of his left hand.

I was alone with him only once. I was with Miko in her room, sitting on the floor listening to Misora Hibari on Mr. Kuroda's transistor radio. The volume was on low because Miko's parents disapproved of the music. (My own parents, had they known what we were listening to, would have been even more appalled.) But still Misora Hibari's voice—it was extraordinary, she was just a girl, three years younger than I was—filled the room with naked, bittersweet yearning of a kind I'd never heard before, yet made perfect, if confusing, sense to me. For once in each other's presence, Miko and I were silent, both with tears in our eyes. The American boogie-woogie that we'd been so enamored of just a year earlier now seemed an accident of silly noise, easily dismissed. This new voice—nostalgic, abandoned, impossibly young—was what we'd become, and it made us weep.

Just then, we heard a loud crash from the kitchen at the other end of the house. I looked at Miko, questioning.

"My mother's trying to cook," she explained, rolling her eyes. At the sound of her mother's voice calling for assistance, Miko sighed. "I'd better go. She's completely helpless in the kitchen."

In a few moments I heard her asking her mother what she could do to help, and her mother complaining that she never did anything to help. Their conversation went back and forth like that for a while. I turned up the volume on the radio in order to drown them out.

And then I heard another sound, delicate as a cat, at the edge of the room.

"Hello," I said.

Kenji said nothing. He was staring at a spot on the floor midway between our feet, his left hand held behind his back. He had neither eyelashes nor eyebrows and their absence made his gaze unnerving. His breath came in shallow animal-like pants, which was how he breathed all the time. Even though he was dressed in two or three shirts—he was always cold, he had so little skin—his body appeared undernourished, almost skeletal, as if the flesh that covered his bones were merely an accident of his survival, rather than the point of it.

Still, I wasn't frightened. I was in awe of him. "Do you like Misora Hibari?" I asked.

His eyes flickered up at me, stopping on my outstretched legs. Looking at his face was like looking at a stone worn smooth at the bottom of a stream; like building a face from scratch.

"Why don't you sit down and listen?" I suggested. Misora Hibari was singing about wandering through streets without knowing where she was going. She was resigned to being alone, if that was her fate, and I was resigned for her. I felt tears welling up again behind my eyes, but I made no attempt to wipe them away. "I'm not really crying," I said. "It's the music, that's all."

His eyes reached my face and remained there like magnets.

"I do wish you'd stop staring," I said. "It's not polite."

"I'm not really staring. It's the music, that's all." His smile was a minnow—small sharp teeth glittered out of the undamaged corner of his mouth—flashing so quickly that I couldn't be certain I'd really seen it.

"Are you making fun of me?"

He brought his hand from behind his back—his left hand; I'd forgotten it was there. Between the thumb and the two remaining fingers, he held a white peony. He bent down and laid the flower at my feet. His deformed hand returned to its hiding place, and he backed out of the room. When he was gone, I picked up the flower and held it to my nose. How he'd found it I couldn't imagine; he almost never left the house.

The song ended with Misora Hibari still wandering alone, the world in infinite silence. Tears streamed down my face. Then an advertisement for my father's sake company came over the airwaves, shocking me like a blast of cold air.

THAT NIGHT, lying on the futon beside Miko, I slept fitfully and dreamed of a boy whose face was all eyes, and they were as white as a crane's feathers. White as peonies. He stood in a garden, the white flowers taller than his head, which was all eyes and otherwise as smooth as the smoothest stone.

And still I could see him bowing.

5

NEW YEAR'S DAY, 1953. I was eighteen. A photograph in the *Asahi Shimbun* stared back at me from the table where I'd settled myself, still half asleep and dreaming of breakfast. Taka entered from the kitchen carrying a steaming pot of tea.

"Good morning, Lazy."

"Taka, where is everybody?"

She was about to put the pot down on the open newspaper when she noticed the photograph; instead, she moved the paper, fetched a folded cloth, and set the pot down on it.

"Awake and busy, that's where. Your mother's seeing to more flowers, and your father's certainly doing something important as usual; I can tell you that without even knowing what it is." She paused to refold the newspaper so that the photograph, which still hadn't caught my attention, was framed to better effect. Satisfied, she set it down again, right in my line of vision.

"Taka, I'm awfully hungry. Is there anything to eat?"

"There'll be plenty to eat later, as you well know. You'll be lucky if you don't end up bursting out of your kimono.

Now drink your tea while it's hot. Your mother's going to want to talk to you about your hair."

"I don't want to talk about my hair."

Taka patted me tenderly on my head. "You should have thought about that before you grew up." Like almost every young woman in Japan, my hair would be turned into a pagoda for the New Year holidays: stiffened with camellia oil, stacked like *kasutera* on my head, and finally pinned with an assortment of decorous ornaments until my neck drooped from the weight. "At least you'll be taller," Taka added consolingly as she left the room.

Bored, and still contemplating the idea of breakfast, I took a sip of tea. In stages, my eyes made their way to the photograph.

The Emperor, the Empress, and the Crown Prince stood looking at a large globe of the type to be found—at least in films I'd seen—in an English gentleman-explorer's library. The antique burnished orb was turned toward the camera, and the Imperial Family configured in such a way that the map was clearly legible. And what one saw was that, though this was a Japanese globe, the United States occupied the position of honor at the center of the world, with Britain smaller and to the right, and Asia hardly visible at all. Apart from being round, the earth was not the same planet whose outlines we'd memorized in school.

As all Japan was aware, His Highness the Crown Prince was to make his first international trip in the spring—a six-month tour especially arranged to include his attendance at the coronation of Queen Elizabeth II in London. In the past months, as the occupation had officially come to an end—General MacArthur had been ordered home by his president for insubordination long before—the Emperor's only son had gone through his investiture ceremony with impressive dignity and self-control, taking his most public step thus far down a road that had been paved for him at birth. The globe in the photograph was the door through which he would now walk out onto the world stage, carrying our tattered, hopeful nation with him.

He was leaning into the globe slightly, as though it were pulling him into its mysterious continents; and his eyes, though unsmiling, looked alive and excited. He was perhaps not much taller or broader than he'd been while riding through the streets of Karuizawa three years before, and yet I sensed in his bearing—in the fullness of his shoulders in the well-tailored English suit that he wore, and in the evident pleasure he was taking in the idea of his first journey abroad—something freshly discovered, and regal.

I poured myself more tea.

"So you finally decided to get out of bed!"

I looked up, smiling. My father stood in the doorway, dressed in a padded dark-gray yukata, his short hair shiny with flaxseed oil. The New Year was the only day that I knew him to get dressed in leisurely stages, almost like a woman.

"It wasn't a decision—more like an accident. Father, you have shaving soap on your ear."

"Do I?" He ran his little finger around his earlobe. "Looks tasty, eh?" He stuck his creamy fingertip in his mouth and slurped as though he were eating a bowl of udon. "The finest."

"That's disgusting!" I laughed.

"Disgusting? What is?" demanded my mother, just stepping through the front door, arms bristling with pine branches and the purple cabbage flowers that filled our house only on the New Year. Pausing in the front hall to slip off her shoes, she called over, "Haruko, help me with these flowers."

"Yes, Mother."

"It's strange, but for some reason everything tastes like soap today," said my father.

My mother eyed him suspiciously—she often thought we were playing tricks on her, and sometimes she was right. "We don't have time for this nonsense. We've got to get going. Where's Taka? Haruko, put down those flowers and let me look at your hair."

THE THINGS ONE MISSES. Call them precious banalities: New Year's soup with toasted squares of *omochi*.

One December before the war, when I was still a little girl, my mother took me to her grandmother's native village to watch the rice being pounded in the raw, early-morning damp of the foothills. Four muscular short-legged men, pants tied above their knees, encircled an old mortar, pounding in wordless synchronized succession the steaming rice with huge wooden mallets, while a farmhand crouched between them, turning the hot glutinous paste with eel-quick flips of his hands. The steam rose like mystical vapor from the wide-awake ground; the mallets pounded their rhythmic wooden heartbeat, calling out the spirits. Now and then my great-grandmother, warming her bunions by the fire, offered technical advice.

Later, the omochi paste was rolled into dough and set aside to dry. I was instructed to sprinkle handfuls of rice flour to keep it from sticking. My mother wiped my flour-dusted face with the dampened hem of her wool jacket. And then Great-grandmother began to chuckle, nodding her trembling head at me as though, just at that moment, I had materialized out of her own distant past and become real.

A few weeks later, properly dried, the omochi was cut into small squares, lightly toasted, and drowned in New Year's soup, where its consistency turned glutinous again. I enjoyed it, knowing where it came from. Seated around our new Western dining table in Shibuya, bowl raised to my lips, I met my mother's eye, and she nodded, confirming our shared experience. I could feel myself start to blush, as across the table my father began an amusing story about the prime minister who'd drunk too much sake and lost his shoes.

WE PLAYED *KARUTA* with the friends and relatives who came to visit after the New Year's meal. Each of a hundred cards was inscribed with a famous poem. To earn the card, you had to recognize the first lines of the waka and recite the rest from memory. The winner was the person with the most cards at the end. I was very fond of the game and not terrible at it. I doubt if this kind of karuta—*hyakunin isshu*—is widely played anymore. It would be like being the last gardener in a city in which the only flowers left are on electronic screens—holographs, I believe they're called: images that appear frozen until you tilt them to the side or move your head, at which they grow second and then third images, yet never do they come alive.

After New Year's soup and visitors and kite-flying and poetry, dressed in our best kimonos we went to the Meiji Shrine. There, walking, we saw other families that we knew. The scene was a festival of pure color: white gravel, red torii, scarlet sleeves, the priests' purple-and-blue *hakama*. Inside the wooden sandals of little girls were tiny tinkling bells. The girls' faces were painted pink and white. Some held hands; others were carried by their fathers as they never would be carried again. Older girls, young women my age, walked with the small, careful steps that we had learned so well.

My mother was smiling. My father still had shaving soap on his ear.

6

THREE YEARS LATER, I was in my last term at Sacred
Heart University. The campus was in Hiroo, sitting like
a decorous postage stamp atop a small hill tucked back
behind the train station. Some mornings, climbing the
freshly scrubbed stone steps to the campus, receiving
the customary bows from the two uniformed guards at
the gate, I liked to imagine that I was entering a Greek
temple of learning, a young women's Academy.

Sacred Heart was an international university, a miniature United Nations attended by the daughters of diplo-
mats and businessmen from many countries. Proper
manners were expected of us, along with a grounding
in philosophy and literature and a fluency in English.
In the spring I was voted valedictorian of my class, and
wrote my graduating thesis on divergent views of the
institution of marriage in the works of Jane Austen and
George Eliot. Of course, I knew virtually nothing about
marriage then.

Nevertheless I had begun to attract suitors. I say this
not as an indication of my own merits—a good number
of the interested young men hardly knew me. Perhaps
we'd played tennis together (I had won a junior tourna-

ment and was considered rather good at the sport); perhaps they or their parents or friends of their parents had heard me play the piano. Undoubtedly they were aware of my family and my father's business. There would have been nothing unusual or demeaning in this. A girl's family was far more important than the girl herself. Parents spoke to parents, arrangements were made or not. There were no painful secrets because nothing was considered personal. Everyone at Seishin knew who the most sought-after girls were, which often had little to do with the girls themselves. And I have to confess that I thought it all faintly ridiculous and wasn't shy about saying so—a somewhat eccentric attitude for the time, which occasionally brought me into conflict with my parents.

"Takeshita-san's father has contacted me about his son's interest," my father informed me one evening during dinner.

"The son is finishing Todai, isn't he?" said my mother. "He'll be going to one of the ministries."

"Do you like him, Haruko?" My father was looking directly at me.

"I hardly know him."

"That is a benefit," my mother said.

"I'm too young."

"You're the age I was when I became engaged to your father. It was arranged for us."

"I'm happy doing what I'm doing."

"Which is what, exactly?"

"Studying."

"That will come to an end soon."

"Perhaps."

"There is nothing wrong with traditional life," my mother declared.

"I am not against traditional life, Mother. Maybe I just don't want to marry Takeshita Masao. They're a good family and I mean no disrespect, of course."

"Tell me, Haruko," my father intervened. "What is important to you?"

The question, so real and enormous and foreign, momentarily silenced me.

"You must be interested in something. An intelligent, thoughtful girl like you. Since you don't seem very interested in poor Takeshita-san, that is."

"There were teachers in Mother's family . . . respected writers and thinkers," I began hesitantly. "One was a student of Fukuzawa Yukichi."

"Fukuzawa Yukichi's most prized student," my mother said.

"That is important to me. The possibility that . . ." My face was burning now. "That perhaps, one day . . ."

"Of course you can, I'm certain of it." A small compassionate smile emerged at the edges of my father's lips, which made me furious. "But, at the same time, let's not be naive. Those esteemed ancestors were men. You must see that."

The room was silent. It felt to me as though someone I'd counted on intimately—a childhood companion, an imaginary playmate privy to my inmost dreams—had suddenly learned to walk, and now was walking away, leaving behind empty shadow.

"Nothing is simple," my father offered as consolation.

I got up from the table. I bowed deeply to both my parents, and then I left the room.

ONE AFTER ANOTHER, the answers went out. My parents were apologetic, practical, annoyed; publicly they settled on describing their daughter as "headstrong"—though not "disrespectful," a word that would have reflected poorly on our family, to say nothing of our illustrious forebears. In this manner two future ministers, three financiers, an inventor, and an astrophysicist were politely turned away, as well as a botanist, a professor of linguistics, a zookeeper, and a man who in time would become one of our most famous and controversial authors.

Again, interesting as all this might have been, it seemed to have little or nothing to do with me. I was left to play tennis and appreciate art. Which is not to suggest that I had no thoughts of men in those days.

One summer afternoon—it was raining and tennis was out of the question—I went to a calligraphy exhibit at the museum. I was to meet some friends from Seishin, but their taxi had punctured a tire and they were late. Alone, I wandered through the galleries. The rooms were almost empty. The rain grew heaviest then, a pounding muffled through the high tiled roof; it felt like being in a tomb, yet awake. In the interior sanctuaries the light appeared finely granulated, filled with sand or spun with gold, making the black brushstrokes of the ancient characters on the walls blacker and more ancient against the white and ivory scrolls and the fragments of handmade paper. They were poems, some of the most beautiful our country has produced in its long history. A few I knew by heart from having played karuta so many times.

In the last room, a young man was sitting on a narrow wooden bench copying characters into a sketchbook with an ink brush. He did not look up when I entered. He had the deeply focused expression of someone who had not moved in a long time, and I avoided walking in front of him so as not to break his concentration. I was behind him, almost past, when without turning his head he spoke to me.

"Excuse me . . ."

I glanced around the room, but there was no one else he could have been speaking to.

"Are you familiar with this poem?" He was looking at me now, pointing to the poem on the wall that he'd been copying. It was the famous tanka by Monk Jakuren, from the Kamakura period:

Ah, solitude—
It is not the sort of thing
*   that has a color.*
Mountains lined with black pine
*   on an evening in autumn.*

"Familiar?"

"Do you know it?"

"Yes, I know it."

"And this is how it really goes? For some reason it doesn't seem like the same poem I remember."

Perhaps I stared at him a little; the remark was so unusual that it made me want to ask him questions.

"May I ask how you remember it, then?"

He sat thinking, as though wanting to make sure he chose his words precisely; I had the thrilling sense that this was the only way he ever talked about things that mattered to him.

"When I was sixteen, my father gave me this very poem to read," he said. "He told me that it was a work of great beauty and sadness. Unfortunately, at the time it made me laugh out loud. It was unspeakably rude of me, and he was furious. He called me stupid and disrespectful, which I suppose I was. But reading the poem now just makes me sad. To speak honestly, it almost makes me feel like crying. I was wondering if maybe the calligrapher had changed the poem." Suddenly his gaze on me turned warm. "What do *you* think?"

"I believe it's the same poem."

"I see."

"Maybe it's you who've changed." I blushed saying this, fearing that I'd gone too far, but he only smiled in return. I noticed how handsome he was then, his hair a bit long over his ears, his brow quite dignified. He was wearing a cotton waistcoat over a white linen shirt, like an Englishman or an artist.

"Yes, you must be right," he said.

"Your father will be pleased."

Slowly, his smile faded. "My father is no longer living."

"Please forgive me." I dipped my head. "I'm sorry, I must be going."

"Wait." Quickly capping his brush and folding his sketchbook, he stood up. He was tall and rather lithe; it required some effort on my part not to watch his every move. "Would you like some tea?"

I shook my head. "I have friends coming to meet me."

"I'd be happy to take them to tea as well."

"That's very kind of you, but I'm afraid not."

"Some other time, then?"

"I can't really say."

"I understand. Well, it's been a pleasure talking to you. I won't forget you. Goodbye."

"Goodbye."

I could feel his eyes on me as I left the gallery: soft eyes, not the sort ever to press on you if you didn't want them to. I went out to the entrance hall. Of course, he did not follow me, and I did not look back. And if he had—or I had—would my life have turned out differently?

A minute or two later, my friends arrived. The heavy front door opened and in they swept laughing, hands covering their open mouths, the sky flashing behind them like glints of clear-blue ice.

So the rain has stopped, I remember thinking to myself, and the poem is unbearably sad. Yes, and funny, too. And no one else has ever said so, or perhaps ever will.

With my friends, I toured the galleries a second time. The poems were all the same; it was the light that had changed.

I never saw him again.

WHAT I MISSED THEN was having one intimate friend nearby to tell it all to; someone who might hold a mirror up to my poor judgments and most unforgivable embarrassments and help me call them what they were, show me how I might go forward as myself and no other.

I missed Miko terribly.

The summer we graduated from high school her father, a diplomat, had been posted to Washington, D.C. The entire family had gone with him. Miko was in her final year at Manhattanville College in Westchester, New York. She had sent me postcards with pictures of the campus—grand, Gothic stone buildings surrounded by green lawns and hedges.

Her roommate Abigail, she'd written me, was descended from a Revolutionary War hero who was supposed to have played a role in giving the Philadelphia Liberty Bell its famous crack. Freedom, I supposed, was the general idea; and in America, even among the nuns, Miko indeed seemed rather free. She ran track and became good enough at field hockey to play on the team. They wore kilts. Her English took on a northeastern American accent, which she was told was like a British accent only not as proud. On weekends she learned her way around Washington, which appeared to her as an enormous museum, and on several occasions she spent holidays with her parents in New York City, which she adored. On Broadway she saw a show called *West Side Story*. Her recounting of it in a letter was typically idiosyncratic:

Just imagine if Tony and Maria were Japanese. They hardly know each other; their parents arrange everything; they get married. Everybody lives! But nobody sings or dances. Jets and Sharks stand around like guests at a cherry-blossom party; nobody wants to offend anybody. The show does NOT go on!

Unacquainted at the time with the show or with that final American turn of phrase, I missed the full dose of my friend's humor, but still found her letter deliciously amusing.

We wrote to each other twice a month, sometimes more often, addressing the thin, almost transparent airmail envelopes in the same two languages, though in reverse order: English-Japanese for her, Japanese-English for me. The tongues of war. How strange to think that my best friend was speaking American with a northeastern accent. Though I myself was fluent in English, I knew that I was not a person who would ever shed my Japanese accent, or even especially want to.

To me, Miko's foreign existence seemed another kind of show—an exotic spectacle one bought a ticket for, returned home from, and told one's best friend about in humorous detail. I was that friend. It never occurred to me that she might stay in America. That instead of returning with her family when her father was recalled to Tokyo four years later, she would remain in New York with Abigail, and later with Abigail's brother, who was to become her husband. That within the space of a few years, by dint of our fates in marriage, our lives might become so profoundly separated.

I deeply regret that I have kept none of her letters from those long-ago days. Her words I carry with me only in my memory.

7

EVERY SUMMER IN THE SECOND HALF OF AUGUST, a tennis tournament was held in Karuizawa. Who was paired with whom, what club one belonged to, whom one was designated to play in which round—these were the truly significant questions of the day. My tone is only half mocking. In fact, by August, whatever level of gravity I'd exhibited at university before my recent graduation had more or less disappeared; I had become quite weightless. My father, who was driving up from Tokyo every other weekend and played golf but cared not a whit for tennis, was under the impression that I had lost my mind.

"All that education, and for what?" he teased one morning as we were finishing breakfast. "A backhand winner? I could swear you used to be a serious girl."

It was not just any morning, and I was too nervous to find any humor in his remark. That afternoon, my partner—a twelve-year-old American boy named Bobby Spencer—and I were to play the Crown Prince and his partner in the quarterfinals of the club tournament. The match wasn't for hours, yet I was already wearing my white tennis dress, and had styled my hair as though I were going to a dance. I'd slept poorly, and had dreamed—intermittently, as though in chapters—that I was standing on a bald, sun-bleached rock in the middle of a fast-flowing river, waiting for someone to rescue me. No one had come, and now it was morning. Soon, the Crown Prince would be standing across the net from me, smiling stiffly as he missed a shot, laughing confidently as he passed me with a winner that always, in the past, had been mine. No, I wouldn't speak to him. I'd let little Bobby Spencer, with his high-pitched voice, do all the talking, and the serving too, while I applied myself to the bare minimum, so as not to humiliate myself beyond repair. He was the Crown Prince. Was he like us? No. Didn't he always win? Was he more, or less, handsome than I remembered? Taller, or shorter? Louder, or perhaps taciturn? I could picture him as in a magazine, yet saw nothing that was real. My palms were sweating, and the match was still hours away. I did not want to care. I did not want to care, but I already did.

THE CLUB HAD PURPOSEFULLY SCHEDULED the match on a side court, so as not to attract attention. As Bobby Spencer and I approached the court from the clubhouse, I observed a man of about my own age, in crisp tennis whites, standing alone to one side of the net, practicing his forehand without a ball. Immediately, my heart began to beat loudly and stupidly in my chest, to the point that I almost believed he must hear it. But His Highness did not seem to notice. His racket was still in its bulky wooden press, giving his strokes added weight, so that when he finally began the match with the press removed he would feel quicker. A steady though not beautiful swing. All this I could see at a glance from a moderate distance. (Over time, I little knew then, would come further confirmations born of this initial impression: his always polite, though irrepressible, competitive spirit, and the endearing quality he has always possessed, at least to me, of never seeming more alone than when in public, like an only child by decree.)

His Highness raised his head then, stopped what he was doing, and came forward to greet us.

"I have been looking forward to this match all morning," he said, looking shyly at me.

I bowed formally and replied that I, too, had been anticipating our tennis game.

"Ah, that is because you are such a good player," he said with a smile. "I've heard about you, you know."

I bowed again, largely to hide the color rushing to my face. "I am afraid that you will be disappointed, Your Highness."

"There is no chance of that," he assured me.

These last words were charmingly delivered to his tennis racket. It was a hot day, and he was already perspiring, as now I was, too. In person he was attractive, hardly taller than I but well-proportioned and fit-looking, his limbs and face lightly browned from a summer of outdoor exercise. His eyes were sharp and serious, warmly intelligent, with an occasional glint of amusement.

Just then, his playing partner arrived, and formal introductions were made. One moment in particular stands out in my memory: the Crown Prince extended his hand to young Bobby Spencer, who clearly did not know how to bow, or, indeed, what a bow was. The boy grinned and pumped the imperial hand like a beleaguered business-man who has just happened upon a most propitious deal. I believe he'd been briefed by his parents that his oppo-nent was an important person, a kind of royalty even, but what that would have meant to a twelve-year-old boy from San Diego, California, who could say.

We took our side of the court. The Crown Prince stood at the baseline, rhythmically bouncing the new white ball as he prepared to make the first serve. But then, moments before the toss, he looked up and met my gaze, where I was standing at the net. The visual contact was so unex-pected, and so immediately warm, that I forgot to look away. My composure was shattered, but so was his: his first serve hit the bottom of the net. His next try was more cautious, looping into the box, where it was met by Bobby Spencer's racket and sent down the line. The Crown Prince's slightly off-balance return floated within my reach; without stopping to think about my actions, I stuck out my racket and blocked the ball, sending a sharp volley into the far corner for a winner. Love-fifteen.

For a moment, everyone on the court, myself included, looked quite stunned. Then Bobby Spencer chirped, "Nice shot!" and the Crown Prince smiled at me, and play con-tinued.

The game ended with His Highness still stuck at love,

though seemingly not unhappy about it. As we changed ends, he complimented my play, and I felt heat rush to my face. The game had passed so swiftly and naturally that I'd almost forgotten that my handsome, courtly opponent, who seemed so pleased to be in my presence, was nothing at all like me, but more, much more, and above me, far away even when close. My heart, recognizing the reality, began its cowardly alarm again, and a vague anxiety suddenly threatened to cloud the lovely day.

There was some stirring from the gallery as we walked past. It wasn't much of a gallery, just a single bench and three folding chairs. On these were arrayed His Highness's surprisingly humble retinue of bodyguards and chamberlains, as well as a gray-haired man, older than the others, the right side of whose dignified countenance, under a wedge of shade cast by a straw sun hat, revealed the scarlet, celluloid smoothness of a burn victim.

This, I knew from having once seen his photograph in the newspaper, was Dr. Takeshi Watanabe, former university president and respected scholar, and for many years the Crown Prince's most trusted adviser. There was nothing His Highness did or conceived of doing, it was said, the potential consequences and meanings of which Dr. Watanabe did not, out of a sense of duty and of something approaching paternal affection, weigh judiciously on behalf of his imperial charge.

In time, I would come to know Dr. Watanabe well. He was a complex and brilliant man, fortified (like many such men, I've found) around a deep reservoir of sadness. In the wartime fire that had left a quarter of his body severely burned, he had lost his only son. Yet never did one hear him refer, even obliquely, to those tragic events. It was the Crown Prince who one day described to me how the doctor had endured the two years of rehabilitation from his grievous injuries only by studying, every single day, a photograph of his son on the occasion of his high school graduation, and by relentlessly, and privately, pondering the unanswerable question of what he, the living, owed the dead.

As I took my place at the net—Bobby Spencer was preparing to serve—I stole a glance at Dr. Watanabe. He had removed his straw hat and was dabbing his brow with a white handkerchief. His gestures were precise, his expression grave. I had the feeling that it was not the heat that seemed to be bothering him so much as the score.

I thought then of Miko's brother Kenji, with his keen, longing eyes and lifeless skin. The flower he'd given me.

8

TENNIS WAS AGAIN THE OCCASION of my next meeting with the Crown Prince, later that autumn.

It was a small tournament for twenty people, organized by His Highness, at the Tobitakyu courts outside Tokyo. The invitation was inscribed on his personal stationery and delivered to our house one morning by imperial courier.

Taka and I were the only ones at home. My mother was out shopping, my father at work. As soon as the courier had delivered his packet and left, Taka asked if she could hold the invitation.

"Eh!" she breathed, weighing the rich handmade paper in her hands. "Pretty fancy stuff, all right."

"Taka, you're not to say one word about this to my parents."

Her calloused thumb repeatedly stroked the Crown Prince's seal, as though she were worried that it might be a forgery.

"Not one word," I repeated firmly.

I took the invitation off to my room. I set it on my desk, then moved a couple of steps away to try to think. Finally, I sat down on my bed. Despite my excitement, I felt unsettled. It was only a tennis tournament. But I could not forget the other time we'd played, in Karuizawa, and the warm look of his before he served, and how, each time we changed ends, he made certain to pass close to me so that we might converse. Mere pleasantries, of course, yet spoken by him in such a soft and inviting manner, with such an attentive eye, that his formal, princely words had seemed more than polite, and had made me blush.

Absorbed in my thoughts, I might have curled up there on my bed, arms wrapped around my knees as I'd been fond of doing as a little girl, but I was soon interrupted by a scratching noise from the hallway.

"Taka, is that you? What are you doing out there?"

Her round face suddenly appeared, floating in the doorway like a peach-colored moon. "Dusting?" Her expression was sheepish. She held up an oilcloth as if to confirm the unlikely possibility.

"Well, please stop."

Taka bowed in apology, while remaining firmly planted where she was. "Haruko?"

"Yes."

"You're going to go to the Crown Prince's tournament, aren't you?"

"I don't know what I'm going to do."

"Oh," she mumbled, looking down at her feet.

I sighed. "Very well, what do you think I should do?"

Her head snapped up, eyes suddenly bright and excited. "Why, accept, of course!"

"There will be all kinds of important people there," I said dourly. "Whether I go or not couldn't possibly matter to anyone."

Of course, I both believed and did not believe this. I see now that I possessed the vanity of the young and privileged in such habitual, unearned abundance that I felt free to spend my trust thoughtlessly, the more so in front of a woman who had uncomplainingly washed my soiled feet as a child. But while my claim of general insignificance was for me little more than an exercise in self-flattery and self-doubt, for Taka, who was guilty only of taking the people she trusted at their word, it was an affront to an instinctive sense of justice. Her cheeks reddened and puffed out as they always did on the rare occasions when she was indignant. She strode deeper into my room, the oilcloth balled in her fist.

"But you're not just anyone," she said, her voice tense and shrill. "Not to me or your family. And neither is the Crown Prince. Neither is the Crown Prince just anyone!"

My first instinct was to burst out laughing: so serious was she, so simple and true, more familiar to me in some ways than my own mother, and yet so completely unlike anyone else I knew or believed in. But just in time I saw the traces of tears in her eyes, and caught myself. To wound her then would have been unforgivable.

"No, Taka," I agreed softly, "you're right. The Crown Prince isn't just anyone. Thank you for reminding me." I embraced her. Her familiar body, compact, a bit lumpy, altogether comforting, soothed my nerves in a way that I can never forget. "Of course I will accept His Highness's invitation."

"Good, then it's settled," replied Taka in a mollified voice. "And we won't tell anybody, will we? As you said, our little secret." She grinned and touched the oilcloth to my cheek as though she were dusting me off for the big day. "Just make sure you win."

THIS WAS RATHER THE OPPOSITE of the advice given by my mother when she found out—it was inevitable, I should have known—about His Highness's tennis tournament.

"Whatever you do, don't win," she said.

"The odds of my winning are extremely slight."

"You said that in Karuizawa the last time, and just look what happened—you beat him. You beat the Crown Prince! I have never been so humiliated."

"It was only doubles, Mother, and I was playing with the American boy."

"The American. They say he's practically a professional."

"He's twelve."

"In America, they grow up faster than we do. That's what everyone says. There are no real children over there."

"You haven't been to America since I was born," I reminded her. "Miko is there now, having the time of her life. She says that people have been wonderful to her."

"Well, I can't say I'm surprised," my mother sniffed. "She's always been a strange one. Attracts attention wherever she goes."

"You used to tell me how much you liked her."

"That was before she went to America."

THE WINNER'S TROPHY for the tournament was a small silver cup. I smuggled it home wrapped in a fluffy Turkish towel given me by the Crown Prince—a thoughtful, spontaneous gift made after I'd confessed to having misplaced my own, less luxurious towel—and hid it in the bottom drawer of my desk, under the rolled piece of sacking cloth, sadly frayed at the edges, that Miko and I had once used to practice handoffs in the halls of Seishin.

I didn't want my mother to know that I'd won the tournament. I didn't want to talk about the fact that, in making my way through the draw, I had beaten His Imperial Highness for the second time in as many meetings; or that, in doing so, we'd had more conversations, and he had continued in his warm attentions, and we had grown invisibly, always politely, more comfortable with each other; that he had begun to seem less strange and fearsome to me—which was to say, less imperial and more like a man.

A WEEK LATER, the imperial courier made a return visit to our house. This time, my mother was home to receive him. She offered tea; her hospitality knew no bounds. But I managed to take the large elegant envelope from the man's white-gloved hand and disappear into my room before she could say anything mortifying.

I closed my door. In private, slowly, feeling a hesitant smile creeping over my face, I broke the seal on the envelope and slid the photograph into my hand. As I suspected, it was of me holding the winner's trophy. There was still a surprise to be discovered, though. On the back, the Crown Prince had written in his clear strong hand:

"A DAY LIKE NO OTHER."

THROUGH THAT FALL and beginning again in the spring of 1958, we continued to meet for the odd tournament or social match. In April, I became a member of the Tokyo Lawn Tennis Club. Joining the exclusive club was my mother's idea, though I went along without complaint. It was a convenient and fashionable place to play as the weather grew warmer and the season grew busy. But mostly it was tacitly understood that His Highness was often to be found there, and that we would have more occasions to play with each other, always chaperoned by at least one member of our widening circle of mutual friends. By summer, we were both in Karuizawa again, playing more tennis and never being alone.

My mother and I were living together in the country, my father visiting on weekends. Uncharacteristically for the two of us, the atmosphere wasn't especially fraught. I was much distracted by my social plans, my tennis games and garden parties, many of which involved the Crown Prince and our friends from Tokyo. But really, though I didn't fully appreciate it at the time, the difference was in my mother.

Perhaps it was the feminine tumult, the unavoidable and disorienting physical adjustment that comes to women in the middle of our lives. Whatever the reason, she was changing. Her gaze, the expression she carried when lost in thought and unaware of another's attention, had turned less sharp. The compulsive need to control my actions, the propensity for anxious watching and meddling that had dictated our relationship since I could remember, had inexplicably begun to ebb. And, paradoxically, as her youth began to leave her, her beauty seemed to ripen. I found myself looking forward to being in her presence, simply so I could watch her. She was less interested in verbal sparring, silent and thoughtful for long stretches. Though she had never been an avid reader, it was not unusual that summer to find her on the veranda with a novel by Soseki or Kawabata. *Snow Country* was her favorite, and it made her weep. Compared with such personal shifts of weather, the tame, publicly chaperoned comings and goings of the Crown Prince in my life, the exalted or humble state of his serve or mine, understandably occupied a less important corner of her thoughts.

This was the house my father kept returning to, and then leaving again. A house inhabited, peacefully and intricately, by two women, each then poised, I think it is not too strong to say, on the cusp of an altered existence.

FATHER ARRIVED BY TRAIN early one Friday evening. Tokyo's heat and relentlessness seemed to trail him like a cloud of brown ether; his brow and shirt collar were damp with perspiration, and he carried a briefcase stuffed with papers and a small valise. Seeing me waiting on the platform, a weary smile creased his haggard face and his shoulders sagged imperceptibly—perhaps only a wife or daughter would have noticed—as he realized that he might, at least for the duration of the weekend, lay down his burdens.

"Well, you look rested and happy, I must say," he observed, embracing me.

"And you, Father, look exhausted."

"A long week," he admitted.

I reached to take the valise from his hand, but he stopped me. "You'll hurt yourself."

I smiled at him. "I've grown strong from all my tennis. Can't you tell?"

He paused, squinting at me as though trying to gauge my true meaning. Then, wordlessly, he let me have the valise.

FROM THE BATH, in his robe, he came to the table for dinner, his hair still wet. He seemed himself again, subtly powerful, and I felt the relief of this simple restoration, the child's faith it never failed to rekindle.

My mother and I had cooked that afternoon in preparation for his arrival: *hijiki*, *ohitashi*, *zaru soba*, the broiled *unagi* that was his favorite. We had bought new pottery glazed with bursts of yellow gold and cobalt blue. My father ate almost fiercely, grunting occasionally, his chopsticks never ceasing, content to listen as my mother and I recounted the important news of the past three weeks.

"I was forced to buy a new lamp," my mother said.

Over the rim of his rice bowl, my father's eyebrows rose.

"The old one was broken," she explained.

"And old," I added.

"Yes, and old."

My mother and I smiled at each other. My father noticed this and seemed surprised, but continued eating.

"And as for these new dishes . . ." My mother gestured over the table.

"Very pretty," I said.

"And not expensive," my mother assured him.

My father looked more closely at the rice bowl in his hand, nodded once, and continued eating.

"And Mizumo-san has died," said my mother, speaking of the old widower who until a few days ago had lived up the street. "I meant to tell you. It was his heart, as expected. His sons have already put the house up for sale." Her tone was disapproving.

"It's the way things are now," my father replied, setting his emptied rice bowl on the low table. "The high taxes leave people no choice but to sell. If you and I were to die tomorrow, Haruko would do the same."

"Not true," I protested. Across the table, he studied me

with something like pity. "I love this house. I would never agree to part with it."

His shrug was resigned. "One must accept that in life anything can happen, and most certainly it will."

"I find this a depressing way to talk," my mother said. "Can't we discuss something else?"

"Very well." My father finished the last of his beer. "Pass me my briefcase."

It was heavy, stuffed with books and magazines as well as business papers. He dug around in the crowded mouth of the bag, making several false choices before finding what he was looking for.

"This is from two weeks ago," he said, holding up a copy of the American edition of *Time* magazine. "A man I know in New York sent it to me. At first I couldn't imagine why he thought I'd be interested. But here, have a look for yourselves." He pushed some dishes aside and spread the magazine open on the table. The corner of the page he wanted to show us was already turned down. "Supposedly these are the final candidates on the list drawn up by the committee responsible for choosing the Crown Prince's future consort. Or perhaps I should call them contestants."

We were staring at photographs of three Japanese women about my own age, all in a row.

"Only three?" I remarked in what I hoped was an amused tone. In fact, my heart had begun to beat unpleasantly fast. Certainly I was aware—I could hardly not have been—that the Crown Prince and his advisers had for some time been searching for a wife for him, and that, be-fitting imperial tradition, their ultimate choice must end with a descendant of one of the noble families and a graduate of the Peeresses' School. Yet until this moment, presented with three aristocratic young women smiling demurely out of the pages of a famous American magazine, I had somehow managed to avoid any troubling reflection on the subject. "They're all quite pretty."

"I suppose so, if you go in for that sort of thing," my father said. "According to the magazine, several hundred have already been rejected."

"How humiliating for those girls and their families to be cast off in public like that," said my mother.

"Exactly why the Japanese press has agreed to stop writing about it until a girl is chosen. The Americans and the British, of course, have no such reservations."

I shook my head at the photograph. "I don't think it right of the Imperial Family to have let their names out. They should show greater concern for people's feelings."

"Why don't you complain to His Highness yourself," my father suggested provocatively. "Don't you see him often?"

"We've played tennis, if that's what you mean. And we have some friends in common. He's been considerate and generous with me, but that's the way he is with everyone. And of course our conversations are never personal."

"Of course."

"You sound as if you don't believe me."

"Whether I believe you or not doesn't matter a bit," responded my father seriously. "The Crown Prince has his advisers, and they'll have their own opinions about what he must do. More than a man, he's an institution and a symbol. I've met Dr. Watanabe on occasion and can tell you he's a most persuasive individual, utterly devoted to his duties. He won't hesitate to do whatever he thinks necessary for the good of the Imperial Family." My father sighed wearily. "Listen, both of you. A reporter came to our house in Shibuya a week ago while I was at work. A neighbor had the good sense to send him away—but then he showed up at my office, pestering me with questions."

"What sort of questions?"

"About Haruko here."

"About me!" It was as if I'd flown out of my body and was looking down at myself, shocked by how small and mundane I was.

"My response exactly," my father said. "I had my secretary tell the fellow I was in meetings all day, until he finally got the message. But then two more just like him showed up. I had to humor them to get them off my back. I was lucky to be able to leave town."

"What did they want to know about Haruko?"

"Oh, anything at all. Can she cook? Why certainly, I said, she can cook seaweed. If you like seaweed, then she's your girl. Can she write beautiful prose? Of course not, I said, she's a terrible writer, just like her father. Can she count? Only when she's spending my money, I told them, which she does very well indeed. Well, what are her good qualities, they wanted to know. Good qualities? Hmm, I said, give me a few days—I'm sure I'll be able to come up with something."

"Thank you very much, Father."

"Don't mention it."

"Be serious for a moment, both of you," my mother pleaded. "I still don't understand what they wanted."

"Don't you? It's pretty simple, really. For some reason, they're under the impression that *Time* magazine got it wrong. They believe that our Haruko here is the Crown Prince's first choice. They're nearly certain she's the one. And moratorium or not, they don't intend to miss out on the story."

THE PRESS HAD INFILTRATED KARUIZAWA, too. We began to see evidence of them directly, though on the whole, out of deference to the presence of His Highness, they were more circumspect in their behavior than they were in Tokyo. At no time was I approached in person. Still, wherever I went I could sense them hovering like birds of prey. It was fresh meat they preferred, but if that wasn't available they were satisfied to feed on carrion. Which of the two I represented I couldn't always tell. That their prurient interest only increased the level of my vulnerability at such an awkward time in my life did not seem to occur to them. His Highness, however, showed no such lack of regard.

I had not been completely honest with my parents. While it was true that I'd never once been alone with him, it was an exaggeration to suggest that the only times I ever saw him socially were on the tennis court. Among our circle in Karuizawa were several of his former classmates from Gakushuin University, people he knew well and trusted completely. It was they who would regularly, and always discreetly, contact me on his behalf to coordinate our meetings, many of which were designed to have the flavor of happenstance. Perhaps as a result, the meetings themselves were often purposefully banal affairs, errands of a kind, such as sitting outdoors with cones of flavored ice, or—once and quite improbably—merely chatting in the back of a small dark shop as sacks of various teas were being opened and sorted. And though no one who was present during these mundane encounters could honestly claim that anything spoken between us was at all inappropriate or in any way personal, nonetheless the air, like the ambient sky that precedes a storm, had a faint but unmistakable charge to it, or so it seemed to me.

Everything he did personally, I noticed that summer, was measured in its effect, thoughtful and considered and sincerely meant. From the age of three, he had been reared apart from his parents and siblings and taught to be what he was. He could be no other, one understood, and every statement he made, in both word and deed, inevitably bore the stamp of his exalted station. Outside that bright sphere, however, in the profound solitude of his affections, he sought to cast his own light no further than the merely human. Born into radiance, he seemed to have no interest in radiance for its own sake. He could be shy, awkward even, when met on the guarded line between his public duties and his private self. At times he could be silent. But his silence had a surprisingly generous quality, which neither encouraged nor demanded silence in return.

He gave a small dance one evening that August. An intimate, carefully planned affair, full of inviting warmth. Paper lanterns lined the entrance to his summer house and the stone path through the garden in which, at dusk, past the soft reaching tendrils of man-made light, fireflies could be seen appearing and disappearing in the humid moss-scented air like tiny apparitions. Inside, uniformed waiters served cups of punch and crustless finger sandwiches as a quartet played American jazz-band songs and couples danced. The music was lively and fun, romantic though not aggressively so. My dress was new; I had dabbed French perfume behind my ears and on the insides of my tanned bare arms. A light but stirring breeze entered the house through the open windows and breathed innocent secrets onto the legs of every woman in the room.

He was careful not to favor me. Partners changed as they always do, well-dressed men approaching one woman and then another between songs, asking if they might, smiling, taking a hand, readying to begin. In this way, conversations were naturally limited, lasting hardly longer than the songs themselves. One danced with everybody, and talked with everybody, and no one was the wiser.

He asked me to dance three times. The last was rather

a slow tune. It was quiet enough, with his mouth not far from my ear, to converse in a kind of privacy.

"I hope you have been enjoying yourself these past weeks?" he began.

"Very much," I replied. "The summer has gone too quickly."

"And I most sincerely hope that your tennis game won't improve any more."

I glanced up at him and found his eyes smiling. "In fact, I'm afraid I'm getting worse."

"Allow me to disagree. But if it were true, then I might have a chance against you in the future."

"A very good chance, I should think. An excellent chance."

"Well, we will have to see about that."

The music turned, and he turned me with it. He was an excellent dancer, nimble and graceful. Beyond the windows darkness had fallen, and the lanterns cast a flickering trail of golden light. Across the room I saw Dr. Watanabe standing by himself, watching us with an expression of keen interest. I was surprised; I had not been aware that he was in Karuizawa. Our eyes met, and he bowed respectfully in my direction.

Neatly, His Highness turned me again. "Do you know your plans for the autumn?"

"I suppose I will be in Tokyo."

"Might I see you there?"

"Of course, Your Highness . . . I would be honored."

His eyes smiled again, this time at my self-consciousness

in addressing him. When the song ended, he stood as though reluctant to let me go, the tips of my fingers still in his hands.

"You and your parents will remain here in Karuizawa for another two weeks or so?" He seemed already to know the answer to his question. And he appeared—it was difficult to tell because of the light—to be blushing.

"Yes, perhaps a bit longer."

"I am very glad," he said sincerely, pressing my fingertips.

Two weeks later exactly, Dr. Watanabe came to speak to my parents.

9

I WAS HAVING TEA at a friend's house. Only much later did I realize that Dr. Watanabe must somehow have been aware of my plans that afternoon—like the Buddha himself, he seemed to have instant yet timeless knowledge of everything—and scheduled his unannounced visit accordingly.

Of course, I had no idea that anything unusual was occurring in my absence. My innocence then was still quite perfect in its way. Walking into the house upon my return, I began to hum, senselessly and joyfully, an airy little tune.

I continued to the back of the house. At that hour the sun was still above the hilltops, yet low enough for its warm, comforting light to bathe the normally shaded area of our veranda; my mother, reading a novel there as had become her habit, was a vision in gold, and I stopped for a moment to admire her. It was only then, standing close enough to her to smell the jasmine in her perfume, that I saw the haunted expression on her face, and realized that the book in her hands was closed.

Her voice emerged as a tremble. "Ah, Haruko."

"Mother, is something wrong?"

"No, no . . . Have you spoken to your father yet?"

"I just came in. Has something happened?"

"Not exactly . . . I don't know what to say. It would be best . . . Your father went for a walk a little while ago, and I know he's anxious to speak with you."

It was not a walk, really, more like a lost penguin's circling. My father seemed to have misplaced himself, there on the narrow earthen road that led past our house; he was shuffling to this side and that, his head down in inconclusive thought, reaching the barrier of the trees and being forced to turn, and so forth. On his third circumnavigation, he looked up and saw me. Standing in the road, blinking in the light, he did not, as my mother had claimed, look like a man actively searching for anyone so much as a man caught in some solitary and painful act.

"Ah, Haruko, there you are."

"Mother said you were anxious to speak to me."

"Anxious? Yes, I suppose she's right," he said vaguely.

"This isn't about that dress I bought last week, is it? It was something I needed, you know."

"Dress? What dress? What are you talking about?"

"Nothing," I said quickly.

We were silent for a few moments. From the gradually darkening trees came the first poignant notes of evening birdsong.

"Shall we take a walk?"

"I've already been walking," he replied—rather grandly, it seemed to me, for someone who'd been going in circles.

"If that's walking, Father, I would hate to see what you mean by running."

He glared at me—but then, abruptly, he laughed. "I suppose I should be satisfied that at least you still have your sense of humor," he said, shaking his head in a kind of grudging admiration. "You will certainly need it when I tell you what has just occurred."

SLOWLY THEN, as the sun began to set and the summer sky to darken around us, my father recounted for me the meeting with Dr. Watanabe that had taken place that afternoon. Already the event seemed permanently woven into his consciousness. He was thorough in his telling, wanting me to see and hear every important detail, the words exchanged and their unspoken implications; as though he considered the story, like so many others passed on to me throughout my childhood, part of my rightful inheritance.

UNDETERRED BY THE AFTERNOON HEAT, the doctor had been dressed in his customary dark suit. He was greeted with appropriate formality by my parents, their shock at his unannounced visit politely hidden. My mother showed him into the formal sitting room. Taka brought out cold tea and what small delicacies could be scavenged from the kitchen on such short notice, and then removed herself. My mother served the honored guest and then my father.

At first there was silence, the doctor acknowledging with a nod of his head the simple, rough-textured cups and the cool bitter taste of the tea. The tension in the room, despite the open shoji and a light breeze, quickly grew oppressive.

Finally Dr. Watanabe set down his cup, then my parents did the same. My father studied the drops of condensation trickling down the side of his cup onto its wooden coaster.

"Respectfully, Endo-san, I have come on behalf of the committee whose solemn duty it is to oversee the choice of a suitable consort for His Highness the Crown Prince," Dr. Watanabe began.

A faint gasp escaped my mother's lips. A stern glance from my father urged her to regain her self-control, and after a moment, in a soft clear voice, Dr. Watanabe continued.

"It is no secret that the committee has been pondering this question, both on our own and in consultation with His Highness, for some years now. If there is a more important question facing the Imperial Family at the present time, I must say that I do not know what it is."

The room was silent. Already the tea—when all, in unison, again took sips—was turning tepid.

Setting down his cup, the doctor continued. "You may be aware—it has been publicly reported in certain irresponsible sectors of the foreign press, despite my entreaties—that in recent months the committee has privately solicited recommendations from the heads of schools other than the Peeresses' School. Of course, this break with tradition has been discussed with the Crown Prince, whose belief it is that we as a nation have reached a stage in our history when certain ancient practices must be thoughtfully adjusted in order to best represent the spirit of the people."

Again the doctor paused to wet his lips with tea. My parents, stricken by paralyzing emotions, merely stared at him without lifting their own cups.

"Last summer, I had the honor of being present at the tennis match where the Crown Prince and your daughter were introduced," resumed the doctor. "As you know, she beat him rather handily. I told him afterward that he'd played poorly, though in truth your daughter was simply better. And while His Highness perhaps suffers from something of a competitive streak"—here the doctor allowed himself an affectionate half smile—"at the same time the event was a revelation to him. One could immediately see that he was greatly impressed with her beauty, her dignified manner, and her lively, intelligent spirit. A feeling which, over time, has only deepened in him, and which those of us on the committee have come to appreciate as well."

My father made as if to speak, but Dr. Watanabe held up a hand asking for patience. His fingers were pale and slender, and unexpectedly long for someone who was not tall; it was indeed, somehow, a patient hand. With sudden and unaffected feeling, he said, "I do not need to list for you your daughter's many charms and accomplishments.

I, too, have a daughter, and can understand how you must feel."

My father inclined his head. Perhaps at that moment, he later speculated, the doctor was thinking not of his daughter but of his son who had died in the fire, for he blinked rapidly as though something were trapped in his eye, and then, avoiding the ruined skin on the right side of his face, he pressed a folded white handkerchief to his brow.

"In conclusion, Endo-san, I have come here today to put before you, in all humility and urgency, on behalf of the Imperial Family, the Crown Prince's most sincere and respectful desire to make your daughter his esteemed and beloved consort."

With that, the doctor bowed once more. When, lifting his gaze, he looked about him again, he could not have failed to take in the shocked pallor of my mother's face, or the agitation expressed by my father's twitching fingers.

"Of course," said the doctor, "you will have concerns. That is only natural. Please feel free to speak to me openly. There is no other way to proceed if we are to make a success of this historic arrangement on all sides, as I sincerely hope we will. You must feel able to express to me your doubts and even, shall I say, your fears on your daughter's behalf."

"In that case," said my father, "with your permission, I feel compelled to respectfully answer your appeal, which does us great honor."

The doctor nodded politely.

"Watanabe-san, we are modest people. Certainly I am aware that, due to my father's efforts and the opportunities he made possible, we are more fortunate than many. Indeed, it would never occur to us to complain about our situation. But, as you have rightly suggested, we are commoners. That is what we are. Our blood is no different from anyone else's. We lead normal, unaffected lives. The sun may pass over our heads every day, but one thing I can tell you with absolute assurance, the sun is not our ancestor. I trust that you will not misunderstand my meaning when I say that, for people like us, the Imperial Family are symbols of the most glorious and remote kind. Which, of course, is what they must be."

"If I may for a moment, Endo-san . . ."

"Please allow me to answer you." My father's face was flushed, and for the first time his voice sounded almost beseeching. (My father did not tell me that his voice sounded almost beseeching then, but I knew that it must have.)

Dr. Watanabe retreated. There was in the room now a sense of barely muted panic, emanating from my parents, which had begun subtly to unman the doctor's confidence; a wavering in himself that came to him as a rude shock, leading him to briefly shut his eyes in search of an artificial peace. "Of course," he murmured. "Forgive me, please continue."

"Thank you. What I meant to say—what I meant to say was simply this: I believe the gulf is too wide. The gulf between the Imperial Family and our daughter. More than a gulf, it is an ocean. And you, of course, as a father, must understand this. Haruko could not possibly swim across such an ocean. She understands nothing about the water—how cold and deep it is, how rough—and she will drown. And when she drowns, we, her mother and I—allow me to say that I don't believe we could accept it. It's a sacrifice that we are not willing to make."

Dr. Watanabe murmured gently, "Sacrifice, yes. A kind of duty."

"Very well, a kind of duty," my father conceded, proudly composing himself. "I understand the meaning of such words and, if I may say, Doctor, I have never shied away from them. Which is all fine and well for a grown man like myself, his life already halfway behind him. But here we are talking about a young woman whose whole life still awaits her."

"And who has her own sense of duty and sacrifice," interrupted my mother, speaking now directly to my father. "A very developed one."

"Precisely," Dr. Watanabe concurred.

My father was staring at my mother—she had been silent for so long that he'd almost forgotten she was there—his expression naked with surprise.

"Forgive me," she murmured, "but it is the truth."

"Of course it is," he admitted rather crossly. He turned back to Dr. Watanabe and in a more level tone added, "Our concerns, however, go further."

The doctor inclined his head. "Of course. Respectfully, I am listening."

"There is in the Imperial Palace—how shall I put this—the old guard. The nobility. You yourself are such a worthy man. It is my understanding that such people make up nearly all of that world, and certainly all of the positions of relevance. Now, I'm the first to admit that I don't know much about any of this. I am a simple businessman—which, I suppose, is precisely my point. If I myself, out in the world fifty years, don't know anything about the ways and customs of imperial life, then how could Haruko? She would be utterly lost, humiliated. More than that, and I mean this sincerely, Doctor, she would be a humiliation to the Crown Prince and the entire Imperial Family. She would be a humiliation to Japan. And yet here you are—honorably, respectfully, on behalf of His Highness—asking us to agree to give her up for a role for which we sincerely believe her to be unfit. A problem that, of course, has little to say about the other kind of loss being asked of us, one that you yourself, as you say, would feel only too painfully. To lose a daughter to another household is comprehensible; to lose her to another world defeats the mind, to say nothing of the heart. And, once she has committed herself, it is for life. She will never be able to leave that world. She will be sealed in forever."

"Perhaps, Endo-san, there are worse places to be sealed in than the Imperial Palace," Dr. Watanabe suggested lightly.

"Perhaps, Watanabe-san, but I don't see how it can be humanely done. Not for our Haruko. And so, respectfully and after painful consideration, acknowledging the great honor His Highness has brought to our household, I must ask that you show us compassion and officially withdraw your interest in our daughter on behalf of the Crown Prince."

My father bowed deeply, and remained in that posture for some time. A soft, regretful sigh from my mother was the only sound in the room.

When eventually he raised himself, he found Dr. Watanabe soberly contemplating a Chinese ink painting on the wall above his head. Though the painting was quite old, it was of no particular distinction; a far superior one hung on the wall opposite.

The doctor's expression, my father later told me, suggested an ambivalent mixture of grimness and compassion. Compassion for all the pitiful human parties involved in such an intractable dilemma; grimness for the possibility and consequence of failure in his imperial mission. How would he explain these unexpected difficulties to His Highness, whose hopes and feelings on the matter had already reached a heightened state of anticipation? What Dr. Watanabe had initially perceived as a mere function of normal good manners on the part of my parents— offered the rarest of gifts, they must certainly appear to refuse it once or twice before at last reluctantly accepting—had upon closer inspection turned out to be a genuine and immediate refusal, and a heartfelt plea for release.

10

I WENT AWAY. Of course, it was my parents' idea, they who sent the telegrams and took the initiative. I was far too stunned and confused by the situation to decide anything on my own. Simply put, I allowed myself to be shipped like a piece of furniture.

The International Alumnae Association of Sacred Heart schools was holding its annual convention in Brussels at the beginning of September. Thanks to Mother Clapp, who had by then become the director of the university (and with whom I had maintained a warm friendship since my graduation a year earlier), I was to attend the gathering as Japan's representative. From Brussels I would travel on to Amsterdam, London, Rome, and Paris, staying in carefully chosen private homes rather than hotels, so that I might gain personal insight into European life.

THE DAY BEFORE MY DEPARTURE, I went to see my former Reverend Mother at her office in Hiroo.

"So," she said briskly in English as soon as we had exchanged greetings, "let me have a look at you." She stepped from behind her desk, her black skirts rustling,

97

the starched and fluted frame of her habit somehow even whiter and stiffer than I remembered. It required significant self-control on my part not to bow a second time, even more deeply, and blurt out, "Reverend Mother, I have a question." But I contained myself and stood still, my face burning only a little as she affectionately surveyed me from head to toe. "Well," she concluded, "despite all the excitement swirling around you, you seem very much the same old Haruko to me, if a bit more grown-up and even lovelier. Tell me, do you *feel* like a princess?"

I was aware that she was partly humoring me, but her words affected me nonetheless: I looked down at my feet, tears blurring my vision. "Mother Clapp," I mumbled, "I feel like a fool."

"Oh come now, child, I wasn't being serious." To my astonishment, she came closer and took me firmly in her arms, her broad hands on my back. "Well, at most only half. But that's no excuse to lose your head. Is this the sort of silliness we taught you while you were under our charge? I certainly hope not."

"A man's head and a woman's heart," I murmured in French.

"Exactly!" she cried, her eyes crinkling with amusement. "I'm so glad you haven't forgotten."

"I will never forget."

"Come, sit down," she said. "You and I have a few things to discuss. I gather from Dr. Watanabe that you've been beating the Crown Prince on the tennis court for almost a year now. Well, you were always a good athlete.

Though I admit that when I first heard about it, I thought perhaps you were being a bit overzealous. There's such a thing as politesse, after all. But then it occurred to me that your approach might really amount to the better indicator of his character. How he takes losing, I mean."

"I do not believe the Crown Prince was ever very pleased about losing," I replied, "though he was certainly gracious about it."

"Gracious is good. I approve of gracious," Mother Clapp said firmly.

"If anything, he seemed to treat me with greater respect each time we played."

"He was probably terrified of you, poor man. All merriment aside, Haruko, I've been wondering what your feelings on the matter have been."

"My feelings?"

"Surely you know that word." Her level blue gaze pinned me to my seat.

"It is simply . . ."

"Yes?"

"That my feelings on the matter, as you call them, do not seem important at this time."

"Not important? How so?"

"My parents have explained their reasons for asking Dr. Watanabe not to make a formal proposal on behalf of the Crown Prince. They have many reasons, all quite considered, though none involve what I believe you mean by my feelings."

"And how do you feel about that?"

"Feel?"

"There you go playing the ignorant Japanese female again! You know very well that I have precious little tolerance for such nonsense."

I bowed. "Please forgive me, Mother Clapp."

"You are forgiven." She paused, and her expression turned warm with friendly pride. "I trust you to know that if I'm hard on you it's only because I believe you to be capable of great things."

I inclined my head to show that her optimism on my account was something that I couldn't share. Then, my curiosity getting the better of me, I asked, "What kinds of things?"

"I don't know yet. And neither do you. That's what makes all of this so urgent. The potential loss is incalculable."

"And the gain?"

"Ah, there you have me. Because I'm not Japanese, I can't properly weigh the meaning of your marrying the Crown Prince and becoming, for life, a member of the Imperial Family, perhaps one day even Empress. What's the value of such an outlandish but suddenly very real prospect—humanly speaking, culturally speaking, and, most of all, personally speaking for you? Only you and your parents can decide such a question. And I must add that I don't envy you the challenge. All I can do is offer what we old teachers always offer our favorite former students on such occasions: affectionate concern, plenty of unsolicited opinions, and a boldly painted arrow pointing you in a general moral direction. In this case, I'd say that for the next six weeks that arrow decidedly points toward Europe. Go there with a full heart is my advice, and live as though each minute were a blessed gift."

I WAS IN PARIS the last week of my trip when a letter arrived from my father:

My dearest daughter,

You have been in Europe some weeks now. From the infrequency of your letters, your mother and I are encouraged to think that your travels must be agreeing with you, broadening your mind and your sense of the world. This is all to the good. Such knowledge can't merely be borrowed after the fact; it must be seen with one's own eyes at the actual moment. You are doing this now, and I am proud of you.

I say all this to begin with because I want you to understand that nothing, as far as your mother and I are concerned, comes before our concern for your happiness and well-being.

I have some news to give you. Through Dr. Watanabe, the Imperial Household has made a formal proposal of marriage on behalf of the Crown Prince. As you know, this is a state of affairs which at first your mother and I tried to avoid. I was nothing if not clear with the doctor at our first meeting that I believed such a marriage would be cruelly unbalanced and unwise for both parties. He listened respectfully and went away. But while you have been abroad he has returned many times, visiting me at home in Shibuya and even, once, at my office. He is persistent, highly intelligent, and beyond reproach in his regard for the Crown Prince's welfare. In short, I believe he is an excellent sort of man. In him, as is so rarely the case with men who have achieved real influence, duty and affection are brought together naturally and wear a human face. Perhaps for this reason I have come to feel that I can trust him to look at this complicated situation with the necessary degree of sympathy, not only for the Crown Prince but for your mother and me, and especially, my dear, for you. It is in this light that I hope you will receive this news.

Of course, Dr. Watanabe understood completely when I replied that no answer to their proposal could be possible without your full and considered consent. We are not one of those families that force their children into the pages of history—nor, I believe, would the Crown Prince or any feeling person of any rank wish us to be.

Your mother agrees with me in all these matters and, of course, sends her devoted love as well. While Dr. Watanabe has been courting me in his fashion, you may be interested to hear that your mother has been receiving constant attention from the estimable Mother Clapp. Believe it or not, your old teacher seems in your absence, with Dr. Watanabe's encouragement, to have come to the triumphant conclusion that you are a most imperial sort of girl.

Yes, we've been having a pretty lively time of it.

Very well, that's enough for you to think about in one letter. You're in France at the moment, I believe, Paris. I trust the Roussards are treating you well and showing you the sights. Dream all you want, Haruko, but keep your head level while *you're at it. When I was a young man, I've told you too many times, I had hopes of becoming a sensei. A kind of wise man, I envisioned grandly. But I was the eldest son and, unfortunately, not very wise, and in the end there was never any question that I must follow my father in his business. What I have done in that line, I make no special claims for myself. The point, I suppose, is that all these years later I would not have it any other way. How could I, not knowing what else in my life might have been different as a consequence? Without you and your mother, I would be a poor man indeed.*

Your loving father

11

UPON MY RETURN, the press installed a round-the-clock
"bride watch" on our house in Shibuya. I could not open
a window or stick my nose outside to smell the flowers
in the garden without having photographs taken of me.
That such photographs were unflattering goes without
saying, though the real punishment lay in the assault on
one's privacy.

The Crown Prince had not given up. As it was quite
impossible that we should ever see each other alone, His
Highness began calling me on the telephone, sometimes
two or three times a day. Phone calls were not then what
they have since become; there was a certain formality to
their execution which cannot now be reproduced, a feeling only heightened when the party on the other end of
the line was heir to the Chrysanthemum Throne. Never
previously had we conversed in this manner, and our
first attempt following my return, given the flagrant, if
still largely unacknowledged pressures of the situation
and his habitual reticence, was perhaps understandably
a bit constrained.

"Ah . . . Endo-san?" he tentatively began.

"Your Highness."

"Ah . . . You have returned, then."

"Yes."

"And your trip? I hope it was . . . Hmm . . ."

"Yes."

"Yes, yes. I hope so."

"Yes, it was, thank you."

"I was in Europe myself a couple of years ago. Yes, on a trip. Quite a long one."

"Yes, I remember."

"Very interesting too, yes. Hmm, well, yes."

"Yes."

And so it went. I can't remember where we got to, if anywhere. By the time we finished, the receiver had left a mark on my cheek and I was exhausted.

In the kitchen, my mother and Taka were waiting to interrogate me.

"Did you discuss the proposal?"

"Certainly not."

"What could you have been going on about, then?"

"I don't know. We said 'yes' a lot."

" 'Yes'?"

"Yes."

"Well, I guess that's better than no," Taka reasoned.

My mother gave her a dry glance but said nothing.

"I'm tired," I said. "I think I'll go to my room."

"Make sure to close the curtains or people will see you."

I sighed. "The curtains have been closed since I came back. I live in perpetual darkness."

My mother's expression grew suddenly tender. She reached up and brushed something from my cheek.

"Don't be so dramatic," she said.

I WANTED TO SEE HIM ALONE. Just once, before giving him my answer. But this was not to be. There were too many people involved. There were too many beliefs. There was too much hunger. There was too much weight. There was too much history. I was just beginning then to see it, to feel the magnitude. But I had no true idea. I was still innocent. I was weak. My arms were unconditioned to the task. I could not even open the curtains.

"WOULD YOU TELL ME SOMETHING that you've never told me before," he said over the telephone one evening.

I didn't answer him immediately. By then I had a telephone in my bedroom for privacy. It was our fifteenth or eighteenth or thirtieth conversation since my return from Europe. We'd stopped saying yes at every turn but had yet to begin saying no.

"There are so many things," I demurred.

"None which speaks louder than any other?"

"Some are too loud. They shout. I find them deafening. And then others . . . Others are no more than whispers. I can hardly hear them myself. Perhaps they don't mean anything at all."

"You might try me with the quiet ones," he said. "I don't mean to boast, but it's been said that my hearing is rather good."

I smiled, knowing that he wouldn't be able to see. "You mean you're famous for your hearing?" I teased him.

"What I am famous for is not what I am," he answered simply.

"Yes, but I also wonder how that can be. What you are, you have always been."

"To truly understand what I mean, you must come closer."

"But there is no going closer without going too far. There is no middle ground."

"Then we will have to build one."

"But would that really be possible? Where you live—"

"Where I find myself."

"All right, if you wish, Your Highness, where you find yourself, things have always been as they are, haven't they? And I'm afraid I don't see how they might ever change."

"They are changing already. I am on this telephone talking to you."

"And I am here, on the outside, in a room in Shibuya with drawn curtains."

"Today that's true, and I am sorry for it," he acknowledged. "But if I may express my deepest and most sincere wish, it will not be true for long."

"I am a commoner."

"That is only a name."

"Forgive me, Your Highness, but it is more than a name. As is your title. These names are the history of our people."

"History is no longer as it once was. The war saw to

that. I believe that some change, in moderation, is necessary for growth and prosperity."

"Again, forgive me, but that sounds like policy, not life."

"I am not a politician," he said, a bit tersely.

"Of course not. Please excuse me, Your Highness."

"Now you are trying to distance me."

I was silent.

"Forgive me," he said, "if I go too far. The moment feels increasingly important to me, and I am not always delicate. I meant before to speak about happiness, that's all."

"That's quite a lot, wouldn't you agree?"

"I would not have thought so before," he said. "But things have begun to appear differently to me."

We were silent for a few moments.

"May I ask you a silly question?" I began again.

"You may ask me anything you like."

"Is the air different where you are?"

"The air?"

"I warned you it was silly."

"It's a perfectly reasonable question," he insisted politely. "The truth is that I've never actually thought about the air. But no, I'm pleased to say it seems much the same. But . . ."

"Yes?"

"Well, I suppose it's the manner of breathing that one might consider different."

"How so?"

"The main goal, I suppose, is not to appear to breathe too hard."

"How do you mean?"

"Well, I've never had much occasion to think about it, but the main thing, I've always been told, is to remain calm. Very calm and still at all times."

I laughed, but he did not. He was joking, yet also urgently serious.

"And do you do that yourself—try to remain very calm and still at all times?"

"I used to. But then, recently, I gave it up."

"What made you change?"

Now it was he who laughed softly, a low gentle murmur.

"I trust you will understand when I respectfully decline to answer that question."

Behind the drawn curtains, through the open window, in the garden where long ago a small yellow bird with gray-and-black wings used to sing, I heard a twig snap under a photographer's creeping foot.

"I enjoy talking with you," I said.

"Then you will consider accepting me?"

"I will consider it with all my heart, Your Highness."

IT WAS OVER THAT SAME TELEPHONE, a few days later, that I gave him my answer. And, a few days after that, my father's formal acceptance in writing was delivered to the head of the Imperial Household Agency.

I had never been alone with the man who was to become my husband. I had never met a single member of his family, or seen with my own eyes the physical world in which they lived.

All that would change, of course, and soon. I would meet the Emperor and Empress, and come to know my way, haltingly at first, like the visitor I was, around the palace and its vast, labyrinthine grounds. In the meantime, a nation waited hungrily to be informed of the identity of the future Crown Princess.

At home, my curtains remained drawn.

12

REACTIONS TO THE ENGAGEMENT were generally enthusiastic, if sometimes bittersweet.

One afternoon I looked up from my bed, where I was reading a magazine (very well, about myself), and there in the doorway stood Taka, her mouth pinched as if she'd swallowed too much wasabi, and her eyes locked on the floor between us. Ever since I'd accepted the Crown Prince, she had been acting strangely in my presence, refusing to meet my gaze. This time I decided to confront her.

"Taka, am I so ugly as that?"

"What?" she mumbled to the floor.

"I've grown two heads and you don't have the nerve to tell me, is that it?"

A brief hiss of laughter as Taka clamped a hand over her mouth. "Two heads!" she cried. Then the amusement drained from her face. "No, believe me, Haruko-san, it's nothing like that. I would certainly tell you if you had two heads."

"I'm relieved to hear it. But Taka, I thought that you of all people were happy I accepted him."

"Oh, I was! I mean, I am. I've told everyone I know in the world. My mother can't stop talking about it."

"And yet you won't look at me anymore. Whenever you see me, you just stand there bobbing your head like a gloomy old crow."

Taka bowed. "Please excuse my disgraceful manners."

"There, you see, you're doing it again."

"I'm very sorry, but I can't help it. You're going to be Crown Princess!" She spoke with sudden, uncharacteristic severity, and her words at that moment struck me like a life sentence from an all-knowing judge.

"I'm aware of that, thank you. But I'm still myself. The same person I was two weeks ago."

"Excuse me, but I can't agree with you there," Taka replied firmly. "I'm nobody, and even I know that."

"Please don't. Not yet. It's too soon."

She shook her head as if to say that her behavior was beyond her control. "I'm sorry."

"Can't you just look at me the way you used to?" I tried to smile. "I promise I won't bite." Slowly, with evident reluctance, she raised her eyes to mine. "There, you see?" I said. "It's simple."

But of course simple was not what it was. This we both could see. Taka stood looking at me, her face flushed and indignant, as if I had cruelly forced her into an unnatural and profane act. Then, too quickly, she turned away.

NOT EVERYONE WAS AS FIERCELY REVERENT as our loyal maid. There were those, I could not forget, who must always stand higher than myself, on a different plane altogether. A matter of birth and blood.

From the back seat of the Mercedes that had been sent for me, I watched the tall wooden doors of Sakashita Gate glide open. We passed between saluting guards and continued along a central driveway with walls on either side, off which branched narrower driveways and higher or lower walls and more smartly saluting guards. I had read and been told about the Imperial Palace, of course—its twenty hectares, gardens, waterfalls, residences, stables, garages, greenhouses, teahouses, hospitals, laboratories, kitchens, and drawing rooms. But I had never been on this side of the moat, within these walls. Here, too, it was late November, the sky the color of dulled pearl. I had the sensation of entering a children's story, though without the comforting knowledge that I could close the book if it turned out to be too frightening, if the forest suddenly came alive or the dragon began breathing fire. My stomach was clenching and unclenching like a phrase that would not speak itself, my heart striking my breast like the hard, frantic beak of a bird attempting to peck its way out of its cage. I sat without touching the seat back for fear of damaging my brocade dress and mink stole. I wished the driver would say something, anything, but he was silently efficient as he stopped the car, got out, and opened the door for me with a bow.

The room in the Imperial Household Building in which I was told to wait for Their Majesties was large and formal, rather sparsely furnished. Beautiful old textiles hung from the walls, and several gold screens gave the room a stately burnished radiance. There seemed to be vast reaches of empty space between each piece of furniture and work of art, as though the room were not just large but cavernous. Though perhaps this impression owed more to my state of mind than to reality.

A chamberlain appeared. Their Majesties were approaching, and I rose to my feet. At that moment in another part of the palace, my parents would be gathering before hordes of reporters and photographers for the press conference to which I would soon be conducted. I thought of them there, camera flashes blinding them, questions hurled, and wondered what legacy it might be that I was leaving them through the decision I had made.

The Emperor entered first, the Empress a step or two behind him. I can no longer recall how many times I bowed. Dr. Watanabe had counseled me. I was careful to appear attentive but in no way direct, my eyes gathering impressions from a series of discreet glances rather than one straightforward approach.

His Majesty was a small, quiet, bespectacled man with a neat graying mustache. His movements were at once dignified and tentative, as though he were walking on rice paper and privately intent upon not making any noise. His voice was soft, his language so formal as to occasionally be impossible to understand. His perfectly tailored clothes were English. To all of these attributes the Empress seemed on first impression a kind of opposite, perhaps even an antidote: full in body and voice, clear in speech, sharp of eye, traditional in dress. Her face was long, as in the paintings of old. Her green-gray kimono was interwoven with delicate crescent threads of gold, echoing the gold screens that themselves seemed to echo an ancestral sun forever in attendance. They were not my ancestors, of course, and I fought the urge to run away.

"Please," Her Majesty commanded, "won't you sit down?"

I had already offered my honorifics and greeting, my bows, all that I had prepared and learned. There must have been a response, but I can't remember what it was. Nods, smiles, a raising of the hand, and we were seated. The Empress had a singular method of seeing beyond one's best attempts to conceal oneself. Even my clothes, specially bought and fitted for the occasion, seemed to tighten and fade under her scrutiny, as though they were mere borrowed finery.

A silence then, like a heavy fog oozing under a closed door. I had grown used to the Crown Prince's manner of not speaking, the expression of a naturally reticent but generous nature. His mother's silence was more like an iron vessel, to be filled only upon command.

Two servants entered carrying tea. When they had gone, the Empress leveled her gaze on me.

"You have been much praised."

I denied this very general compliment as humbly as I could.

"As you are aware," she continued as if I had not spoken, "Watanabe-san has been our son's most trusted counselor since he was a boy. We have all come to rely on his sound judgment concerning the next generation of our family. His sense of tradition is entirely honorable."

"Extremely so," agreed the Emperor with a vague smile.

"Yes," said the Empress, "the search for you was long and thorough. And quite unprecedented."

"I will try my utmost, Your Majesty, to be worthy of this honor and of the trust placed in me," I replied.

At this, the Emperor nodded benevolently, gazing at one of the gold screens behind me, while the Empress studied me matter-of-factly over the rim of her teacup. "Yes, well, the choice was much—I will not say debated, but discussed, certainly. Much discussed here in our little circle. Of course, whenever there is a break of this magnitude with the past, there will be concerns. The question of lineage, for instance. For a tradition such as ours, the question of lineage is unavoidable. For the sake of history and continuity, it must be well considered. Yet in the end, as I have already said, the choice was made. I cannot confirm that everyone's opinion was taken into account equally. Still, the choice was made, and our son has informed us that he is content."

"My most respectful wish, Your Majesty, if it is within my power, is to make His Highness happy as well as content."

The Empress was regarding me with dark shining eyes, a half smile fixed on her lips. "A very noble wish indeed."

This veiled reference to my lack of noble blood was not

lost on me, nor did I suppose it was meant to be. I inclined my head. "Your Majesty."

"You may have noticed," the Emperor broke in, his eyes boyishly animated behind his spectacles, "that Emperor Meiji's Phoenix Hall is no longer with us."

Having noticed little thus far beyond the car and the moat and the walls and the policemen and now the room, I could only smile ambiguously at this curious declaration.

"Since the war, we have lived in Obunko, above the library," the Empress elaborated, rather proudly it seemed to me. "It is very simple, made of concrete, but more than adequate for us at a time when the people themselves have so little."

"It was not one of the bombs that did the damage, you know," said the Emperor, seeming to warm to his subject. "No, we were spared all that. Rather strange, when one thinks about it. Well, across the moat there, the War Ministry was burning. Yes, it was burning all right, everything—papers and documents, and so on. Bright orange it was. Terribly hot. There was a strong wind that day. Very strong. And—here's the thing—the wind carried the burning papers over the moat and onto the palace." He smiled his vague, benevolent smile, as though he were telling me a bedtime story. "I thought your father might be interested to know some of the history. Now that we are all going to be . . ."

He smiled once more; his hand opened and closed. And I realized that he had concluded.

"Thank you, Your Majesty. I will tell my father."

The servants entered and whisked away the tea things. Then a lady-in-waiting appeared with a lacquered tray. The gift from my future parents-in-law—a figurine carved out of ivory—was held up for me to inspect. I saw that it was a dog, beautifully made, accompanied by a carved ebony stand and a silk-lined wooden box.

"For your collection," the Empress instructed.

I bowed and expressed my humble thanks. I was born in the Year of the Dog; at home in my room, behind drawn curtains, I kept a cabinet overflowing with dogs in every manner of material. This, I supposed, must now have become public knowledge. And yet what no one, not even the Empress, could possibly have known was that those tender inanimate creatures had seen me through the trials and joys of my childhood. Of course, none in my possession were as exquisite or rare as this new one, and as my first imperial gift was taken away to be wrapped and put in my car, it was hard for me not to consider the cost.

WITHIN WEEKS OF THE NEWS that the Crown Prince was to wed the "accomplished," "beautiful," "graceful," "athletic," "discreet," "eminently normal," and "highly finished" daughter of the "renowned and respected businessman Endo Tsuneyasu" (no longer in the press was my father referred to as the "Sake King"), "scion of an old family of both intellectual and economic prestige, and distant cousin of Fukuzawa Yukichi" (in fact, Fukuzawa was on my mother's side of the family), an entire industry of weekly magazines dedicated to the event and its aftermath burst into life. In *Sande Mainichi,* for example, there appeared an article, "On the Courts of Kuruizawa," describing with certain piquant inaccuracies the doubles match at which the American boy Bobby Spencer and I had "trounced" the Crown Prince. From there, the piece continued, with rather greater attention to truth, to list the measurements of my height, weight, bust, waist, hips, and neck. In conclusion, the unnamed author applied himself to the "larger meaning" of the upcoming nuptials:

> The Crown Prince selected a princess from among
> the people. It appears that there was a movement
> among one faction in opposition to this. However,
> both of them love and respect each other from
> their hearts, and if they become Japan's ideal
> couple and establish a model home life, then for
> their countrymen there could be no happier thing.

The epitome of this sort of journalism was a weekly magazine called *Josei Jishin,* which began publication the month following my engagement. The tone was chatty and informal. The goal, apparently, was to try to win back some of the print readership already being lost to television. Every day, a female *Josei* photographer with a little snub nose would appear at the Kojimachi, where I had begun my all-consuming lessons in the many imperial functions and ceremonies—the duties of the Crown Princess, Japan's new constitution, imperial protocol, waka-writing, calligraphy, to name but a few of the many categories of specialized knowledge that I was required to learn before my marriage.

Several months later, during "Haruko's last days as a commoner," the photographer was transferred to a rented room on the second floor of our neighbor's house in Shibuya (our neighbor, one could not help remarking, had that same day driven home a new Toyota). From there, it was a clear view over the wall and into our garden, in which, five days before her wedding day, Haruko was photographed "playing a ball game with her father."

WE WERE IN THE HOUSE THAT DAY, all of us, under siege. Earlier, my father had come home from work in the middle of the afternoon—an occurrence without precedent in our family's history—simply appeared like the postman, his face flushed, his eyes riddled with rubied blood vessels caused by stress and sleeplessness.

"There's nothing one can do in this madness!" he'd muttered in response to our worried questions. "I'm not going back to work until this thing is over and done with." It was the voice of defeat, or something more serious still. He disappeared into his bedroom and did not emerge again for hours.

By then I was sitting at my desk, studying myself in a hand mirror that had been passed down to me by my grandmother. In finger-shaped grooves on the handle, the lacquer had worn thin, revealing the grain of the original wood beneath. I was staring at my face as if I'd never seen it before. Many minutes had passed.

"May I come in?"

In the mirror, dwarfed in the glass, I saw him standing in the doorway. If he'd knocked, I hadn't heard. I lowered the mirror and turned to face him.

"I was just staring at my face."

I would not have made such an embarrassing confession to my mother, but I felt the need, that day, to make it to him.

"A fine face," he said.

I shook my head, perhaps too vehemently.

"And I know faces," he assured me.

"Did you sleep?" I asked, wanting to change the subject.

He made an ambiguous mothlike gesture with his hands. "I closed my eyes. Half the battle, no?"

"Is it a battle?"

"Isn't it?"

He came farther into the room. He'd splashed his face with water and slicked back his hair, as he often did, and the effect was heartening, as he'd intended it to be. He was an important man, a man of influence, a natural conciliator between board members, shareholders, bureaucrats. He placed his most eloquent hands on my shoulders, his boardroom hands.

"Let's see that mirror again."

"No, Father."

"I insist."

"Please don't."

"A father has the right to see his daughter admiring herself before she's married, don't you agree?"

"It wasn't admiration," I said.

"Then what the magazines say about you must be true. You've lost your mind."

"I've tried, but my mind refuses to let me go so easily. It's too stupidly attached, I don't know why."

"Stubborn mule."

"Old goat."

He smiled, kissed the top of my head, rubbed his chin. "I think I just got some of your hair oil on my face."

"You can use it to shave."

"Smart girl." He squeezed my shoulders. "You know," he said, abruptly turning away and beginning to pace the room, "we will miss you."

"You mean you won't be delighted when I'm gone?" I replied with forced levity.

My father stopped pacing, and looked at me with the greatest seriousness I had ever seen in him. "You will not be gone, Haruko. You will be somewhere else."

We were silent. Perhaps an entire minute passed before his pacing resumed. The void of language between us was like staring at that little mirror had been for me earlier—the time simply disappeared into it, never to be seen again. Only to be felt, never explained.

He turned away. "I had a meeting planned for this afternoon, a man I've been trying to meet for quite some time. I believe our two companies would have a lot to say to each other, given the chance. The opportunities could be extraordinary for everyone involved. It would be good for business, and for the future. A great deal of persuasion was needed to get him to agree to see me."

He sounded like a businessman, a chairman. At the window he stopped pacing and put his hand on the hem of the curtain. Slowly but without hesitation, he drew the curtain back until the room was filled with daylight and we both could see the garden, with its two weeping cherry trees—and the wooden garden wall, and above it the neighbor's house, at whose window the snub-nosed photographer from *Josei Jishin* sat poised with her camera.

"But then, you see, this morning for some reason I got to thinking. It caught me by surprise, I won't lie to you. Usually at the office I'm far too occupied to think about much other than the business at hand. But today, for some reason, none of that seemed to mean very much. The reporters were hanging about, photographers, but it wasn't that. My secretary handed me my schedule for the afternoon. I knew all about the big meeting, of course, and was well prepared."

Still facing the window, he paused. On a table at his side, in a basket woven of reeds from the rivers around Karuizawa, were three loose tennis balls, relics of the previous summer. My father picked up one of these and began to squeeze it compulsively, as one might who hoped to strengthen his hands.

"I called the fellow myself to tell him I was canceling

our meeting," he said. "It was the least I could do. It was bad enough without me hiding behind my secretary. He was angry and offended, of course, but he was polite. Well, of course he would be. I'm going to be the Crown Prince's father-in-law, and who knows how useful it might be to do business with me someday in the future. But the point is, today—the point is I simply couldn't have cared less."

"Father—"

"There's one more thing, Haruko. Perhaps I should say the only thing."

"What is it?"

"Tomorrow or the next day, you understand, things must start being different. They *will* be different."

"What do you mean?"

"Between us and you."

"Us? Who is us?"

"Your mother and me and all of your relatives."

"You mean yourself. You will be different."

"I mean all of us."

"How will you be different?"

"We will be farther away."

"Stop saying 'we.' I'd prefer it if you spoke for yourself. How far away will you be?" I could not keep the panic from my voice.

"As far as is appropriate to your station."

"My station is here, with you and Mother."

He shook his head with a violent sadness.

"I can still change my mind," I told him.

"No, Haruko. You must listen to me now. If I didn't think you could do what you must in your new life, I never would have agreed to let you go. But you are more than capable. You are rare. You will bring honor to the Imperial Family as well as your own. Never forget how much I believe in you."

AND THAT BALL in his hand as he spoke to me in my room five days before my wedding—that ball, with its white felt worn almost to uselessness, souvenir of my strange, sporting courtship with the Crown Prince?

We played catch with it in the garden a little while later. The "ball game" referred to in the magazine.

It was my father's idea. He saw the photographer sitting like an assassin in the second-floor window of our neighbor's house. Turning to me with a smile, he said, "We may as well give them something to remember us by."

13

WE WERE TO BE MARRIED on the second Friday in
April—an auspicious day, it was declared; or, at any
rate, the only day approved by the Imperial Household
Agency. My final weeks as a commoner I spent at my
Court lessons and in endless clothes fittings: clothes for
luncheons and dinners, clothes for teas and receptions,
clothes for leaving and entering—if not the world, exactly, then at least every manner of ceremonial room,
including the occasional tomb.

One afternoon at the end of March in the Imperial
Household Building, after hours of standing like a
stuffed flamingo on a small raised platform before the
imperial tailor—a devious and thick-fingered fellow, forever bowing and scraping while constantly pricking me
with pins—I suddenly felt my spirit leaving my body, my
eyes rolling up into my head, my sense of smell so pre-
posterously heightened that it seemed I could distin-
guish every individual cherry blossom in the pale-pink
garden beyond; and then I fainted. There was a cry not
my own and a rending of light, followed by blackness
and infinite repose. It didn't hurt or frighten me, and it
was all over too soon. I found myself on the floor in my

silk gown, pins expelled, cheeks flushed from mortification (and something else, some glimpse, indescribable and heart-lifting, of a pure world beyond the reach of tailors and bureaucrats), propped into a sitting position, and much attended to by various ladies-in-waiting and imperial taskmasters, whose skeptical eyes reflected a general reckoning that perhaps this young bride-to-be was not up to the historical challenge before her.

That evening, His Highness came to see me at my home. As the winter had warmed to spring, we had been allowed to see each other alone once a week, usually at Tokiwamatsu, where he then lived. (He, too, I was learning, was powerless over many of his own actions, which made me want to protect him.) Once in a long while, I found the courage to call him by his personal name, Shige, as he'd asked me to do. Our stolen visits, always faintly rushed, always proper, felt new to us both—a feeling that in turn expressed, or exposed, a certain undesirable formality in our relations from which we could not seem to escape.

Hours after I'd fainted, I was standing in the kitchen with my mother listening to her explain why as Crown Princess I must be sure to request extra amounts of daikon in my diet (something to do with iron in the blood), when from the streetside of the house there suddenly arose a commotion of shouted voices punctuated by the popping of flashbulbs, as though an electrical storm were passing over our neighborhood.

"What could those reporters be up to now?" my

mother complained, tossing the daikon she'd been wielding during her impromptu nutrition seminar into the sink, where Taka would retrieve it later. "They're coming to the door. Don't they know it's dinnertime in the homes of respectable families? This really is unacceptable!"

Her indignation was heroic but fleeting. The moment she opened the door and saw who it was, she exclaimed, "Your Highness!" and bowed deeply without the slightest hesitation.

The Crown Prince bowed in return, raising a shy questioning glance in my direction. "Please forgive me for disturbing you at home without proper warning, Endo-san," he said, greeting my mother. "I was most concerned about your daughter's health and wanted to check on her myself."

"How very considerate of Your Highness. Haruko is much better, thank you."

"Yes, Your Highness," I added, bowing myself. "I'm fine, as you can see. My mother and I were just having an animated discussion about daikon."

"Haruko!" hissed my mother under her breath.

The Crown Prince looked amused. "Daikon?"

"Its medicinal properties."

An expression of polite confusion overtook his handsome face. "Ah, well, yes of course, I've heard that it can be . . . hmm . . . well, quite medicinal."

It was so silly, I laughed out loud. My mother stared at me in horror—but then the Crown Prince burst out laughing, too, a lovely exhalation of freedom, and a kind of order was restored among us.

"Won't you please come in, Your Highness?" my mother said. "We would be honored."

"Thank you. If you are certain I am not disturbing . . . ?"

"You could not disturb us, Your Highness, if you were to arrive in the middle of the night with a retinue of forty men."

"No fear of that." I noticed that he'd begun to blush. "I go to bed on the early side, and prefer to travel lightly."

He entered the house, followed by one of his chamberlains and a manservant. The chamberlain's name was Mado and, as his head of sparse gray hair suggested, he'd been with the Crown Prince in various capacities since His Highness was a boy. The manservant was Igawa; he was dressed in impeccable livery, and he, too, had been with the Crown Prince for many years, though he was tall and strong and still youthful-looking, perhaps doubling as a bodyguard. There must have been another man or two on the street running "crowd control," for the din among photographers and gossip reporters stirred up by the unexpected imperial arrival had died down to the normal veiled murmurings of residential Shibuya: a barking dog, a pestering crow, a man with a cart selling for dinner the remnants of what earlier had almost certainly been the makings of breakfast.

Inside, the Crown Prince slipped off his handmade

English shoes and stood looking at our well-appointed but otherwise ordinary house. I watched his features alight with that expression of general interest familiar from countless published photographs of him on scripted visits to the houses of his subjects: Yes, his face naturally declared, he understood and cared. But now, directly behind that pleasantly engaging, if superficial, mask, there appeared a more pointed curiosity, verging almost on the rude, led by impolitic eyes that hungrily ferreted out whatever tiny details of my past might be claimed in a few seconds.

Finally, his flickering eyes moved to me, and grew still. "I hope you didn't injure yourself during your fall?"

"I fainted, as you probably heard," I replied, careful to hide my expression, not wanting him to know he'd been discovered. "It was like being asleep and falling stupidly out of bed. I landed softly, and have no memory of how I got there. The flowers smelled very sweet. I apologize for being ridiculous."

"You are many things, but you could never be ridiculous. I'm afraid you are exhausted."

"Perhaps I'm a bit tired. But then, I remind myself, I am not alone in this."

"No, you are not alone." His gaze had turned intimate and knowing—a doctor administering to a favored patient. I felt at that moment extraordinarily safe. "It's my greatest hope that you will tell me if there's anything I might provide to make you more comfortable," he went on. "Anything at all."

My mother stepped forward. "You have already been more than generous with Haruko, Your Highness."

"Forgive me for disagreeing, Endo-san, but what little I have done for your daughter these past months has been merely selfish: I want her to share my life with me, because it is what I have to offer. Her gift, far outstripping mine, has been to accept."

My mother inclined her head. "She is certainly most grateful."

"No more grateful than I, I assure you."

"There *is* one thing I can think of," I broke in rashly.

"Of course," he said, smiling. "Please tell me."

I chose to ignore my mother's hooded glare of warning. "About that horrible tailor, the one with the sharp pins . . ."

His face fell—a leaf disturbed by a sudden breeze. "Ah yes, I see what you mean. For that, I'm afraid, I will have to speak with my mother."

THE HISTORIC DAY WAS FAST APPROACHING, a mountain rising out of the sea. I stood on the shore, watching in permanent disbelief, knowing that soon I would be living on the far side of the mountain.

More than a thousand guests had been invited to witness the ceremony in the Kashikodokoro within the palace grounds: members of the Court, the government, the Academy of Arts and Sciences. My family would be present, straining along with the rest in the inner courtyard to achieve anything more than a fractured glimpse of the arcane ritual taking place within the shrine nearby. It was not then fully clear to me that no such glimpse would be possible, on that day or ever. Many centuries earlier, an appropriate separation between worlds had been prescribed (by whom, I could not say), a degree of mandatory concealment, and despite the new constitution and the Emperor's official demotion to human status, that ancient distance could not now be either bridged or ignored. To be invited to sit within the Kashikodokoro and "witness" the wedding of the Crown Prince, then, was to be reminded of what could not be seen by the mortal eye.

The only non-Japanese invited to the ceremony was the Crown Prince's former tutor, Mrs. Pine, the tall and honorable Quaker from Philadelphia. For four years of his isolated childhood, she had been a constant in his life, a wise and feminine counsel, a teacher of English, and, above all, as befitted her religion, a pacifist. The values had lingered, and the connection. And so it was that, three days prior to our wedding, His Highness arranged a luncheon at which Mrs. Pine and I could meet.

By this late date the entire country was in a state of intense, barely contained excitement, like a pearl diver with breath held to bursting, swimming up, up, treasures clenched in both fists, toward a shimmering sun hovering high above the water's filmy top. In a few short days the surface would be ceremoniously breached, the old air expelled in a gasp of reverent national exultation, the lungs refilled with fresh oxygen so that the people, all together, might once again dive into deep unknown waters, secure in the belief that the past was continuous and the future miraculously intact. Mrs. Pine, though a foreigner, had already played a role in this ongoing myth through her relationship with the Crown Prince, and her return to Japan for her old pupil's wedding had been widely reported in the newspapers. She was said to be modest, articulate, and self-possessed, as traditional (or, in the American parlance, "old-fashioned") in her way as many Japanese were in theirs; and, as I have already mentioned, she was impressively tall. I could well imagine her towering over me like the Statue of Liberty. As the day of the luncheon approached, my breath grew increasingly short, my anxiety reaching a pitch that, I both hoped and feared, only the neighborhood dogs would be able to hear. Their imagined howling already haunted my dreams.

The hosts of the luncheon were Dr. Watanabe and his wife, old friends of Mrs. Pine's. Unfortunately, His Highness could not be present; at that very hour he was at Tokiwamatsu, awaiting the arrival of his mother. It was the day when my trousseau was to be delivered from my parents' home to my husband's: three trucks of maquillage tables and garment boxes, dresses and kimonos folded in rice paper and packed into wooden trunks, to be joined on the other end by the dozens, perhaps hundreds, of purchases already made by me or on my behalf in Tokyo's most exquisite shops and delivered directly to my new address. There, under the Empress's sharp and knowing eye—aided by Her Majesty's men in contrasting uniforms special to the occasion, her chief lady-in-waiting, and her Mistress of the Robes—my belongings would be inspected and put away in their appropriate places. (After the wedding, my own ladies-in-waiting—all chosen for me, I had been told, with particular attention by Her Majesty—would, if I was interested, show me the whereabouts of my things in my husband's house.) At this ritual I was by custom not welcome, just as the Crown Prince's attendance could not be excused. Indeed, Dr. Watanabe had made a point of mentioning to me Her Majesty's excitement at the prospect of spending several hours alone with her son in his own house before his marriage—an occurrence of informal familial visitation, I was to understand, of singular rarity in the history of the Imperial Family.

"I hope you won't mind," the Crown Prince had said during our previous visit together (the last before our wedding), a week earlier.

"Why should I mind Her Majesty taking a personal interest in her son's life?" I replied mildly. "It's the way things are."

"Yes."

"And always have been, I suppose?"

"Yes, I suppose . . . Though, to speak honestly, I'm not certain."

"You mean this is a new tradition?"

"Not new . . . But perhaps, hmm, not ancient."

"From Emperor Meiji's time, you mean?"

"Yes, I suppose . . ."

I was silent.

"Well, as long as you don't mind," he'd said with poorly disguised relief.

"Why should I mind?"

And so that conversation had ended, one of the least satisfying of our relationship thus far.

Such recollections were unpleasantly with me in the back seat of the car that took me to lunch with Mrs. Pine that Tuesday in early April. As the driver turned into the little lane framed by high walls that led to the Watanabe house, we were met by a crowd of old ladies and young children who had gathered to wave to me as we passed. Also in clamoring attendance was a phalanx of photographers, following me like my own unblinking conscience. They were always there—or, to put it another way, as if describing one's shadow, they were never *not* there, except in darkness. And like one's shadow, but unlike one's conscience, they lacked that third dimension of the naturally living, the compassionate, and the brave.

I had dressed that day in a pale-pink kimono sparingly highlighted with gold threads and braced with a rose-colored obi. Mrs. Pine, waiting with the Watanabes on their doorstep, dressed in a gray wool skirt and jacket ensemble, stepped briskly forward and took my hand as I emerged from the car, saying in perfectly enunciated English, "Miss Endo, you look a perfect cherry blossom."

It was a lovely human gesture. Dr. Watanabe, left behind on his doorstep with a bemused smile on his face, appeared rather stunned by this spontaneous display of warmth, no less than I. I smiled at her; she wasn't as tall as I'd feared. "A cherry blossom's beauty is so brief," I murmured.

"Yes, Miss Endo, but immortal. As the poets so often remind us."

After such a greeting, formal introductions would have been redundant. And yet for the next few minutes Mrs. Pine and I stood slowly shaking hands, like Bunraku puppets or merely people who weren't very smart, for the sake of the photographers, as they kept shouting for us to greet each other again, American style, and again and again.

AT THE END OF LUNCH, my driver appeared at the door, and I rose to take my leave. Once again Mrs. Pine and I shook hands, though this time no camera was there to capture us.

As I was getting into the car, she appeared by herself on the doorstep and motioned for me to wait. "I will be seeing His Highness this evening," she told me.

There was to be a reunion of his old Peers School class at the Akasaka Prince Hotel, and Mrs. Pine, as a former teacher, had been especially invited.

"I'm aware that you have not been able to see each other very often of late," she continued. "And I merely thought I would mention how much pleasure it would give me to carry a message to His Highness from you, if you were so inclined."

I could feel myself begin to color.

"Excuse me," she said. "I might be a Quaker, but my

friends tell me that I can be rather forward when stirred up."

"And you are 'stirred up' now?"

"Oh, yes."

She smiled, and then I did. "In that case, I think I have a message."

"Very good."

"Tell His Highness, please . . . Tell him that I don't mind."

"You don't mind?"

"That is right. I don't mind."

Smiling, she reached for my hand again and shook it. "Very well, he shall be told. Miss Endo, you are a lovely mystery, and you will make a beautiful princess."

14

THREE DAYS LATER, I woke to the rustle of my mother's sleeping robe as she knelt in the darkness beside my bed.

"Haruko, it's time."

"Is it still raining?" Those were my first words on that momentous morning. For two days it had been pouring; during the night, I had dreamed of swollen rivers and floods.

"Your father assures me that it will stop soon. Now come, we must begin getting you ready."

"What time is it?"

"Half past three."

She started to turn away, but impulsively I reached for her hand and pulled her back. "Mother, I'm frightened."

"Of course you are. It's natural to be nervous on your wedding day."

"I'm not nervous. I'm frightened."

"Then you must be brave."

"I am not brave," I pleaded. "You know I'm not."

Beside me, she stiffened. "I won't listen to any more of this. You're my daughter—courage isn't a choice for you. Consider it an unreturnable gift from your ancestors. You might think you don't want it now, but when you're my age you'll be thankful. If you were a coward and weak, do you think your father and I would let you go?"

She went out, and I lay in bed remembering a day at kindergarten when I'd wanted her desperately to stay with me and how, one by one, she had peeled my fingers from her arm and left me in that strange and frightening place to fend for myself. It seemed as if no time at all had passed since then.

I was standing looking into my cabinet of dog figurines when she returned. The recent gift from the Emperor and Empress was on the topmost shelf, resplendent on its ebony stand.

"Your bath is ready." There were blotches on my mother's cheeks and forehead; I could see that in her absence she'd been crying.

"Thank you."

We stood in each other's gaze longer then, I believe, than at any time in our lives. There was a quivering in the shadow-filled room, in the air all around us, and I turned to check on my friends in the glass cabinet, thinking that perhaps there had been a tremor. But all was still. The tremor had been in my imagination, that deep underground cavern where hope and feeling need not live in fear of each other. Briefly, it seemed, and with what heartrending surprise, I had encountered my mother there, and we had spoken to each other in the only language that we truly shared.

FINALLY AT SIX O'CLOCK, the rain stopped falling. A cool morning sun broke through the gray roof of clouds as through a window, and a light breeze arrived to keep us mindful of the invisible spirits.

A car navigated its way through the crowds and television cameras gathered on our street, and soon our house was filled with my new ladies-in-waiting and many others from the Court whom I hardly recognized. The entrance hall grew crowded with strangers, and harsh voices called out orders and questions about things that had never mattered to our family in the past. My home had been taken from me before I had been allowed to part from it.

I saw my father, dressed in a morning suit, walking through his own house like hired help. His true feelings were cruelly revealed by his posture—as though he were fastened to a pillar of wood—and the small, rather aimless steps he kept making, turning himself in half circles of evasion, as members of the Court attempted to engage him in conversation. Despite his best efforts, he could not restrain his eyes from darting in my direction, his brows raised in questions that he did not seem conscious of asking.

Since our talk in my bedroom, he had been true to his word. Virtually overnight, I had been forcibly elevated by my parents to the position of most important person in the family. It was well meant, a grave and generous sacrifice, exquisite in its way. But it was crushing to be reminded at every moment, by the two people I loved most, of the title I would now wear. At every turn, sometimes subtly and sometimes crudely, the same lesson was driven home: the world would greet me with abject deference not because I deserved or wished it but because of my station, which in all things would stand above me, and indeed would outlast me.

Those were not my parents' words. Their words were kind, their eyes loving, if fearful. But we were running out of words, and soon no one would look at me.

It was a quarter past six. There came a moment when several people were talking at once and no one was paying attention, and I took the opportunity to slip away to my mother's room.

She was alone in front of her dressing mirror, attending to the sleeves of her dark kimono. Makeup had covered all signs of permanent regret. With a somber reflected smile, she reached out a hand and guided me in front of her. I stood looking at myself in my new French clothes—pale, full-skirted dress, mink stole, small white hat—in my mother's mirror, and felt the cold tongue of despair begin licking at the back of my neck. I shivered.

"Are you chilled?" my mother asked me, with such tender solicitousness that tears, or perhaps merely the childish longing for them, pushed against my eyes before receding.

So much I might have said to her then! But life is not an echo, endlessly returning the past to us so that we might read and reread in its fading variations the meanings we cannot keep ourselves from wanting.

At that moment Mrs. Oshima, my chief lady-in-waiting, entered the room carrying a gold pocket watch that, it was widely known, had once belonged to her father, the late Count Oshima.

"Are we progressing?" she asked. She peered at the watch as though it were her own feudal history of daimyos and shoguns she were proclaiming, rather than the most banal of questions.

"We have progressed," replied my mother coolly, adding the merest suggestion of a bow. Then she turned her back on my chief lady-in-waiting, drawing an invisible cloak around the two of us, and stood close to me again, her eyes holding mine in the mirror.

"My daughter, you are beautiful."

"The time has come," Mrs. Oshima insisted.

Regally, my mother turned from the mirror. It seemed to me that I could hear Count Oshima's watch ticking like a weapon. We returned to the front of the house and joined the others.

It was twenty-eight minutes past the hour. His Highness would be watching the television at his house, waiting, like the rest of the country, to witness my departure.

Much later, of course, I was struck by possibilities that I was too confused to conceive of at the time. I might have found some way to step secretly out of the house that morning and hold up private handwritten messages to the television cameras, messages meant for my fiancé's understanding alone:

If you find that you don't like the way I look today, please con-
sider that Oshima-san informed me of Her Majesty's particular
desire that I wear these clothes. Oshima-san, as you must know,
has served your mother loyally for almost forty years, and one
can be quite certain that when she speaks she has your mother's
interests well in mind.

Where are you? In your house, I know, watching me; but
that is not what I mean.

Who are these people who have come to claim me on your
behalf, I wonder, who now stand behind me in what was once
my home?

I can no longer feel the false smile where it sits on my face.

Can you protect me?

"Haruko-sama," Mrs. Oshima announced. "We are
ready. Let us arrange ourselves and proceed outside."

I was in the entrance hall, surrounded by people. I
thought to respond, but no sound came from my mouth.

"Haruko-sama," Mrs. Oshima repeated.

"She is here, and perfectly ready," answered my father.
He was right behind me. I had not known he was there.
His voice was steady, and I felt his strong, comforting
hand on my back. "Haruko, I am here behind you," he
whispered in my ear.

"Then I am ready, Father."

The door was opened. By arrangement my parents
went out first, then I followed. The soft breeze caressed
my face; I felt the tentative rays of the morning sun. Above

the garden wall I could see television and photographic cameras perched like mechanical heads on pikes, and the clicking of shutters sounded as though we were being attacked by a multitude of pigeons. But the air was clear, the weather sublime. I took a few more steps, and noticed tiny new green leaves on the trees.

I have never known a goodbye that was as it should be. In my dreams, the rivers are swollen and the animals swept away on their backs; or the sun shines high and brightly, my hair whips in the breeze, and in the intimacy of our unspoken losses my parents and I wave to each other across a fortified moat, as though the separation that threatens us were but for an hour, a day—come tomorrow, at the very latest, we would be a family again, as we once were.

15

I BOWED TO MY PARENTS, and left them.

In the first of two large automobiles, deep maroon with the imperial crest, I was driven down the narrow street on which I had lived for most of my life. Through the faintly darkened windows I waved to the people gathered along the way, here and there recognizing faces that seemed to have aged a dozen years since I had last seen them. Reaching the main avenue, we turned in the direction of the palace, our police escort pulling along-side to form a caravan. I held on tightly to the door handle to keep myself from trembling.

Mrs. Oshima, seated on the jump seat with drawn-together knees, regarded me with thin-lipped suspicion. It was an expression that in time I would come to know better.

"You must bear yourself with greater control," she said.

"Of course, you are right, Oshima-san. I will try harder."

"And before the cameras you must not allow your head to droop in that coarse manner."

"Forgive me, I was not aware."

"Evidently not. In the newspapers tomorrow, the photographs will prove what I am saying to you."

"I have no doubt."

"Her Majesty will share my opinion."

I stared out the window at my neighborhood reeling into the past, twinned feelings of helplessness and terror patrolling my shoulders like two sharp-beaked crows. They knew me by sight and could attack at will; there could be no outrunning them. It seemed incredible to me, I will not deny it: that the roads on which I had innocently walked as a child, however incidental, had somehow led me to this morning, gliding through the streets of my home city toward a country at once closer and more unknown than any I had yet encountered, on a journey that, if I were not to fail utterly, must be for life.

At that early hour, with few people about, the streets appeared like mouths waiting to break into smiles. Wherever I looked, I saw flags and paper cherry blossoms adorning doorways, lampposts, subway signs, parked cars, bicycles. From shop windows everywhere blown-up, beribboned photographs of His Highness and me in formal attire or tennis clothes stared out, unblinking. Only after the car, with its smoothly oiled machinery, had carried me by did I recognize in those framed and cropped images two people of my intimate knowledge.

All the while, owl-like, Mrs. Oshima was hunting me from her perch on the jump seat, the raised and demonstrative angle of her chin declaring her condemnation of my performance in those ubiquitous photographs, as well as her personal indignation. How wrong it was, how un-natural, that a mere commoner should be thus raised above her in the hierarchy! My comportment would not do, it would not do at all. One click of her steel shutter, one stamp of her family's noble seal, would capture me for all posterity. I would be exposed.

There was nothing to do then but set my own chin, re-lease the door handle from its death grip, and turn away from my keeper. The frozen smile on my face not for her but for the unseen television cameras set up along our route. If His Highness, watching at home, happened to catch sight of me in the back of the car, I would give him no cause for worry.

Closer to our destination, one began to see more peo-ple in the streets. Later, during the imperial procession following the marriage ceremony, there would be many occasions for commerce, and those who hoped to profit were stirring now, already establishing their carts and wares for the crowds to come: taxicab drivers, pedicab pullers, women tying bunches of flowers and sticks of in-cense, a man in a pointed bamboo hat pushing wooden skewers through squid. With my motorcade some dis-tance away, they would still be going about their prepara-tions with habitual skill, memories alive in the rote muscular actions of hands and feet. And I envied them, I confess—their mornings of labor and industry, difficult as they no doubt were, yet continual and routine, days with-out end.

And then, over Mrs. Oshima's shoulder, one by one

through the windshield, I watched awareness of my approach dawn like the sun on these good citizens: the police, my motorcade, the imperial crest. I watched heads turn and hands fall useless. In the air, that dense stillness which swallows sound. And, as my car came abreast of them, I watched my future subjects drop to their knees on the pavement as though struck down in battle. Their reverent backs my final glimpse of the jumbled, striving, visceral world with which, I suddenly understood, I had never been well enough acquainted.

I looked away. Mrs. Oshima did not pass up the opportunity of catching my eye. "When we arrive, you understand, there will be no time for sightseeing," she informed me.

Along the wide curving moat surrounding the palace, rows of cherry trees announced the end of their seasonal beauty. Some of the trees were weeping: blossoms in white and palest pink, ponderous with decrepitude, eddying on the brown water, stirred by the paddling of ducks. Beyond the moat were the massive walls of gray stone, the tiled rooftops of guard towers. At the Double Bridge, our motorcade slowed to a halt. We were waved across to enter the palace grounds. There, too, blossoms littered the edges of paths and lay windswept where they'd fallen.

The House of Bamboo had been built for the Crown Prince's two sisters, though only Princess Midori, the younger and unmarried sister, still lived there. I had met her several times during the winter—slim and pretty, with an oval face and small aristocratic hands, fond of orchids and cormorant fishing and the movies of Doris Day. I did not see her that morning, or anyone else from her family. My ladies-in-waiting met me at the entrance to the house and immediately herded me upstairs to a private chamber. The spacious, elegantly furnished room in which I was to be purified and dressed in the twelve-layer costume was cool and faintly damp from the night. A chill was in the air as the women began to undress me.

Tiny bumps rose on my naked arms and breasts, and my nipples, to my mortification, grew prominent. I remembered being with Miko and her family in Hakone one winter holiday before the war. In a bath house beset with frigid drafts, we'd pointed in giggling disgust at her mother's dark, furiously erect nipples—edamame, we'd called them, never imagining that one day we might involuntarily produce our own. And now that my own time had come, physically exposed like this, my mind couldn't quite grasp the horror. I was stripped naked, my arms positioned like a mannequin. During the anxious months of preparations for the wedding, I had lost too much weight, and was only too aware now of the jutting planes of my hips and pelvis, the earthly disappointments of my corporeal self.

I stood gazing into the stone basin of purification water, trying not to weep.

"Respectfully, Haruko-sama, we must begin," Mrs. Oshima said.

I looked up at her, her face a mask of imperial propriety. And so, at least, the situation between us was clear

enough: in her public language to me she would be duti-
ful and correct, while in private she would speak more
critically for the Empress and their kind.

I reached for the stone dipper. I scooped the warm water over my body, felt it splash and soothe my chilled skin.
The warm clean water ran down my legs to the floor. For
generations, empresses and princesses had purified themselves in this manner; briefly closing my eyes, I received
the sanctity of their collective awareness. A sense not so
much of welcome or sisterhood—never had I felt more
alone—but of an intricate web of ancient history, invisible
to the outside world yet unbreakable, to which the thread
of my destiny was about to be irrevocably joined.

OVER THE WHITE PADDED SILK KIMONO, a magenta skirt,
then the *nagabakama,* pleated and divided, falling to the
floor. Then, in succession, five unlined silk robes, their
gaping, elaborately bordered sleeves each shorter than the
one preceding. Next, a long kimono of exquisitely embroidered crimson silk, followed by a kimono jacket, hip
length, of embroidered violet silk. Finally, the train, a pale
sea-green, laced with intricate patterns.

Before Lady Nijō, before even the time of Genji, this
was how women of the Court had dressed in ceremony. I
would be no different. Like theirs, my hair was molded
with a viscous pomade into a wide heart-shaped frame,
a black winged halo for my whitened face. Pressing
painfully on my forehead was a three-pronged golden or-

nament. At my breast, half hidden among the deep folds of silk, I held a bouquet of special handmade paper.

This was not my first time. There had been rehearsals for both hair and clothes. Such aspects of tradition could not be left to chance or to my own ineptitude. Awkward as a foal's, my feet had been trained over weeks to master the necessary childlike steps under the silken tent of robes: forward and backward, forward and backward. A harsh discipline, with its pain and punishments, its small terrors in the dark. One would be able to travel no great distance under such restrictive conditions. I was to discover, though, that one could yet go far enough to disappear.

16

INTO THE SILENCE of more than a thousand witnesses—
of costumed Court musicians holding instruments mute
in their hands; of verbose politicians and scheming bureaucrats; of television cameras attempting to see what
could not be seen and radio microphones to hear what
could not be heard; of centuries upon centuries of ritual
contained like a single poem in a day—His Highness and
I, led by separate priests, entered the Kashikodokoro.

He went first, as always he must, preceded by the
Chief Ritualist in his long white robe. Like the priests,
His Highness wore a cap and a headdress of black lacquered silk. He held a scepter of polished wood in his
right hand, representing his authority over our worldly
domain. His robes, as ancient as mine and nearly as
elaborate, were the deep burnt orange of Amaterasu
Omikami's first rising over the earth. Walking a few
paces behind him was Mado, his grand chamberlain,
in violet trousers and a robe of deepest black, carrying
the long white train that extended from His Highness's
waist. Following was a second chamberlain bearing His
Highness's sword, for a thousand years passed from one
Crown Prince to the next at the time of investiture.

The silence was not complete. Fine-grained white pebbles covered the floor of the courtyard, and our feet crunched softly. Sparrows trilled high notes in the pine trees overhanging the walls, and from farther off, beyond the hallowed enclosure, one heard the muffled snap of firecrackers and the low lumbering of a jet plane flying over Tokyo.

I held my gaze straight ahead, as I had been instructed to do. My clothes weighed fifteen kilos, my hair perhaps three. My feet, groping along beneath the silken shroud of the *nagabakama,* were as tentative as the hands of the blind.

I was to see none of the twenty members of my family who were in attendance. But I felt them with gratitude, their looks of wonder and compassion, the silent wringing of their hands, their suppressed exhalations, like the last warming rays of the sun before it sets. *Haruko, I am right behind you.* They kept my blood from freezing when the temperature was coldest.

At the same time, forty-six members of the Imperial Family sat observing the procession. All but the Emperor and Empress, who, just as they had acquiesced in allowing their son to be reared apart from them, were by tradition not present at his wedding. They would be in their residence watching on television, limited by camera placement and screen size to the same inconclusive pictures as their subjects, to say nothing of the citizens and other monarchs who would be watching in countries all over the world.

Nonetheless, shuffling along the perimeter of the courtyard, glancing neither right nor left, I could not help feeling the cool discrimination of Their Majesties' gazes on my shoulders, and imagine what it was that they were seeing.

Here, first, came their own kind, a true prince, chosen by destiny and blood, the mantle firmly carried on his shoulders, the crest centered on his back.

And here, then, came another, fundamentally not of their kind: tottering like a lamb just given life, chest heaving like a newly caged bird's, the splendor of her borrowed robes and appropriated symbols finally too misplaced to be overlooked.

Did she not know better? Had she no respect?

The Chief Ritualist had reached the entrance to the sacred shrine. Bowing deeply, his white robe pooling around his feet, he went inside. Then His Highness did the same. After he was gone, I found myself searching for his footprints in the fine white gravel. I was moving ever so slowly, following the second priest, Mrs. Oshima and another lady-in-waiting bent at the waist and scuttling along beside me with uncanny discretion, pulling and straightening the excess material so that I would not trip and fall. And, though I knew little as yet of imperial silkworms or their habits of existence, the shuffling of my feet within the voluminous tide of cloth sounded to my ears like a haunting amplification of their mysterious spinning in the softly glowing darkness in which they passed their lives. As though, in making this honored pilgrimage, I had already been reduced, becoming no more substantial than a silken thread spun by unknown hands and soon to be woven into a pattern in some larger tapestry not of my conception.

My feet, impervious to such premonitions, kept moving; before I was ready I found myself standing at the entrance to the shrine. On either side were smaller, subsidiary shrines for the many gods of heaven and earth and the souls of all emperors and empresses. But this most sacred place, containing a replica of the Divine Mirror kept at Ise, was reserved for veneration of the Sun Goddess alone. The mirror is believed to be the agent of Amaterasu's spirit, and in its concentrated light one cannot but be struck by the miracle of imperial creation and the abiding life force of our people. And indeed it was so, or nearly.

The wood of the shrine was unpainted, smelling of forest. I thought of mountains in the early morning in the north. I thought of my great-grandmother's village, and the morning that my mother and I had spent pounding rice to make omochi for the New Year's feast. My great-grandmother had been dead eight years, and I had not returned to her village since. And now, I thought, if ever I am to return, it will not be as myself but as some other.

A low warning hiss, like a tire puncture, pulled me out of my reverie. I glanced toward my feet, from which the sound seemed to be emanating, and was brought up short by the piercing stare of Mrs. Oshima.

I bowed deeply to the shrine, and went inside.

WE STOOD FACING A WHITE BROCADE CURTAIN. Beyond the curtain lay the most sacred space, entered by none but the Emperor, the Empress, the Crown Prince, and the Crown Princess, and then only on one's knees. Here, at the point of worldly separation, our attendants laid down the folds of our garments, which they'd been carrying, and stepped away. The shrine was quiet enough for us to catch from the outer courtyard the sound of more than a thousand people rising wordlessly from their seats in unison, like birds rising from a dusky plain. The shrine was quiet enough for us to hear the thin curtain being raised at its center. Through this sacred doorway the Crown Prince, holding the wooden scepter, entered the inner enclosure on his knees. One could hear the slow, difficult passage of his raiments as he moved across the floor, and then the cessation as he reached the square mat with the brocaded border resembling the thrones used by the ancient emperors; and there he knelt in utter stillness, his back to the earthly world.

Half a minute later, holding the crimson Court fan carried by the Empress at her wedding and enthronement, I followed. The fan felt unbearably heavy. The floor hurt my knees. In short, my journey seemed interminable. The brief distance was a desert, and it was the sky. But I could travel only like this, on my knees, so slowly and awkwardly, so much like a bewildered lost child, as to experience with indelible recognition every last centimeter of my journey.

Finally, I reached the Crown Prince's side. He did not look at me, and I did not look at him. Our robes gave off the poignant smell of the past, innumerable silk-filled palaces lost to fire and ruin. Our faces, beneath their coats of creams and oils, felt inhuman. Before us a bamboo curtain was raised, revealing the altar. The Chief Ritualist handed to each of us a cut branch of *sakaki,* the sacred tree, adorned with red and white ribbons. Four times we bowed low together, then returned the branches, which were offered at the altar. And then His Highness removed a scroll from his belt and declaimed our marriage pledge. He asked for Amaterasu's divine blessing. His voice was clear and strong, loud enough to be heard by the hundreds gathered under pagoda roofs in the courtyard. They would be standing again, unable to see us, yet bowing in our direction.

On our feet this time, we returned to the outer sanctuary and, with a few sips of sake from a bowl of white unglazed pottery, I became Her Imperial Highness, Crown Princess Haruko of Japan. My husband and I announced our marriage to the imperial ancestors with all due solemnity.

It was then that I heard the crows. Two or three of them, perched on the roof of the shrine, haranguing the esteemed captive audience, their black laughter at the foolishness of men drowning out with equal irreverence the noble gods and the poor cowardly sparrows who would not leave the shelter of the pine trees. Flagrant spirits and malcontents, the crows had no respect. Or perhaps they were merely wise. My husband did not appear to notice them, though I was not so blessed. Long after I have forgotten the exact words of my marriage pledge, I continue to hear their mocking cries.

BACK IN THE HOUSE OF BAMBOO, the wedding costume was removed layer by layer, the golden ornament lifted from my head and my hair scoured with odious-smelling benzene and redone in my usual modern style. An evening dress was slipped over my limbs and fastened in the back, and the decoration of the First Order of the Sacred Crown, inlaid with pearls, was pinned over my breast. The tiara placed upon my head was reportedly set with a thousand diamonds.

All this took time. I missed the opportunity to eat a small sandwich with my husband, already dressed in formal white tie and decorated with the Grand Cordon of the Chrysanthemum. I missed the opportunity to exchange with him words and smiles of a private nature. We had announced our wedding to the imperial ancestors but not as yet, unofficially, to ourselves.

WITH SLOW AND STATELY GAIT, unsmiling, Their Majesties entered the West Room of the Imperial Household Building and were seated in front of two baize-covered tables on a dais. Behind them were the same golden screens I remembered from our first meeting in that building five months earlier, radiating the same burnished light, and among the retinue of attending chamberlains, ladies-in-waiting, house servants, and footmen, I remarked a few half-familiar faces. I made no sign to anyone. In the palace, I was learning, recognition was not necessarily a gift, and often best kept to oneself.

At a signal from the master of ceremonies, my husband and I approached the dais and together made a bow of respect. He reported to his parents that our marriage pledge had been affirmed before the Sun Goddess and, in words of formal reverence, humbly thanked them for their guidance and wisdom throughout his life. The Emperor, his dark eyes blinking rapidly behind his spectacles, expressed his congratulations and sincere hopes for our happiness. And then my husband addressed himself to his mother—I cannot remember his words to her—and she offered him her blessing. She was looking at him, and speaking to him, and that is how it was. I watched his noble straight back and his hands of resolute calm as he exchanged the Cups of Parent and Child, filled with sake, with Their Majesties, and once again it did not escape me that my husband had been born to be exactly as he was.

Then it was my turn. I did as he had done, with my back perhaps not as straight and my hands rather less than resolute, though still managing, I hoped, a successful imitation.

"Let us step onto the balcony to acknowledge our guests," the Emperor said. Already, as though in preparation for the encounter, his smile had begun its habitual slide into vagueness.

"One must not be late," the Empress warned.

A chamberlain with a gold pocket watch stepped forward. "Five minutes still remain, Your Majesty."

At two o'clock, the Crown Prince and I were to be driven in an open-air imperial coach in a procession through the streets of the city to Tokiwamatsu, two and a half kilometers away.

"Very well, then. Five minutes."

Curtains were parted, glass doors opened. The sound of excited voices, sun-warmed and sweet, entered my consciousness like a letter sent by an old friend. In this case, the friend was many people and could not—indeed, never would—be isolated and embraced. I turned and looked at my husband. He, too, had felt the stirring of sentiment and was smiling back at me, his eyes naked in their joy. And I was reminded again of his particular expressions of feeling during the autumn of our telephone courtship:

What I am famous for is not what I am.

To truly understand what I mean, you must come closer.

I might have touched him. Instead, I merely smiled. The doors were open, and first the Emperor and Empress, and then the Crown Prince and I, stepped onto the balcony. From the height of the trees we peered down like zoo-kept birds at the privileged guests who'd been invited to see us off on our procession. I waved to my parents, uncles, aunts, cousins. I saw the prime minister, the director of the post office, a celebrated surgeon. I saw Mrs. Pine standing with Dr. and Mrs. Watanabe, all looking extraordinarily pleased. I heard murmurings of approval over my dress and the diamond tiara, which did not belong to me.

I felt my husband's touch as he raised my hand in an impulsive tribute. From below came bows of homage and smatterings of applause.

Then a man I didn't recognize, his face red with exultation or perhaps too much sake, called out "Haruko-sama!" and bent himself sharply at the waist, apparently prepared to hold that humbled position all day. Another took up the man's cry, and another.

"Haruko-sama!"

"Haruko-sama!"

The Empress's smile, I noticed, grew fixed.

"Haruko-sama!" cried another voice.

"What is that fellow going on about?" the Emperor complained under his breath, still waving and smiling to his public, his expression by now as vague and muddied as a roadside puddle. "I can't understand any of these people. The young speak so poorly these days."

"They are enthusiastic," the Crown Prince replied.

"It is the fate of mere novelty that at some future date it ceases to be new," remarked the Empress in a low voice, finishing this cryptically oracular observation—while continuing to wave and smile at her subjects—with a cool sideways glance at my tiara, as though it were too large for my head. "In any case," she concluded, "I believe the carriage is waiting."

At this, His Majesty brightened. "Yes, yes, one must not be late," he said, giving one last wave and ducking back inside.

We followed.

The old does not accept the new. Not, at least, the new that never was old. Among my ancestors I could count three samurai of distinction, two renowned scholars of Emperor Meiji's day, a famous mathematician, and a handful of notable civil servants, to say nothing of my grandfather and the business he began. But old my family would never be.

We were led downstairs through long rooms and corridors. No one spoke a word. But for our clothes, we might have been on our way to an execution. Amid the echoing of our footsteps, my stomach began to churn with nerves and my heart to clamor. Never since have I had to wonder what the musician approaching the concert stage or the athlete walking through the dark tunnel into the light of an Olympic stadium endures on her short but solitary journey to the challenge of her life.

The throng of invited guests, transported to the driveway, hailed us as we came down the steps. Once again my name was called out in loud and repetitive celebration, compelling me to wave and smile in acknowledgment. Once again the Empress appeared unhappy at the degree of adulation I was receiving, as though she suspected me of being its source as well as its object. I did not know how I might correct such a mistaken impression, nor was there a moment when I might have consulted my husband about my behavior. We were marching relentlessly forward. Waiting for us was a handsome carriage, foreign and anachronistic, deep maroon with golden seals of chrysanthemums painted on the sides. Crystal lanterns raised on brackets floated above the front wheels, and two elaborately costumed footmen, heads covered in gold-braided, cocked hats like nineteenth-century British admirals, stood at attention on a platform at the rear. At the front of this grand formation, policemen and imperial guards sat astride magnificently groomed horses, with two more carriages filled with chamberlains, ladies-in-waiting, court officials, the imperial physician, and still more imperial guards prepared to follow. It was a remarkable sight.

I was handed up into the carriage to sit beside my husband. It was not an especially elevated position, and yet it was like looking down on the world from a cloud. From such a remove, I had no difficulty locating my father at the back of the crowd of well-wishers. He was holding a camera in front of his face, his fingers twisting the focus ring back and forth without apparent success. The lens was pointed at me. I was aware that it was a new camera, a Nikon, because I had seen him with it the other evening at home, in the hours after dinner, deeply immersed in the instruction manual, a look of grateful concentration on his face. I was waiting for him to take the photograph. But somehow I understood that he would not be able to press the shutter.

A sign of the hand then, a clipped military order, the clopping of perfectly shod hoofs on stone, and our imperial procession began to move.

17

BETWEEN CRYPTOMERIAS AND TWISTED PINES, moss-covered stone lanterns, celebrated guests, and humble volunteers from the most distant villages standing four-deep along both sides of the road, we crossed over the Double Bridge and out into the teeming modern city. As the guards on horseback and then our carriage turned onto the first of the long, broad avenues that would eventually take us to Tokiwamatsu, cries of "Banzai!" rose up from the throngs of spectators. They were not shouts, as one might have expected, but half-whispered, almost strangled exclamations.

"I'm afraid they don't sound very enthusiastic," I murmured to my husband, smiling and waving to the left as he did the same to the right. It was our first chance to converse all day.

"They've been warned not to startle the horses," he explained through barely moving lips. "But I know their feelings well and can tell you that they are happy."

Earlier, with the carriage waiting in front of the Imperial Household Building, he had committed two unprecedented acts of radical husbandly consideration, which, unbeknownst to us, would be talked about for decades. Leading me, as was his rightful custom, several times he'd glanced back to see how I was getting along; and then, as we were arranging ourselves in the open carriage, he'd reached across to tuck my voluminous skirts under my legs that I might be well wrapped for the journey. At the time, neither of us gave a moment's thought to these gestures. But to the ever-observant palace watchers, for whom we are but polished stones in an endless game of imperial *go,* these two minor courtesies by my husband on our marriage day resounded like the first shots fired in a revolution.

"Are you very tired?" he asked solicitously out of the side of his mouth. "You must have hardly slept."

"And you."

"Oh, I'm used to it."

"Then, as your wife, I must become so."

"As my wife." His public smile, like a glass filled with wine, grew privately enriched with his happiness. "Do you know, I watched you on television, leaving your house."

"I could feel you watching," I confessed. "Just a certain . . . presence. I even thought about sending you messages."

"What messages?"

"May I tell you later?"

"I look forward to it with pleasure."

As did I, though it never took place. Other messages, real enough, intervened. There were so many things to talk about, and precious little time. And so few of the things there were to talk about had anything to do with who we were or might be becoming. It was hard to keep one's eyes and ears open. It was hard to speak of important things.

The procession had left the wide avenues and moved in among the narrower streets. Here the crowd, densely contained behind police lines but always polite, felt more visceral, more like a living being in its own right, with personal expressions to offer and a will of its own. Yes, the people. Though I did not mind this forced proximity: it felt, at least, like life.

The carriage moved at an imperial cadence. And all the while my husband, with his kindly deceptive gaze at his subjects and his ventriloquist's lips, managed to converse with me about our plans.

"I've arranged with Watanabe-san that on our return from Ise we will dine with your parents at their home," he said.

"My parents?" As we were in public, I had no choice but to restrain my outward surprise, though it was intense. Many times over the past months Mrs. Oshima had informed me that visits by female members of the Imperial Family to their parents had in former times never been permitted. The current Empress herself, however noble of blood, had not been allowed to visit her father even on his deathbed.

"Would that please you?"

"Very much." I smiled at a group of schoolchildren.

"Then I will see to it that it happens."

"I would be grateful." I inclined my head, aware once again of the jeweled weight of my tiara.

"Giving me the chance to witness your happiness will be more than enough for me." He turned and waved to an especially vocal section of the crowd. I did the same, copying his gestures, as he went on: "I would like you to think of ours as an ordinary marriage."

"And if my parents are strange with me when we see them?"

"Certainly they will be a bit awkward at first," he said. "But in my experience I've found that good people can grow used to the strangest circumstances."

"Perhaps, then, we are the ones who are strange."

My somber words appeared to catch him off guard. He was in the middle of waving and smiling to his people when involuntarily he turned to stare at me—as though I'd called his name and woken him from a troubled sleep.

"I can't disagree with your observation," he said. And then, as if to soften his rather stiff reply, he reached for my hand.

At that moment a hard object slammed into the carriage on my side, leaving a dented gash in the maroon paint.

"Eh!" one of the footmen exclaimed in a low voice behind me.

Our carriage continued rolling forward as if nothing had occurred. I turned to look in the direction from which the object had come. I saw a young man with long, unevenly cut hair and baggy makeshift clothes slip through the police line and begin running toward us. In his hand was a large object, and as I looked he sharply checked his momentum, planted his feet, and hurled it. There was no time to react. The stone passed within an arm's length of my husband and me; I heard the faint sibilant hiss of it flying overhead.

He was running again, charging at us, and now with a jolt of incredulity I could see that his goal was to gain the carriage where we were, to jump up and lay his hands upon us. He was clutching the low door on my side when two guards leaped at him from behind. A brief scuffle ensued while he continued to hold on desperately to my door, and for a startling few seconds I found myself staring directly into his eyes—black eyes filled with a contempt so absolute it rocked me backward like a blow, sending me against my husband's knees. And then the guards had him, and were dragging him roughly away.

"Are you all right?" My husband's voice was anxious. He helped me compose myself on the carriage seat with as little sign of distress as possible.

"Yes, thank you. I was not touched."

My heart still fluttering, I looked back over the rear of the carriage, whose stately progress had never ceased, and saw the assailant surrounded now by guards and policemen, his arms pinioned behind his back, his long ragged hair gripped by a hand, forcing his chin skyward. I felt a brimming, unexpected pity for him and quickly looked away—remembering at the same time to wave and smile at the lines of people ahead who, ignorant of the danger just averted, continued to celebrate us with unbridled enthusiasm.

I became aware of light hands on my shoulders: it was my husband, helping discreetly to straighten my stole. Once again, he managed to speak to me without appearing to do anything so personal.

"You mustn't worry. I'm certain his violence was directed at me."

"It's you I'm concerned about."

My words seemed to please him; his posture relaxed, and I sensed the full expression of his weight against my side. With an imperceptible smile of gratitude, he murmured, "Then that will be the only point of our marriage on which you and I can never agree."

We rode on. The river of people closed round us and renewed itself, and soon it was no longer possible to see the place where the assailant had been.

COLORED PENNANTS AND BLOWN-UP PHOTOGRAPHS of our likenesses twitched in the breeze, and puppets made in our image danced atop waving arms. Flags and balloons and dogs with ribbons tied round their necks, old women grilling yakitori, peasants in heavy trousers and round straw hats, schoolchildren in dark-blue suits, and rows of uniformed veterans in wheelchairs, war medals gleaming on their chests, their heads bent over the cloth-covered remnants of their amputated limbs. Our horses turned a corner onto a new street, and our carriage followed obediently. The crowds behind the police lines turned with us, never leaving our sides, the river flowing onward, infinite. We smiled and waved, as we always must.

In the crowd to our right, a mother was holding her infant girl, dressed like a cherry blossom, straight above her head, short crooked legs kicking, so that His Highness might notice her child above all others. Dutifully, my husband waved and smiled.

His face then was a mask. And so was my own face a mask: I could feel it resting there obscurely, heavily, across my cheekbones and nose, holding together my practiced smile and astonished eyes, making me a picture to the world and myself.

We rode on. The procession took a long time. It was historic, every moment intended for posterity, though we were still living it. And so the life I had left behind began to disappear from the world.

It was then, on the final leg of our route, looking out into the crowd and expecting to see only the vast blank face of the masses, that I happened to catch sight of an old friend from my previous life. I had not seen Kenji Kuroda, Miko's brother, in years. A young man incongruously wearing now, in the early April sunshine, a heavy winter coat, the padded cotton hood fitted snugly over his head. Like a thinly stuffed chick fallen out of a tree. The hood an attempt, one had to suppose, to keep insulated his smoothly barren face, which was missing an ear and several layers of skin. It was a face, still eerily the same as the picture in my mind, stripped of the requisite layers of protection that might normally allow such a man to wait for hours among so many strangers (their diseases, their staring eyes) to catch for a single minute a view of the imperial couple, the Crown Prince and Princess—the latter especially, an old dear friend of his sister's, the formerly Misora Hibari–obsessed teenager on whom he'd once bestowed, with no explanation, a white peony, mysteriously procured.

Kenji was a painter, Miko had told me in her letters. He still lived at home and rarely ventured out. He had staked out a position for himself in the first row of onlookers, on a street corner, wrapped in his padded coat like a bundle of wheat in a peasant's *furoshiki,* his narrow chest squared bravely up against the police line. Of course, he was taller than I remembered. A grown man with a grown man's features half wiped away, as though by a child's eraser. He wore his painful strangeness, like his unseasonable coat and his skin lost to fire, as a flag not of suffering but of distinction.

He said not a word as we passed in the carriage, and my husband took no notice of him. But as we made the turn and pulled even with his position Kenji ducked nimbly in front of the police line, pulling his hands from his pockets and raising his arms above his head, palms facing the sky as though basking in the unfamiliar sun. That was his gesture in its entirety. One could see that his left hand was missing two fingers. He never took his eyes from my face.

By then I had acknowledged him. I smiled and waved,

overcome with the happy astonishment of seeing him again. Over the years, if I'd thought about him at all, I had assumed him to be a sort of prehistoric case, frozen in time, another lost victim of the war. It seemed inconceivable that he should have surfaced on this day. Yet here he was, palms raised to the sky, his naked gaze like a voice stripped of lies, compelling me to speak for once with equal conviction.

And I almost did. I almost said something, looking down on him from my moving carriage of unsurpassed elegance. Some wishful phrase sincere and true, I console myself by believing. Some sentiment of timeless resonance, heart, delicacy, rippling circles of association. Some part of myself never to be relinquished or forgotten. Yes, I almost called out to him—to his courage and his love, his blazing disfigurement, his unrequited longing burning holes in his palms. . . .

Until I remembered who I had just become, and stopped myself.

PART TWO

18

THE DOOR TO OUR BEDCHAMBER closed with a sound like a heavy lock falling into place, and for the first time we were alone as husband and wife. In the awkward silence that followed I sank onto the edge of the bed, my silk jacket rustling in protest.

"Are you very tired?"

I looked at the kind, decent man standing a few paces away, his suit coat in his hands, and offered him what felt to my face like a terrified smile. "A little."

Silence again. Unsure what to do next, I remained perched uncomfortably on the bed, my jacket buttoned too tightly over my breast. All evening long it had been too tight, and now with clumsy fingers I undid the top button of polished bone and attempted to breathe.

"Here," said my husband, coming to my side, "let me help you." Gently he began to struggle with the buttons himself. I could feel his hands trembling faintly, his warm quickening breath against my cheek. A button came free, the undersilk gaped a bit more; and soon my breath began to quicken, too. "I'll have this last one in a moment . . ." he breathed. The last button came undone, my jacket spilled open, revealing more layers of silk and cotton, and he stared at my underclothes in respectful silence.

"You are certainly well protected."

A firm knock on the door startled us both. He waited until I had rebuttoned my jacket before calling out in a clear voice for the visitor to proceed. An elderly couple entered, carrying between them a lacquered tray of silver dishes.

"Good evening, Your Highnesses," the man greeted us in a high raspy voice.

Both the man and the woman were tiny and wizened—as if, neat in their imperial uniforms, compact as funereal figurines, they'd been buried alive in a previous century and recently dug up whole. They managed a synchronized bow without disturbing the dishes on the tray.

"Good evening, Shizuoka-san," my husband said. "We have been expecting you." His cheeks were flushed, either from the small lie he'd just told or from the activity preceding it.

"Very good, Your Highness." With shuffling steps the couple carried their delivery to a table by the bed. The tray was painted with many storks, and each of four silver dishes contained six delicate rice cakes. Shizuoka addressed himself to me with a bow.

"Your Highness Haruko, if I may say on behalf of my wife and me"—from behind a wrinkled, upraised hand the old woman smiled and performed a bow of her own—"welcome to Tokiwamatsu. I hope Your Highnesses will forgive me if I am repeating that which Your Highnesses already know. The omochi here on this tray—the same number as the honorable age of Your Highness Haruko—bear with them certain instructions, which I will now deliver. Every night for four nights running, Your Highnesses will pray together for a baby—a boy, of course—after which you will each consume a single omochi. Four mornings from tomorrow, the sixteen remaining omochi will be buried along with the lacquer and silver in the most auspicious plot within the palace gardens. If these instructions are followed exactly, pregnancy will result in short order. So instructed, please allow my wife and me to offer Your Highnesses our most respectful congratulations on your marriage, and to pray for the speedy arrival of the next generation."

Bowing and shuffling, they left us. The door closed behind them, and we were alone. But this time our married silence was not so easily banished. The tiny rice cakes on their silver trays, overseen by storks, sat before us like witnesses.

"Do you remember the prayer, Haruko?"

"I think so."

"Then let us pray."

We did so. I said the words with him as best I could, asking for a son. And, as instructed, we ate one rice cake each. They were smaller and not as good as those made in my great-grandmother's village and eaten in my parents' home on New Year's Day.

And then my husband, sitting beside me on the bed and cautiously resuming his ministrations, murmured,

"Let me help you again," as though it were my shoes he was talking about removing. But it was not my shoes. The buttons keeping me hidden from him were stiff under his fingers, and this time our breathing would not be hurried. One had first to recover from the prayer, the imperial instructions, the old lives bowing down before one, the burial, and the hope.

The moment we'd both been waiting for, and distantly apprehending, occurred later in the night than either of us had imagined. In the dim flickering candlelight of the ages, he removed the last of my garments and put his hands on my bare skin. Not as a prince but as a man. He whispered my name. My real name, soon to be lost to the world.

19

AND SO LIFE BECAME A SERIES OF RITUALS written in another age. And rituals became life. A month passed, then two. Every day, without fail, I entered a room too quickly, spoke too often or too loudly, waved my hands in a coarse fashion, scratched an itch, offered an opinion, bowed to an angle of less than sixty degrees before my parents-in-law, and so forth. Some of these gaffes of courtly etiquette were due to nerves, some to ignorance, others to innocence, still others to experience of a kind that no longer counted for anything. Whenever possible, my husband attempted to counsel me on how to improve myself, and in the process to shore up my depressed spirits. But his responsibilities lay elsewhere, and I had handlers enough to educate me. They were women—my ladies-in-waiting, Mrs. Oshima chief among them—who in all cases and at all times spoke on Her Majesty's behalf. In their strict adherence to a long-established body of rules and a willingness to punish the smallest signs of lax discipline, they were like the nuns who had taught me in school, though the soil in which this higher calling was planted was too thin to sustain even a trace of the nuns' compassion. It took me some time to register this crucial difference. I was, at first, under the illusion that my mistakes would be viewed as temporary surface flaws, nicks and scratches easily healed. But as the weeks passed and the harsh judgments poured in—always in private, in the coded language of feminine Court disapproval that was to be my new mother tongue—I was gradually disabused of my naïveté and made to understand that in a world constituted entirely of surface, all flaws run deep.

I had expected that my husband and I would to some degree be separate; that we would have the opportunity to establish our own lives. We lived two and a half kilometers away from the palace, with our own residence, staff, and busy schedules. But these logistical facts were like pieces of movable scenery on a stage; a larger drama, written by another's hand in a mythical century without end, was at work, in which we were mere players. Even my husband, the Crown Prince and heir, had his lines to learn. The drama was told not in acts but in rituals. And rituals, more than the calendar, were the markers of our days.

Every Sunday we dined with my husband's family. These meals were long and tedious, and out of fear of saying the wrong thing I usually said as little as possible. Regardless, every fourth Sunday without exception His Majesty would end our time together by inquiring about my "condition." And every fourth Sunday, following my report that as yet there was no sign of pregnancy, the Empress would admonish me for spending too much of my time on selfish pursuits and not enough time on my duty.

Invariably, on the following morning Oshima would pay a call on me in my private study, bearing a new list of Her Majesty's "observations."

"Your Highness," the daughter of the late Count Oshima would begin, "I paid a call on Her Majesty an hour ago and found her most unhappy."

"I am sorry to hear that."

"Her Majesty has asked that I speak to you about your behavior, which she believes is in danger of reflecting badly on the virtues and beliefs of the Imperial Family—a family, she hoped I would impress upon you, that was here long before you arrived, and will be here long after you depart."

"Please tell Her Majesty that it is my deepest regret to have disappointed her yet again. Though it might be useful to know exactly which mistake I committed this time."

"Did you not enter the room before your husband last night?"

"To be honest, I can't remember."

"And speak before him?"

"We were in private."

"Do you mean to say, Your Highness, that you consider being in Their Majesties' presence the same as being alone?"

"Forgive me, but I can't remember."

"But you must remember; that is precisely Her Majesty's position."

"I do not remember, Oshima-san, and I am sorry. I entered the room—whether before or after my husband, I entered it. And now, as I say, I am sorry that I entered that particular room."

"You say that you are sorry, but you certainly do not seem it."

"Perhaps, respectfully, that is because your constant criticism gives one little opportunity for reflection."

"Her Majesty will be most unhappy when I tell her that you feel her criticism to be unwarranted."

So it went. The argument was circular. There was no topographical point against which I might take a stand, however pathetic. Oshima's condemnations were delivered to me only, leaving no eyewitnesses to corroborate my sense of injustice, or even to assure me that I was not losing my mind.

Of course, I did not burden my husband with my problems. He had enough to think about. Above all, I did not want him to think me weak, to feel that he had made a mistake.

THE REWARD FOR MY STOICISM arrived some weeks after our wedding: the dinner my husband had promised to arrange for us at my parents' house.

I missed them painfully: my mother and her moods; the wet-clay scent of her lipstick; her tyranny in the kitchen and soft girlish joy when shopping; even the compulsive way she lined up shoes at the entrance to the house. I missed all that she had never been able to bring herself to say. More than anyone, though, I missed my father. Missed him so much that I forced myself to ration my thoughts of him, knowing that there would be no new memories to replenish the old ones once they had been consumed in time's slow fire.

The days immediately before the dinner passed with agonizing slowness. Every hour, I imagined how it might unfold. Again and again in my mind, I dressed for the occasion with care and confidence, wanting my parents to see me in the best possible light—wanting it for them, and for me. Yet when the evening finally came I could not decide which dress to wear or what jewelry. Finally, I allowed my third lady-in-waiting to dress me in cold silence, in clothes of her choosing, until I hardly recognized myself.

We arrived with a small retinue of guards, who remained outside throughout the meal. Inside the house— once so warmly familiar, now like an austere museum of regret—the air seemed sapped of oxygen; in the awkward silences that plagued us from the start, our strained breathing possessed a despairing eloquence. Even Taka, normally so voluble, was struck virtually mute, and would not look me in the face as she served me my food. It was, finally, too much for my father's sense of dignity. After an hour of stilted conversation (so many topics one could not discuss)—most of it from my mother, whose agitation led her to talk too much to my husband about things of no consequence—Father excused himself from the table and left the room. He was gone so long that I decided to look for him. It was in my recently vacated bedroom that I found him standing by himself, staring at, but not into, the lacquered hand mirror that had been passed down to me by my grandmother. I had left it behind rather than include it in my trousseau; without saying so, I had left it for him.

Seeing me in the doorway, he set the mirror down on a desk that, like the rest of the furniture in the room, must have been purchased since my departure, for I did not recognize it.

"Ah, Haruko." His face was mildly flushed—it might have been the wine at dinner, or embarrassment at being found alone in my old room.

"You were gone so long I began to worry, Father."

"Nothing to worry about," he said.

"You're not feeling sick?"

"No."

We were silent.

"Is this new furniture?" I asked.

He nodded without looking at me.

"Well," he said, rubbing his hands together desperately, "we should be getting back to the party, don't you think?"

"Father . . ."

He turned to me, his expression suddenly naked in its unendurable loss. We both understood that an evening like this was impossible and would never happen again.

"I am still your daughter," I said in a broken voice.

Picking up the mirror again, he began to twirl it joylessly in his strong hands. "I've been meaning to telephone you. I might, if they'd ever put my call through, which they won't." With false casualness, he held the mirror out for me to take. "Here, I want you to have this. It belongs to you."

We were standing close together. For all its history, the circle of old glass was still clear and brilliant. As I took it from him, before either of us could protect ourselves, my father and I glimpsed our joined reflections on its surface, and saw there the end of something that had once been beautiful.

20

THE EVENT WAS ARRANGED by Dr. Watanabe: a carefully
staged foray into the public sphere by the imperial newly-
weds, to build upon the natural bonds of goodwill the
people seemed to have for someone like myself, born and
reared in Shibuya-ku, Tokyo. We toured the grounds and
inspected several inhabited apartments of a sprawling
municipal apartment complex. Crowds of reporters and
spectators followed us everywhere we went. My husband
wore a white summer suit and a fine straw hat. My own
hat was small and French, turban-like; my bag was from
Hermès. I'd been feeling a bit out of sorts lately—a sensitive stomach and some minor fatigue—and had taken
special care with my makeup and dress to appear suffi-
ciently lifelike. We waved and smiled and answered questions. My husband thoughtfully remarked how every
manner of modern convenience—television sets, washing
machines, electric rice cookers, refrigerators (the most
prized and expensive of all)—seemed to be more and
more available to the people, and how this was good for
the country as a whole. Asked my opinion of the wealth
of appliances on display, I merely observed that such machines made the lives of women easier, allowing them

greater time to look after their husbands and children. Which original wisdom was duly written down, edited, and soon spread across the land.

One of the apartments in that huge labyrinth was lived in by a young salaryman named Matsui and his family. As the mayor and the president of the corporation that had built the complex led us through the three small rooms (each identical to the rooms in the previous apartments we'd seen), I saw the backs—all in a row, from tallest to shortest—of the Matsui family as they bowed before us: father, mother, son, daughter. Their bowing was excessively nervous, and after a few moments my husband asked them to rise.

The boy was six or seven, the girl two or three years younger. They were dressed as for a relative's wedding, the boy in his best short trousers. There was a tidy bandage on one of his knees. I asked him what had happened to his knee, and his mouth popped open in excitement, the answer tumbling out in a single long squeak:

"A-dog-chased-me-it-was-very-scary-I-tried-to-climb-a-tree-to-get-away-it-was-tall-there-was-a-big-bird-very-big-with-a-long-sharp-beak-I-got-scared-and-fell-down-but-I-am-fine-thank-you-very-much-for-the-nice-question-Your . . . Your . . ."

"*Highness*," croaked his father in a whisper—to the floor, for he was bowing again, deeper even than before.

"Highness!" squeaked the boy. He looked up and grinned, pleased with himself, and I saw that he was missing two front teeth.

"Please excuse my son's terrible manners, Your Highnesses," said the father desperately to the tops of his shoes. "We have tried to teach him respect for trees and animals, all creatures—including Your Highnesses, of course. Please excuse us—but, well, as you can see . . ." He threw up his hands in defeat. "May I speak honestly? This is the worst day of my life."

"Please, you must stop bowing," my husband insisted. "You will harm yourself."

The man straightened, but his eyes remained on the floor. His face was square and clean, framed by square black spectacles, his hair cropped squarely to his head, adding to the initial sense of a plain but solid geometry currently under invisible assault. Behind his present state of mortification, however, one had the impression of a ruddy good humor. His cheeks were flushed, as if bowing too much had had the same effect on him as drinking too much sake.

"Well," the mayor announced in a loud voice, "this has been most interesting. But I am certain that Their Highnesses—"

"Why do people bow?"

The high-pitched tone, sweeter and rounder than the boy's, identified the surprise questioner as the little girl.

"Really, now!" the mayor huffed. "This won't do."

"It's all right," murmured my husband.

Regardless, the girl was not finished. She pulled on her father's trouser leg for his attention. He tried to brush her off, but without success.

"Daddy, why do people bow?"

"Please be quiet, Little Bean," the man mumbled helplessly, looking as if he might decide to prostrate himself a third time.

"A very good question," my husband said, praising the girl.

"You think so?" demanded her brother.

The boy's skeptical tone proved too much for the mayor—a rather crude man, to whom there had attached rumors of minor dealings with the yakuza—who barked, "Hey there, little fellow, don't speak to His Highness disrespectfully if you know what's good for you!"

"Yes, an excellent question," my husband went on, ignoring the mayor's outburst as though it hadn't occurred. "And not simple, you know. Not simple at all. Much better than that typical one we always get about why is the sky blue. You know that one, don't you?" My husband smiled; rarely before had I seen him enjoy himself in public. "That question about the sky has a scientific answer, which I leave to your wise parents to explain to you when you are old enough. The question of bowing, on the other hand, now that's something else altogether. It speaks to the issue of how we as a people behave and regard each other; how, in a sense, we show respect both to our heritage and to one another as human beings. Do you understand?"

The children nodded silently.

"Very good, then. It has been a pleasure for me to meet you both. It gives one confidence to know that our nation's future lies in such inquisitive young minds."

With that, my husband nodded to the open-mouthed parents and, with a glance meant for me alone, turned to leave.

I followed, passing in front of the wife. She was pretty, rather tall and slim, with soft eyes, long straight hair, and a little pink bud of a mouth. And she was trembling, her face as flushed as her husband's.

I smiled, hoping to calm her. "Your kitchen is lovely, certainly the nicest I've seen today," I said.

I kept my voice low so that my words would not be overheard and recorded, and I attempted, unsuccessfully, to meet her eyes with my own. She looked aghast that I'd spoken to her in such a personal manner; the color in her cheeks deepened to a burn. But as I turned to leave I was pleased to see that her trembling had stopped.

It was at that moment, entirely by accident, that our eyes happened to meet. Two women standing on opposite poles of the round earth, our lives so distant from each other in practice and purpose that one would have thought it impossible for any sight line to be drawn between. And then, over the course of two or three seconds, without the slightest spark of anticipation, over the heads of a prince, chamberlains, government officials, untold numbers of functionaries, we saw each other. That was all. No longer did her eyes seek to hide from me the dread of forced exposure and the raw pride at having survived, however imperfectly, the trial of it, or the continual awareness of walls and boundaries—in her case, three rooms; in mine, too many to count—and the mute wonderment at finding oneself permanently trapped inside.

I stared at her: another life.

"Twenty minutes behind schedule," I heard an official mutter irritably.

"Yes, a good visit," my husband announced. His voice was faint, and I realized with a start that he and most of the others were already in the corridor.

A bodyguard appeared at my elbow. "Your Highness?"

"Yes, let us go."

It was finished. Had I imagined the connection? From the doorway, I took a last look back.

Already the family seemed to have reconstituted itself, forgotten us. A nascent smile was beginning to creep over the husband's square face: he would cuff his son on the head, not for his insolence but for the sweet relief of having made it through. The son was picking at his knee bandage and chattering on again, in his engagingly squeaky voice, about the dog that had chased him up the tree and the frightening bird with the long sharp beak that had been waiting for him there. What a boy he was: free from punctuation, he was free from everything. And his sister was practicing her bow in a mirror hanging above the cat bowl. And the young mother was staring at a spot on the floor.

On the following day, I learned that I was pregnant.

21

I GREW ROUND. Wise with its own biological counsel, without regard for rank or title, unwilling to wait for permission, suddenly my body knew no goal but the giving of life. Overnight I'd become a woman with a single purpose, in which lay my only power. As a symbol as well as a body, I grew ever larger. It was said that the child I carried in my womb belonged to everyone. How many people was everyone? Many, many. Extra food was piled on my plate. I was encouraged to sleep more. My husband was kind and solicitous, hovering over me. The imperial physician hovered, too; specialists were called in. I was probed and palpated. The baby's heart was listened to like an ancient instrument; his music was pronounced good. He was growing, changing, getting nearer, unable to fathom what he was, how he would be different, what would be asked of him.

Infinite hands were already reaching to claim him, while he was still inside me.

ONE EVENING LATE IN THE YEAR, my husband and I sat watching the television news after dinner. It was a terrible time in our country, the most terrible since the war.

There were riots against the security treaty with the Americans—tens of thousands charging the Diet Building, breaking windows and urinating in the streets. Shouts of "Yankee go home!" The prime minister dispatched the police, who gathered and charged. In the ensuing mayhem, a little girl was crushed to death. The riots were not shown on the news, only the aftermath. What we were looking at on the black-and-white screen was the chalk outline of her body where she had lain dead in the street. Then a picture of the girl's mother, sobbing.

My husband turned off the set.

"Why did you do that?"

"It's not healthy for you."

"I'm not the one who lost her child."

He was silent, studying me like a psychiatrist.

"Aren't we removed enough as it is?" I demanded. "Don't you want to know what's happening outside?"

"Haruko, there's nothing we can do about this. It's already happened. It may go on, but in the end it will be all right. The country is strong. Now, you should get some rest."

"I won't."

"You're needlessly upsetting yourself and the baby."

"The baby needs to know, too."

"Know what?" he said impatiently. "What are you talking about?"

"Others!" I shouted at him. (Never before had I raised my voice to my husband, the Crown Prince, in this defiant manner.) "Other people, Shige! Day after day, we sit here and do nothing while people are dying. We are useless! No—worse—we are pathetic." Suddenly I was sobbing like the grieving mother on the news.

"Haruko, be reasonable . . ."

"I think I'm going to be sick . . ."

I stumbled to the bathroom and lowered myself like a collapsing cow onto the cool tiles, my taut belly pressed against the front of the toilet.

Within moments, the door to our bedroom was opened; behind me I heard the hushed voices of our caretakers.

"Go away!" I cried. "Shige, send them away."

"I think you'd better go," my husband directed quietly. "Let me know when the doctor arrives."

"Yes, Your Highness."

The door closed. The voices were gone.

I was crying again—slowly, patiently, as though time belonged to me now—embracing my white porcelain throne.

"Haruko, listen to me." He was right behind me, speaking in an urgent voice, his hands on my shoulders—like my father on my wedding day, trying to urge me forward. But he was not my father. "We are not among them. We never will be—never. We are above. That includes you now, and our child. All we can do is try to make them feel that we are with them in spirit."

I gripped his hand desperately. "Hold me, Shige. I'm afraid."

22

I GAVE BIRTH TO OUR SON in the Hospital of the Imperial Household. The news of the successful delivery and the triumphant sex of the child was conveyed to Their Majesties by the Emperor's grand chamberlain, who for a man heading into his latter years of wisdom and serenity proved, on that historic day, to be surprisingly fleet of foot. The infant prince was officially measured at a length of 53.2 centimeters and a weight of 3.864 kilograms. He was declared in robust health, washed and purified, and made presentable for viewing by the Crown Prince and myself, Dr. Watanabe, and an assortment of chamberlains and ladies-in-waiting. Then a nursemaid took him away.

The lights in my room were painfully bright, though not so bright that they kept me from drifting in and out of sleep over the next few hours. I could feel myself smiling like an addled goose who after long flight, and by sheer hopeful accident, has found the only cloud in the vast blue sky on which to rest. There came a moment when, through this floating pillow of ethereal cotton, my husband reached out and touched my hand—a breach of precedent, Oshima later informed me. Our son, meanwhile, still too shocked by the change in his surroundings to register this foreign conceit of joy, or indeed its opposite, could not yet know what he was. One minute his head was purple, the next a ferocious pink. His tiny shuttered eyes, glazed with light and wonder, were unable to see me clearly, yet would not let me go.

By imperial tradition, it is the Emperor's privileged duty to name the children of his eldest son and heir. Our newborn would be given two names, one for himself and one for history. This would take seven days. Until that time, he would be called *Shinno*—Imperial Prince. And so it was that on the day of Shinno's birth, as a team of six expert doctors looked on, Buddhist priests delivered a paper amulet, and the *haken-no-ji* was performed in defense of the child's health. A messenger from the Emperor arrived with a thirty-centimeter-long sword crafted by a master swordsmith, embossed with the imperial seal, in a crimson case lined with white silk. The sword was placed beside Shinno's basket as a totem of divine protection.

On the morning of the seventh day, one of Her Majesty's ladies-in-waiting ritually bathed our baby in a cypress wood basin, while an eminent professor personally chosen by His Majesty read an auspicious passage from the *Nihon Shoki*, written in the classic Chinese style; and two men from His Majesty's staff twice plucked at the taut strings of traditional longbows to ward off malevolent spirits. This was the ceremony meant to instill excellence in Shinno, and also, once again, to ensure his good health. I watched from my bed, and the Crown Prince watched from a place nearby. And our son was indeed excellent. And we prayed.

Later that day, at the palace, the naming took place. Three more professors had been picked to make recommendations derived from the Japanese and Chinese classics, from which the Emperor would make his final selection. After the ceremony, our son's name and title, inscribed by the Emperor himself on handmade *washi* paper, were carried by imperial messenger to our Togu Palace and presented to the Crown Prince. From there, they were announced at the three shrines of the Kashikodokoro, and at the Imperial Household Agency. Finally, rather late in the day, the washi paper was delivered to the hospital.

Since sunrise, it seemed, my room had been filled with people coming and going, none bearing the name I was looking for. But now, as the day had begun to darken, as though I had stepped into a clearing in a dense forest, I found myself alone with my child. He lay asleep against my breast, his feeding for the moment completed, one tidy burp achieved, his glazed half-open eyes twitching contentedly in their sockets. Beyond the drawn shades of my room, I could see dusk beginning to descend. A momentous day, but a day all the same. And then I heard footsteps in the hallway. At the door, a nursemaid was bowing.

"Your Highness, the imperial messenger has arrived."

I pulled my robe closer about my son and me. "Give me a moment, then tell him he may come in."

"Yes, Your Highness. He is not alone."

"No one is, it would seem," I murmured into the curled pink shell of my baby's ear.

"Your Highness?"

"Nothing. You may go."

Bowing, she went out. We were ourselves again, Shinno and I. Yes, it was rather perverse of me: now that he was finally about to receive his name, I found myself beginning to grow fond of that dull generic moniker, that Shinno, if perhaps for no other reason than that, on the verge of being replaced, it had suddenly become precious.

"Shinno?" I whispered to him.

His eyes opened.

The imperial messenger appeared in the doorway, accompanied by various officials. I could see the washi paper in his hand. Then he was standing at the foot of the bed, his chest puffed out like a glossy toad's, declaiming the new Prince's name and title. My son's name was Yasuhito, to be known, as he grew, as Prince Tsuyo. Yes, it was all properly done. History had been served. And yet the messenger's inhuman droning frightened my child: Yasu began to whimper and then to bawl, his tiny bunched hands grabbing ineffectually at my face. This unseemly burst of noise caused, in turn, a ripple of helpless anxiety among the clutch of imperial officials. One of them called for a nursemaid, it being assumed that I would want to give my son up only to receive him again, hours later, docile and wrapped in a blanket. But I had no wish to give him up. That is what they could not understand. I hungered for him just as he was, vivid, against me, his hot sweet breath fluttering like a butterfly under my chin. And so I sent the nursemaid away—an act of maternal independence that only caused further consternation among His Majesty's representatives.

This was not entirely unexpected. Already, of course, there existed certain tensions. Privately, over the months before the birth, my husband and I had come to various half-professed conclusions regarding the upbringing of our children. On one point especially he had been resolute: that our children not be separated from us at the tender age of three as he had been, and that they not be brought up entirely by chamberlains and ladies-in-waiting.

Lying in the hospital bed with Yasu whimpering into my neck, I silently recalled a conversation with my husband earlier in the winter.

"And Their Majesties?" I'd asked, as we sat over cups of green tea one night after dinner. My belly by then was rounder and heavier than I could ever have imagined; I felt the steady discomfort of being anchored like a leaky battleship to whichever chair I happened to be sitting on. "Have you expressed your thoughts to them directly?"

"Watanabe raised the matter in their presence. And, as you know, I paid them a visit yesterday."

"And were they sympathetic?"

"I believe my father understands the necessity for both symbolic and practical change in a changing world."

"That sounds rather abstract."

"Do you mean that as a criticism?"

I glanced at the servant standing by the door. Simply by raising his chin, my husband arrested the man's attention. "Thank you, that will be all for the moment," he said. As soon as we were alone, I was gently admonished. "They are our people, Haruko."

I did not offer my opinion that they were his people, perhaps, or his parents' people, but hardly mine. The woman who cries out "Spies!" in the middle of the holy temple is not a woman likely to be attended with much sympathy by either gods or humans. And sympathy was a dream that I was not yet prepared to abandon entirely.

"It is important that you feel comfortable in our life," he continued. "I'm aware that things can be difficult for you here—I'm not blind—but I would like you to feel my support at all times."

"You are my *only* support."

"Things will get better."

I was silent.

"Haruko . . ."

"You have yet to describe Her Majesty's views about our children's upbringing."

He sighed. "My mother agrees that the world is changing. But in her opinion many of the changes aren't necessarily for the good of our people."

"And if we intend to keep our children with us and raise them at home?"

"Naturally, my mother sees her role in the traditional terms of a woman of her generation. She considers it her duty to support my father in his views without reservation."

"I see."

"Nonetheless, it's expected and understood that I have my own life. We live apart, with our own duties and obligations. We are meant to be copies, but also, you might say, originals."

I paused for a moment to allow the notion of an original copy to speak for itself. "And our children? Who are they meant to be?"

"I will see to it that our children remain with us for as long as possible. That is my promise to you."

Once again, we were silent. The informal dining room (an old converted sitting room) echoed our wordless thoughts. On the other side of the door, the kitchen was empty; the servants, reading our moods, had left us for the night. I lifted my teacup—like so many of the things around us, an object of exquisite beauty, its marbled emerald glaze like the shell of a sea turtle—turned it aimlessly in my hands, and set it down again without having truly seen it.

I said, "Sometimes I wonder if my being of different background is not too heavy a burden for you."

He patted my hand, but did not otherwise reply.

IN THE HOSPITAL that late winter day, after the imperial messenger had placed the washi paper on which the Emperor had written with his own hand the name and title of the new prince beside his sleeping basket, I was again left alone with my son. He'd stopped crying but was still whimpering like a half-asleep puppy, disturbed by some lingering presence in the room, the nature of which I believed I could fathom well enough, for it was with me, too.

I rocked him gently in my arms. And soon I found myself beginning to talk to him in a low voice, a private whisper meant for his ears alone.

With regard to his name and its intimations of official peace, I told him that the history of the war and its horrors belonged to others before him, and that while of course he must steep himself in its lessons I prayed that he would not bear the burden of its truths too personally. To comfort him, I told him stories of my grandmother and my mother as children; of the pounding of omochi in the mist-shrouded hills at dawn; of my school years in Gunma Prefecture during the worst of the bombing. I told him about Shanghai eggs, octopus holes, my cousin Yumi losing her father to the fires. I told him about Miko and the sign of the crane. I told him about the physical misfortunes of Kenji Kuroda and Dr. Watanabe, so that seeing their scarred faces for the first time in his life would not frighten him. I told him that, after I had become engaged to his father, Taka could no longer bring herself to look at me and even my own parents were different with me—as if I, too, had been disfigured.

I talked to my infant son, and when he stirred and whimpered again I fed him from my swollen, aching breasts, and finally we both slept.

THE MORNING OF THE EIGHTH DAY dawned brightly. Despite my incessant fatigue, a bubble of anticipation floated within my chest. I had my hair washed in the bathroom sink by a nervous young lady-in-waiting whose nails kept digging into my scalp. I was dressed in suitably fashionable clothes, attractive but not too pretty. A gold brooch in the shape of a wild chrysanthemum—the emblem chosen for me by the Crown Prince before our wedding—was pinned to my lapel. And somewhere in another room, I was aware, Yasu-chan, too, was being bathed and powdered and dressed.

I was very nearly ready when Oshima walked in.

"Good morning, Your Highness." She was faintly out of breath from her brisk walk down the corridor, the remnants—or beginnings, I could never be certain—of a scowl teetering on her thin upper lip. "I have been to see Her Majesty."

"So early in the day? Thank you, that will do," I murmured to the lady-in-waiting, who had just pricked me with the brooch. "Would you see to it that Yasu-chan is ready for our departure?"

"Immediately, Your Highness." The young woman bowed and left.

"Her Majesty," continued Oshima, "as you are no doubt aware and would do well to emulate, has such an abundance of responsibilities that virtually no hour is too early."

"Her conduct is impressive."

"Indeed it is. Today, however, I found her very distressed."

"I am sorry to hear it."

"Then why do you insist on being the cause of Her Majesty's unhappiness?"

"I am surprised that I should be so much in Her Majesty's thoughts—I haven't seen her in several weeks." I moved to the bed and, lifting the sheet, peered underneath. "Have you seen my gold bracelet? I'm afraid I've lost it."

"I have seen no bracelet," Oshima answered coldly. "And I would strongly advise you, Your Highness, not to be flippant over matters of such vital importance."

"I assure you, Oshima-san, that nothing could be of greater importance to me than Their Majesties' regard."

"And yet you insist, against Their Majesties' wishes, on breaking imperial precedent by carrying the baby out of the hospital yourself?"

I stopped moving about the room and looked at her directly. "He is my child."

"He may be yours, but he does not belong to you."

A shiver passed across my skin. "You have children yourself, Oshima-san, do you not?"

"That is a separate matter, of no consequence to this discussion."

"A separate matter to you, perhaps. But here you see me attempting to feed my baby with my own milk, hold him in my own arms. I am speaking to you now as a woman who has given birth to children of her own. Can't you understand my feelings?"

"Your feelings are immaterial. Imperial tradition takes no account of feelings. So my father, the late Count Oshima, often told me. And so it shall ever be."

"In that case, I must humbly thank you and your illustrious father for your counsel."

"You are most welcome to it."

I turned away from her. Already ingrained in me was the sense that I should not leave a room on my own terms, without accompaniment and plans for future movements and a careful recording of the moment. No, a Crown Princess, regardless of how she might have come to her station, could not simply walk out of a room.

And so I waited, Oshima looming in my peripheral vision like a stone monolith. I again pretended to look for my lost bracelet; I stared out the window. I felt the corrosive shame of remaining in a room with a woman who considered herself above me and wished me harm as a consequence.

It was my husband who rescued me. I recognized the distinctive light-footed rhythm of his steps approaching along the hallway, harmonized by those of his attendants. Oshima recognized them, too: the statue of herself, carved in a mountain face by the ancients, began to crumble and shrink, until soon she was little more than an average-size tortoise.

The Crown Prince entered the room, Dr. Watanabe

just behind him, both dressed in dark suits. "The car is waiting," he told me. "Is everything ready? Where is Yasu-chan?" The name rolled off his tongue with ease, and I wondered if he had been practicing it at home.

When I remained silent, he studied me for a moment before turning an uncharacteristically hard eye on Oshima. "Is everything in order, Oshima-san?"

I watched the small residue of color in her cheeks evaporate. "Of course, Your Highness."

"Then you may go."

"Yes, Your Highness." She went out.

"We will be home soon," he said.

I nodded, not trusting myself to speak.

"Give me your hand. I have something for you."

I held out my hand. In it he placed my lost bracelet.

"I spotted this on the floor when I was here the other morning. You seemed so tired I thought I'd better keep it for you."

A crowd had gathered outside with the cameras and the television crews. Gleaming purple-black crows, drawn by an auspiciously brilliant sun, had appeared in unusually large numbers in the tall pine trees, their harping, full-throated cries sharp enough to puncture, once again, the most sentimental platitudes. A cheer went up from the assembled celebrants, and I walked with my husband out into the cold luminous air. A nursemaid holding our son met us on the front steps, and as the shutters clicked and whirred I reached out for Yasu and took him, wrapped in blankets, into my arms.

23

MY TRIUMPH WAS PAINFULLY SHORT-LIVED. I had been home from the hospital for only a few weeks when I asked that Yasu be brought to me in bed for his first feeding of the day. Those twenty minutes that I looked forward to as I did to nothing else in my life—his fierce attachment to my body; the soft rhythmic beating of his hands against my sides as he took from me all the nourishment he needed to grow. On this morning, however, it was not the usual nursemaid who brought him to me but my third lady-in-waiting, a woman only a few years older than I named Aoki. Just the sight of my baby in her indifferent arms made my full breasts ache. I took him from her and settled him in the crook of my elbow.

"Is he all right?" I asked. "He seems quiet." Yasu was not crying from hunger, as I'd expected, but lying placid and half asleep in my arms, hardly aware of my presence. Something felt wrong to me, but I could not yet say what it was.

"He is well, Your Highness. He has already been fed."

I asked what she could mean, and was told that he had been given a bottle of infant formula half an hour earlier.

I stared at her. "By whose authority was this done?"

"By Her Majesty the Empress, in consultation with the imperial physician," said Aoki. "Oshima-san delivered Her Majesty's instructions last night after you had retired for the evening."

"Send Oshima-san to me immediately."

"Yes, Your Highness."

"You may go."

She left, and I retreated to the bed, my baby in my arms, his lips moving in a dreamy half sleep. One of my tears fell into his open mouth. The salty taste seemed to please him, for he smacked his lips.

My husband entered the room in his robe, toweling his hair from the bath.

"What is it?" he asked.

"They are weaning him from me without my consent, Shige."

He looked confused. "Weaning him?"

"With a bottle."

I waited for his reaction. He touched the towel to a damp place on his cheek while he considered the issue.

"Perhaps it's not such a bad idea," he said. "You've been tired and run-down lately, and your schedule allows no room to spare. This would give you the chance to get more rest."

"I don't want more rest, Shige."

"They say that the formulas are very advanced now. Better, even. Boys grow faster on it."

"Is there no one you can speak to about this?" I pleaded.

"I'm sure it's for the best, Haruko."

He said nothing more, and began to dress.

WHILE MY HUSBAND ATE BREAKFAST I went, unannounced, to the nursery. The room was unattended, and I entered. Yasu lay asleep in his crib, his body a curl of tenderness, the back of one tiny hand pressed against a cheek. I leaned down over the crib's railing to breathe in the warm, moist puffs of air that he was breathing out. The smell of him. I wanted only to sit by his side and watch him sleep. That was my intention: to be the first face he saw on waking.

"Your Highness," a voice said. "Is something wrong?"

I turned—quickly and almost furtively, as though I'd been caught spying—and was met by two identically dressed nursemaids.

"No, I was just . . ."

The two women were beside me. What I perceived at that moment may not have been literally accurate, but it felt absolutely real: they'd insinuated themselves between me and the crib, forming an exclusive circle around my baby.

"Has he everything he needs?" I mumbled, in submission.

"Of course, Your Highness. He has been fed and changed, and now he is sleeping."

I said nothing more. But I could not bring myself to

leave. There is no telling how long I might have remained there, powerless but stubborn, if a new, more strident voice hadn't broken the silence.

"Your Highness, why are you here?"

I turned around. Oshima was standing in the doorway, with Aoki behind her.

"Your Highness, the head of the Red Cross is already waiting for you in the Imperial Household Building," she said. "We must go at once. Our entire schedule depends on it."

Oshima stepped to one side, making room for me to precede her. She knew already that I would go with her. Which I did—without a murmur of protest, as though my tongue had been cut out.

So was I weaned—not my child, but me.

24

EARLY ONE OCTOBER EVENING, we were driven to the Kaintei—the intimate pavilion in the heart of the palace grounds, where for many years family gatherings were held—Yasu on my lap in the back of the limousine. After several minutes of listening to our son's concert of high-pitched chirps and half-phrased syllables, my husband observed, "Do you see how excited Yasu is to be visiting his grandparents?"

I was silent, not wishing to contradict him. I lowered my window, beyond which the dark evening was rising through the clear dusk like shade filling a crystal lantern. The breeze from the car's motion caused Yasu to smile at the world.

"Don't you agree that he enjoys these visits with my parents?"

His determination to receive confirmation on this point touched a bitterness that had been growing in me, and I turned from the window. "Whether Yasu wants to visit Their Majesties or not would seem to be irrelevant. Today is the second Sunday of the month, and on the second Sunday of the month at exactly six o'clock we are driven to the Kaintei for the pleasure of Their Majesties' company. Isn't that so? No amount of discussion could change the routine."

My husband stared at me. Then I watched his eyes dart ahead to see if the driver had been listening. There was no sign; there never would be. In a low voice he said, "Has something upset you?"

I was silent.

"Are you feeling sick?"

"I am well enough, physically."

"Then what is the matter with you?"

I shook my head. There was some little light in the car and Yasu grabbed excitedly for one of my jeweled earrings, hitting my throat with his soft fist instead. It didn't hurt, but briefly my eyes filled with tears. I lifted him and buried my face in his belly until he giggled once more.

"We are going to arrive shortly," my husband said. "If you've had some recent communication with my parents, you'd better tell me about it now."

"There have been many communications."

"My mother has spoken to you directly?"

"That is not her way."

"You're referring to Oshima, then. Has she bullied you?"

"I'm referring to no one . . . and everyone."

"Now you are talking in riddles."

"I only want to be understood."

"We're here," he said coldly.

A slowing as our car passed between the pillars of the gate. The veranda lights of the Kaintei flashed intermittently between the thickly leafed trees like the probing beacon of a ship, and the sight of that fractured illumination filled me with a sense of dread for which I was unprepared. Every muscle in my body seemed to constrict. Yasu must have felt my internal rebellion, for he began to whimper, and then suddenly to cry. My husband was close at hand, though far away and silent. The car entered the driveway and stopped in front of the pavilion; the driver climbed out. My door was opened and there to greet us was one of Her Majesty's ladies-in-waiting, whose expression of shock when I all but shoved my wailing baby into her arms gave me a certain rueful satisfaction.

I could hear Yasu crying behind me as I went through the door and into the pavilion, three steps ahead of my husband.

A SMALL INFORMAL FAMILY AFFAIR. The Empress, who whenever possible eschewed Western dress, wore a kimono of her own design, and silken wildflowers of at least a dozen varieties appeared to have taken root in her padded figure. Her oiled hair shone, her face was expertly painted; that pale elongated face, those smallish black eyes that never rested. The Emperor, meanwhile, as was his custom when "at home," was dressed in tailored Scottish tweeds. The flaming torches burning on the terrace, where the Jenghiz Khan grill had been prepared for us, could be seen reflected in his round spectacles, suggesting a blaze of personality not entirely in keeping with His Majesty's general demeanor.

Out on the terrace, attended by two chefs in white jackets and stovepipe toques, we moved purposefully around the cooking fire with our chopsticks and saucers, grilling pieces of marinated lamb for ourselves. The air was redolent with the scent of seared meat and the spices of a barbaric age. His Majesty, languidly turning a piece of lamb with a pair of long mahogany chopsticks, noted that Jenghiz Khan's original name had been Temu-jin. Princess Midori, waiting behind her father, wondered aloud about the meaning of the name.

There was a pause. Beyond the terrace, a light breeze stirred the reeds at the edge of a small viewing pond. Looking out at this intimate vista, one could see the reeds and a stone lantern and the brightest of the evening's stars floating on the gloaming mirror of the pond. Then the breeze came again to crack the water's surface, and the picture was flooded.

"I believe this needs more sauce," the Empress announced to no one in particular, sending a servant hurrying inside.

"Jenghiz Khan," explained my husband to his youngest sister in a confiding voice, "conquered the Chin of northern China. He took Peking."

"But this doesn't taste Chinese," said Princess Midori.

"Yes, well, he conquered many other territories besides."

"That would explain it. I suppose they must have brought a lot of sheep with them?"

"It was the essential part of their diet," her sister Takako informed her knowledgeably. Takako, the former Princess Sorano, lived on a dairy farm an hour's drive from Kobe. By marrying her husband, she had officially become a commoner. A strange phenomenon, certainly: one couldn't be said to be returning, because one had never been in that particular country to begin with. And yet there could be no denying that one had been expelled from one's native territory.

The servant reappeared with a bowl of the dark fragrant marinade, and began brushing it over the pieces of raw lamb that were still to be cooked.

"You are slow," the Empress said, reproving him. "His Majesty could not wait."

The servant bowed low, excused himself, and continued his work.

The Emperor held the piece of lamb in his chopsticks up to the torchlight to see if it was cooked to a sufficient degree. Concluding that it was, he placed it carefully on the white saucer in his other hand. "The meaning of Temu-jin . . ." he declared in the whispered, slow voice that he reserved for historic utterances, "is Jenghiz Khan."

One waited for more, but there was none. Some moments were needed to recall the original question, though His Majesty himself did not appear to notice the general confusion. He proceeded to cook a second piece of lamb, showing the same solemn care in his attentions as he had with the first. Having completed his task, he carried his small rewards—he was known to suffer from irritable digestion and rarely ate more than a few bites at a time—inside to the dining room.

IN THE DRAWING ROOM LATER, tea and sweets were served. The Empress asked to see her grandson, and Yasu was brought in and held up before her to be inspected. He neither smiled nor cried, merely dangled there in the arms of the lady-in-waiting like a fallen parachutist stuck in a tree, staring with wide unblinking eyes at Her Majesty, as though trying to decide whether she was a novel species of bird or fish, or perhaps a threat.

"He is not bad-looking," she concluded finally.

"I think him quite handsome," offered Princess Midori.

"It is too early to tell," said the Empress. "His comportment is what one must look to. We recall that our own son began receiving his lessons at an appropriately early age."

"Yes, a fine boy." The Emperor nodded vaguely, studying the teacup in his delicate hands. It was not clear which boy he was referring to.

"It's true that I was separated early on, as was the custom at the time," my husband remarked seriously. "But as you have informed me subsequently, Mother, that was not done without certain reservations."

The Empress frowned. "It is His Majesty's belief that knowledge of the traditional past is our people's most precious asset." She looked at her husband as though for confirmation, perhaps received it, and then, though she was speaking to her son, finished her reply with a serrated glance at me. "We are the embodiment of that knowledge and that past. We are the source, and the source must not be corrupted. Do we not agree?"

My husband sipped his tea and was silent.

"Times have changed, it is true," the Emperor broke in mildly. "The Olympics, for instance . . . Well now, there's a case, I suppose. The Olympics coming to Tokyo in, what is it, three years' time? Really quite encouraging, when one thinks about it. Equestrian events, for example . . . Very invigorating and correct. Full of tradition, as you said. Yes, I hope that boy is going to be taught the proper way to sit on a horse. There can be no tradition without proper training, as everyone knows."

"Proper training," the Empress repeated. "Precisely what is required."

Yasu had begun to kick his legs like a frog being dangled above the beak of a hungry crane. I signaled the lady-in-waiting to bring him to me.

"That must of course be right," I said. "But it's rather confusing how nearly every time one picks up a newspaper of late one finds oneself reading the opinion that Japan has entered the age of progress and technology and must not, cannot, turn back. I wonder what one is to make of such statements."

"You should consider reading less," my mother-in-law said.

For an instant, I met her cold eyes; then I surrendered to her greater power. "No doubt you are right."

217

"Then we are in agreement on at least one count."

"I am certain that my wife intended no disrespect," said my husband.

"And I am equally certain that your consort could not possibly offend me, even if—and this would be most foolish—she were so inclined. My disappointment comes simply from the fact that she seems to have so many ideas of her own. Yes, so many crude ideas, so poorly used."

"If I may respectfully answer Your Majesty—" I began.

"I was not aware that I had asked a question," she interrupted, speaking to her daughters as though I were not in the room. "But she may continue."

I inclined my head, my face on fire. "Thank you for your condescension, Your Majesty. I merely wanted to say in my own defense that my ideas are not fixed. They change constantly. That is the manner in which I was educated."

"So it would seem. I could not have phrased the problem better myself."

"Yasu-chan seems tired," said my husband, getting to his feet, his voice brittle with tension. "We will take him home now."

"An excellent idea," said the Empress.

"What, leaving already?" murmured the Emperor to a blue vase on a table some way across the room. "Pity. A nice evening, I should think. That lamb—really quite delicious. Now, the main thing is to listen to the people who know what they're talking about. That is certainly the main thing. Precisely why the teaching must start nice and early. Yes, nice and early. There's only one way to do things, as everyone knows."

WE RODE BACK to our residence in unbroken silence; even Yasu, not yet asleep, withheld his wordless thoughts. Though my son would make noise soon enough. And soon he would be gathered up by his caretakers. And then my husband would speak to me, a few neutral words to see us through the night. And we would sleep. And morning would come—the sun, or its simulacrum, would enter our window, and in that light I would stand before my mirror and see myself.

25

THAT AUTUMN PROGRESSED by gravity alone. The sky
grew heavier by the day. The light grew dimmer. Winter
would follow, that was all one could say. Weeks that left
virtually no memory; like the dead leaves falling over the
paths of our private gardens, time was being swept up
by white-gloved hands almost before it could touch the
ground.

I was finding it harder and harder to speak to people.
Apart from official correspondence, I had not written a
letter in many months. After Yasu's birth, Miko had
written with warm congratulations, her letter filled with
lively, amusing descriptions of her life in New York, the
apartment she shared with her friend Abigail, the interesting people she was meeting. She ended on an uncharacteristically somber note, though, expressing her deep
regret that she had never seen me pregnant, or met my
son or husband. "To speak plainly, Haruko, sometimes
I fear that I will never see you again; you are so far away,
not just in miles but in every aspect of life. When you
can, please write and tell me that you understand my
fear, and perhaps even share it."

Her letter lay in my desk drawer, among my few personal papers, under lock and key. Not a day went by that I did not begin—and fail—to imagine in my mind a reply that would somehow do justice to the feelings expressed. As autumn wore on, and her letter remained untouched in the drawer, its truth scalding the dark, I began to despair of ever being able to write to her again.

BEFORE BREAKFAST ONE MORNING, my husband suggested a walk around the grounds. We would take Yasu with us, bundled in his pram against the chill. I agreed, and the usual heart-sapping preparations were made. We had to wait while, in other rooms and by other hands, our son was fed, changed, and wrapped in blankets. Only then, laid in his pram, was he delivered to us outside the residence. It was annihilating—the cold-blooded repetition, the mechanical orchestration of routine, like picking up a car one has ordered—and before we'd taken a step with our child, all desire to move or speak had left me. A woman with whom I had never exchanged more than a dozen words stood behind my baby's pram, ready to push it alongside us as we walked. When she was told that her services were not needed, there was some brief confusion, which I settled by taking the pram from her and following my husband along the path.

A walk, a family: I could not see my baby because of the pale-blue canopy extended above his head. Under the canopy he was very still and quiet, and after fifty meters or so I stopped and peered at him to make sure that he was all right. His eyes were open, staring at me without light or expectation, as though I were just another woman sent to look after him. I said his name and smiled at him, and he blinked a few times. And then he began to cry. I took hold of the pram's handle and began to rock it back and forth to soothe him. But he would not stop crying.

My husband joined me on the path, peering anxiously at our son.

"He is cold."

I shook my head. Yasu was not cold; if nothing else, I knew that much.

"He should be taken back inside."

No, I thought, but did not attempt to say the word aloud.

A mistake. My silence was misconstrued, or simply ignored. Out of the corner of my eye I saw my husband signal to our minders, who, all along, had followed us at a distance, as though the three of us were not a family, after all, but just more dead leaves for them to sweep up. The woman whose services I had previously rejected approached at a brisk pace. Yasu began to cry louder.

"Take the baby back to his room," my husband instructed.

"Yes, Your Highness." The woman stepped forward, but with my hands still locked on the pram she was forced to halt.

"Haruko," urged my husband in a low voice meant for my ears alone. "Let her have the pram."

I stayed as I was. And the woman stayed as she was, unable to back away. We were deadlocked, and Yasu's crying was turning hysterical, and my husband was growing embarrassed and impatient.

"Haruko."

I could stand it no longer: I reached into the pram and picked up my baby. He stopped crying at once, just as I had known he would.

"Have you forgotten yourself?" my husband whispered.

He took our son from me himself and handed him to the woman. Yes, like a very small, very quiet, unheralded death, my hands lost their courage, and I allowed my child to be taken from me.

26

"YOUR HIGHNESSES, morning has arrived."

I heard the familiar knock on the door to our bedchamber—three times, a pause, then once more—through
a muffled dimness of consciousness; followed by the respectful greeting of Igawa, my husband's manservant.

My eyes must have opened, for I took in the near-
darkness of the room that November morning, half
past five. And immediately afterward my eyes must have
closed again, for the routine sounds of waking—my husband stirring and turning on the lamp, his rising from
the bed and muttering, "Yes, yes, I'm coming"—came to
me out of a greater darkness, as though a blanket had
been thrown over my head for the purpose of abduction.
And yet I was not asleep.

In this attenuated state I heard my husband enter the
bathroom. I heard the imperial plumbing. I heard him
come back into the room, say my name in greeting, and
continue past the bed without stopping. I heard him
open the door and inquire whether there had been any
news during the night, and on learning that there had
been none he received the day's papers, neatly folded,

along with copies of our daily schedules. All this I heard and faintly comprehended.

He returned to the bed. It was then he must have noticed that I had not risen with him as was customary, but continued to lie under the covers, apparently insensate. He said my name again, though it was not a question yet. There was still time. I lay as tightly curled as a wet spider, my eyes closed.

"Didn't you sleep?"

I heard his question, felt his eyes on my covered back—and could not reply.

"Are you sick? Should I call for the doctor?"

Unable to speak, I managed to shake my head. My husband was by nature a man of certain discretions, governed by established preferences and quiet routines, and my stubborn silence would have struck him as vaguely anarchic, and certainly disrespectful.

"Would you mind telling me what this is all about, then?" In the sharpness of his demand, I could hear his confusion beginning to clarify into impatience.

I began to sob and shake—soundlessly.

"Haruko?" he said in alarm.

Then he, too, was stunned into silence.

IN THE TOGU GOSHO THAT MORNING, the newspapers went unread.

After recovering from the initial shock of my suddenly altered condition—what would eventually, in unofficial circles and the West, come to be referred to as my "breakdown" or "nervous collapse"—my husband attempted to comfort me in the privacy of our bedchamber. That his attempt did not on that morning, nor on subsequent mornings for months to come, meet with success (or, indeed, with any sound at all) should not reflect on him. He offered me everything he possessed in the way of husbandly concern. And the hurt frustration he showed on realizing his insufficiency—the wounded perplexity of a deeply practical man in the face of irregularities of a female nature (that apparently sound mechanism which nonetheless may decide, for whatever reason, simply to cease functioning)—could not contain itself.

Soon enough, however, he accepted the present reality. Of course, he had no choice. He did not leave me behind during the days and weeks that followed so much as wisely decide—or, more likely, accept the counsel of his chamberlains—to conduct his affairs (and, where possible, mine as well) from an adjoining room. I could be aware of his presence in the vicinity, and he could be aware of mine; and we might go on that way for as long as it might take for me to return to myself.

Thus was my husband's support for me expressed: his frustrated faith that, despite my inexplicable breakdown, I would eventually return to the stage. As if the self that had so unfortunately collapsed on that late-autumn morning could not really have been mine.

He tried comforting me. And when, as I've mentioned, that proved futile, he summoned his most trusted adviser.

I BECAME CONSCIOUS of Dr. Watanabe's presence a few hours later when, after knocking on the door to our bed-chamber and receiving no answer from me, he cautiously entered, closing the door behind him.

By then, still dressed in my nightgown and wrapped in a blanket, I was lying on a nineteenth-century chaise longue, a wedding gift from the French ambassador. It was indicative of my condition that I could remember the provenance of the chaise longue but not how or when I had moved there from the bed. I had sobbed for a while, and then I had stopped. I had sat staring at a spot on the wall, which seemed to wax and wane as I looked at it. Twice I had attempted to speak a single spontaneous word to myself—the first was *Taka*; the second was *tennis*—and in both instances had failed to make a sound.

"Please forgive me for intruding on your privacy, Your Highness," began Dr. Watanabe with a brief bow. "His Highness summoned me rather urgently to say that you were unwell. I was most troubled to hear it. It was His Highness's hope—a hope to which I humbly add my own—that I might somehow be of service to Your High-ness in a difficult circumstance."

There followed a pause. I could not bring myself to look at the doctor for long. This was not personal. His dark suit and tie were elegant and correct as always, though on this occasion they put me in mind of funerals and death. It hardly mattered whose. My head on its frag-ile stalk seemed to turn ever so slowly, until I was looking at the wall. The familiar spot—an indentation in the plaster—began again to wax and wane like a small secret moon of my own, and from this familiar oddity I found that I might draw a moment's comfort.

With a light practiced clearing at the back of his throat—the sound of a tailor's lint brush discreetly applied to one's shoulders—Dr. Watanabe continued. "His Highness thought it best that I confer with you alone. Of course, he remains nearby, ready to attend to you himself should you wish it. As well, our finest physician has been called—"

I shook my head.

"Merely as a precaution, of course. Quite unnecessary, perhaps. And Oshima-san—"

The sudden violence of my reaction seemed to catch Dr. Watanabe off guard.

"Naturally, she is as always at your disposal, should you require her," he added quickly, amending his plan as he spoke. "She is aware that you are not feeling well, and has hastened to clear your busy schedule of all obligations. That is a practical matter, and it has been attended to. More than that, allow me to suggest that there appears to be no conclusive reason why Oshima-san should be brought more intimately into this delicate matter at present," he concluded.

I fell back against the chaise longue, exhausted.

"Yes," Dr. Watanabe added weakly, but said no more.

The ensuing silence was of a type with which I was to become familiar. Even Dr. Watanabe, that sophisticated and humane wizard of the Court, could not know what to do with a princess who had collapsed and gone mute. I could not be traded in, returned like a faulty appliance; therefore I must be treated. But how to treat what one could neither fathom nor respect?

"If I may, Your Highness," Dr. Watanabe began again. "My personal recommendation would be that the imperial physician examine you for signs of laryngitis, pneumonia, or one of the viral diseases known to affect the lymph system. There are quite a few maladies associated with the loss of the ability to produce speech, and likewise with the . . . Allow me to say, Your Highness, an association with the depression of the spirits."

I turned away, seeking again my moon of consolation; for a moment, unable to locate my little friend on the wall, I began to sob. Then it shed its disguise and emerged, smaller than I remembered, and to this poor planetary illusion I latched on like a baby to her thumb.

I remained in that position, a nun devoted to her god, which was but a spot in a false universe. Time became fluid. I assumed that Dr. Watanabe had left the room. But when I turned to look again he was still there, the scarred right side of his face subtly angled away from me, his hands clasped before his waist.

"Your Highness, I am here," he said humbly, with quiet respect, inclining his head.

I closed my eyes. When I opened them again, I was alone.

27

WHEN MY VOICE DID NOT RETURN, a kind of routine was established around me. Which is what happens when one falls down and is simply too awkward to be moved: the flow of traffic, the river's current, the wind where it strikes the hillside—such living forces will find their way, without a trace of sentiment, around any dead obstacle in their path. That is the law of nature, and it is our law, too.

During this period, my husband and I continued to share a bedroom. I intend by this no suggestion outside the logistical. If the nights then seemed endless, it was not because of him. Indeed, those hours of habitual quiet suited me best. One could be voiceless in the night without appearing to commit treason. But to remain silent throughout the day—never to utter "Yes"—was to actively contradict the duties of the realm.

Often during that difficult time, he would come to see me in the company of Dr. Watanabe. The older man seemed to afford the younger some security in the face of a most perplexing dilemma. It is very hard, after all, to be always the sole source of a conversation meant for two. Back in November, I had received a diagnosis from the imperial hospital which was psychological in its terminology and, consequently, rather obfuscating—a thick mist on top of an already existing fog. And so my husband, uncertain in the matter and rather helpless, came to rely ever more heavily on the counsel of his most trusted adviser. Like two eminent conferring physicians, they would knock on the door of my study—a private room thoughtfully designed for me in the English feminine style, with tall iron-case windows, high bookshelves, stuffed chairs, and an antique writing desk—and await my primitive signal to enter, which was a single, rather soft, handclap.

Several months had passed like this. And then one evening they came again. Beyond the casement windows I could see dusk rapidly knitting together the lengthening shadows into a single curtain of darkness. Seated at my desk with a blanket over my lap, I was engaged in the profound act of rolling a heavy gold fountain pen from one side of my palm to the other. I had been doing this for the better part of an hour.

I looked up and they were in the room. My husband, as usual, came forward and sat on the edge of the chair nearest me, his worried eyes probing my face with touching hope—had there been any improvement in my condition, any change at all? The shuttering of his expression as he realized my silent answer in the negative was always a difficult moment for us both; and yet, at the same time, perhaps the only moment of the day that we could honestly claim to share. This was not so with Dr. Watanabe, who remained on his feet near the door.

"I am sorry to see your condition isn't improved," began my husband, who then waited patiently for nothing. It was evident to me that he was no longer surprised by anything I might not say. My lack of response had *become* my response, something understood implicitly between us, something he almost seemed to depend on. "Though I'm pleased to say your color looks a bit better. Wouldn't you agree, Watanabe-san?"

"Yes, better, a bit," Dr. Watanabe agreed. It was at this point in the conversation, directly appealed to, that the doctor decided it was appropriate to venture farther into the room. "Did Your Highness find it convenient to take some fresh air today?" he inquired.

To him I offered a nod of my head: Yes, Her Highness had found it convenient. Her Highness had brought her lap blanket and a cup of hot tea into the frozen garden. Her husband's garden. A chair had been provided for her, and for some half an hour Her Highness watched the starlings entering and leaving their colored houses. She hoped they were the correct houses, so that no domestic trouble would ensue. And she hoped that they were heated. At this time of year, so many of the trees without leaves, the birds appeared small, stubborn, and brave. Were they aware that their instincts were outwardly perceived as established patterns of complex behavior, rather than as basic needs? Her Highness doubted it. She had sipped her tea and the minutes had passed.

"Soon the weather will be better," my husband observed.

"Perhaps I will find the time for us to go to Hayama for a few days. Yasu would enjoy that, don't you think?"

Here I attempted to nod again, or believed I did. But, from the flash of frustration in my husband's eyes, I understood that I had not managed even so small a gesture as that.

The mention of our son had unintentionally set my thoughts adrift. I had seen little of him of late. A mother must be able to speak to her child, tell him of her love and prepare him for the world. Especially a child like ours, of whom, as I was constantly being reminded, we were merely custodians. And if the mother cannot speak, if silence is her only means of communication, if she cannot find the courage and strength to master herself, then she must be prevented from frightening or confusing the boy. For the good of the nation, mother and child had been separated.

"Well," murmured my husband, his voice, as it inevitably did during our visits, beginning to lose its natural belief in progress. "I'll inquire about your schedule . . . Concerning a visit to Hayama, I mean."

On the palm of my hand, the gold pen rolled from one side to the other. Together, as children may sit rapt before the pendulous workings of a clock, we stared at it with fascination.

Then my husband cast a discreetly questioning glance at Dr. Watanabe, and the gray-haired consigliere raised a finger of the hand resting on his knee, silently cautioning patience and maturity in his young charge. Yes, raised a finger, as though merely being in my presence had drained them both of words, leaving them, in their consummate wisdom, to sign and gesture like mutes.

Schedule? I imagined myself declaring. *Your Highness, I have no schedule.*

"Your Highness?" prompted Dr. Watanabe in a low voice. "One's parents . . ."

He was addressing my husband, speaking in a code they had worked out beforehand with regard to the palliative direction of the conversation. I saw my husband receive his cue. Inclining his head, he gathered himself and faced me. "Now, Haruko . . ."

It was the nature of things that I rarely heard my real name. Almost never. And in this spirit of withholding and perpetual detour my name, suddenly spoken aloud, took on a power that hardly seemed plausible; a power, perhaps, that it was never intended by the gods to have.

"Watanabe-san has convinced me that it might do you good to spend a few days in a different . . . What I mean is, a *simpler* environment. Something less structured than what we're used to here. We'd like you to feel more like your old self, you see. Look, I was speaking a moment ago of Hayama. That's only one possibility—there are others. In fact, Watanabe-san just now spoke on the telephone with your father about the prospect of you resting with your parents in Karuizawa for a few days. . . ."

The gold pen dropped from my hand and rolled beneath the desk. Sinking to his knees, my husband retrieved the precious instrument. He offered it to me but I shook my head, and so he slipped it into his pocket for that future time when I might be strong enough to ask for it back.

AT THE BEGINNING OF MARCH, I found myself being driven to Karuizawa, which I had not seen since my marriage. Dr. Watanabe had thoughtfully provided me with an ordinary-looking car—lightly tinted windows were the only hint of its true purpose—so as not to attract undue attention on the road, and a new driver, a young man named Okubo. Dressed in a black suit rather than the usual imperial livery, Okubo kept his handsome, strong-jawed head fixed patiently forward, content to check on me only with occasional eye darts into the driver's mirror. It was as though this man of twenty or so precociously understood what degree of exposure his broken charge could tolerate. For two hours, speech was not simply what I could not perform—one more failure among many—it was beside the point. With my new driver's unspoken support, the ride to Karuizawa became my rolling sanatorium, in which I might do nothing but lose myself in the once-familiar landscape outside my window.

We approached the town in the late morning. In the cold sharpened light of winter's end, after a night of heavy rain, the dirty tin rooftops appeared like the rusted blades of old swords. Tennis courts, netless and dull, were still covered with tarpaulins. A few fashionable tourists strolled about the narrow streets in the latest ski fashions from Switzerland, though there was no snow on the ground and very little on the mountains. The town appeared smaller and plainer than my memory of it.

"Your Highness?" The instant I found Okubo's eyes in the mirror, he shifted his gaze back to the road. "Would Your Highness care to go directly to her destination? We are twenty-two minutes early."

With a trembling hand, I gestured for him to go on.

"I understand, Your Highness. We will go slowly."

Slowly, we began to climb the curving dirt road to my parents' house. I had not had a private moment with them since the dinner in Shibuya more than two years earlier. They had lost their only daughter, and had laid eyes on their grandson only in photographs. In the view of many, Yasu was not truly their grandson. He belonged to the Imperial Family. To the people.

"If you will allow me, Your Highness," Okubo said, "I would like to wish you a happy and healthy spring, and all good health to your respected parents. My maternal grandmother was born in this area and still lives here. As I recall, the plum blossoms should appear any day now. In my humble experience, plum blossoms are always good for raising one's spirits."

The car slowed; the entrance to my parents' house came abruptly into view, and my breath caught in my throat. Okubo turned off the engine. He climbed out and opened the door for me. The air reached my lungs—the cool, bracing, lost air of Karuizawa. And through my tears I saw my father, looking years older than I remembered, emerging on the front steps of the house.

28

A HUSHED WEEK. My parents walking in their own home as in a temple, speaking softly. I did my best not to let them see me weep. Coming to them from my distant planet, voiceless, I was someone else. They stared, and wondered who I was, and wept their own invisible tears.

Karuizawa was a dream that none of us would ever have again.

And so we made it through that week, and into our last evening together.

"MORE RICE, HARUKO? You must eat something." My mother reached across the table for my bowl, which was still full. I covered the bowl with my hand. "You see? She has no appetite."

"I see that she's already big enough as she is," replied my father. "Do you want her to go back to the palace stuffed to the gills like a carp?" His tone was teasing, but the forced paternal wink was contradictory, haunted by the foreknowledge that any attempt to wring humor from my present condition must be like trying to draw water from stone. He reached for the bottle of sake on the table—his own special brand, one of the finest produced—and poured a fresh cup for himself.

My mother, with a tight mouth, watched him finish the wine in two swallows. Already his cheeks were deeply flushed from the alcohol.

"One merely wants her to keep her strength up," she insisted. "She has so many important responsibilities."

"Come now, Kikuko. Five hundred journalists follow her every move—if she were really disappearing before people's eyes, wouldn't somebody have the guts to say so?"

"They don't see her as we do."

It was a simple remark, but he stared at her as if she'd just ripped the blinders from his eyes.

"That is true," he said quietly.

And with that, his own strength seemed to have gone from him.

IN THE MORNING, his knock on my bedroom door was so soft that I almost missed it. I was still in bed—not because I thought I might sleep more but because I could not envision getting up.

"Am I disturbing you?"

He was in his sleeping robe, his hair uncombed. Unlacquered and unprotected. Older than I had ever seen him. He did not expect an answer from me, and I had none to offer. Beneath the covers, I slid my legs aside to make room for his uneasy weight on the corner of my narrow bed. He reached awkwardly to pat my leg under the covers, but found only emptiness. I moved my foot closer to his hand. Though by then we were both too aware of the effort required; through the layers of cotton and wool his once-comforting touch turned mechanical, and soon was taken away.

"When you were born, Haruko," he said, "my male friends were full of sympathy for me, because you weren't a boy. And then, when it turned out that you were going to be our only child . . . Well, you can imagine the looks of commiseration I got. No one to carry on the company, the end of my name—they did everything but send flowers of condolence to the house. But the fact is, I never agreed with any of that. Not in my thoughts and not in my heart."

He fell silent, his breathing husky with memories that would never be told. Hands against the bed frame, he pushed himself to his feet. And then he turned to me, bending down, his face emerging from its own shadow into the day's light, and kissed me on the forehead. His lips were dry, and his warm breath smelled faintly of last night's sake.

"Haruko, you have been the best child a father could ever have hoped for," he said. "No one could have made me happier. But now you must go back."

Tears sprang to my eyes, and I shook my head no.

"Yes, my daughter. Home is with your husband and child now. No one understands better than I what you've sacrificed, or regrets your suffering more. But you made a commitment. For the rest of your life you are bound to honor it. I'm sorry."

On that final word his voice died, and, mute like me, he stepped away from the bed. Quickly he walked to the door and, without looking back, left the room. I heard his footsteps fade down the hallway, and the sound of him shutting himself in the bathroom as in an early grave. Then, but for my own tears, which I could not stop, there was a terrible silence in that house that once had been a sanctuary for us all.

29

"YOUR HIGHNESSES, morning has arrived."

I was awake to hear Igawa's customary greeting through the door of our bedchamber at half past five. As usual, my husband stirred beside me and swung his legs out of bed. He scratched himself and switched on the light.

"Good morning," he murmured vaguely.

He was facing away from me, already shuffling toward the bathroom. He had long since given up expecting a reply.

"Good morning," I whispered.

At the sound of my voice he stopped as though a dipper of freezing water had been poured over his head; his shoulders were raised nearly to his ears in hope or alarm. Slowly, he turned around.

"Haruko?"

"Good morning," I repeated in a stronger voice.

His smile was uncertain. "You've come back?"

"I believe so."

"I'm very glad."

"My voice . . ."

"A little out of practice, but still familiar."

"Not to me."

"It will be again. I've been waiting for this a long time." He paused, staring at me as though I might disappear. "Tell me, what has brought you back?"

I shook my head, knowing that the answer could not be put into words he might understand.

"Well, it doesn't matter, does it?" he concluded hopefully.

NEWS OF THE RETURN of my voice spread quickly through the Togu Gosho, from there to the Imperial Household Agency and, by midday at the latest, into the imperial residence. Each group of Court denizens seemed to have its own special point of interest. Among the volunteers from the mountain villages who tended our lawns and gardens, I was told, there was speculation that the recovery of my strength of mind was in some mystical way connected to the successful season of cormorant fishing on the Nagara River. In recent years, the *ayu* had all but stopped spawning; now, for no apparent reason, the fish had returned in large numbers, and lured by the fires hung from the sterns of the old boats, were being caught in abundance in the restricted gullets of the leashed imperial birds.

And the Crown Princess was again speaking. And once again decent people everywhere might be able to go forward, inspired by a meaningful vision of the bright future of our glorious past.

NOT EVERYONE WAS IN HARMONY with such sentiments. The richer the blood, the cooler the eye. Her Majesty the Empress had her own theories about the loss and renewal of my vocal capacities, and these her minion Oshima was most generous in sharing with me at our first meeting since my collapse the previous autumn.

"I was speaking with Her Majesty yesterday," she began. "As is our habit."

We were in my study. On this spring morning the room wore the fresh sunlight filling its windows like a disguise; Oshima was the thundercloud hidden in plain view.

"I am very glad, Oshima-san, to find that throughout my illness you and Her Majesty have maintained that level of intimacy which I know you value so highly."

"We are in communication most days of the week." Oshima did not attempt to keep the self-congratulation from her voice, and for this I very nearly felt embarrassed on her behalf, but was saved from my mistake by the piercing arrogance of her smile.

"And a very full week it must be," I murmured.

My chief lady-in-waiting colored angrily. Like the Empress herself, she was an elegant, if full-waisted, woman of a certain age, and she always delivered herself of her words as though she were about to sing an aria. Music, however, was not her passion.

"How pleasant for you that you have recovered your voice, Your Highness," she said. "Their Majesties are certainly relieved. Your clever insinuations have been much missed around the Court, I can assure you, as well as your common touch. In fact, as I began to say before you interrupted me, yesterday Her Majesty and I shared quite an agreeable exchange on just that subject."

"And I suppose that you do not intend to keep me in suspense any longer about the details of your discussion?"

"As you wish. Her Majesty was wondering, now that you have your voice back, as to the probable causes of its abandonment in the first place."

"That is most considerate of Her Majesty. Please tell her that I have no idea why I lost my voice."

"You sincerely claim that you do not know the reason?"

"It is not a claim, sincere or otherwise. It is the truth."

"Forgive me, but is that wise?"

"Wise not to know the cause of something unknowable? Who can say?"

"I must warn you, Your Highness, that Her Majesty is not at all fond of riddles or jokes."

"That must be a genetic disposition. My husband doesn't much like riddles either, though he's not bad with jokes."

"Are you trying to amuse me?"

"You or myself, I'm not sure which."

"You are giving me cause for offense."

"Please forgive me, then. I mean merely to give you cause for thought."

"I, for one, am beginning to regret the return of your voice."

"That would make two of us."

"And when I have informed Her Majesty of the tenor of your mind—"

"Forgive me for interrupting, Oshima-san, but you are referring to my conversation, I believe, not my mind."

"Once I have informed Her Majesty of the tenor of your conversation, I am certain that she will have regrets of her own."

"I don't doubt it," I confirmed. "But I'm afraid that there's nothing I can do to change that prospect. Her Majesty's regrets run deep, and have been fixed in place since she first met me. I consider that a shame, but on the point of whether it is my shame or hers, I don't believe that you and I will ever agree."

"You forget yourself."

"On the contrary, I have remembered myself. That was the great, the only consolation of my months of silence. You might try it yourself one day. I recommend it. One says not a word, utters not a sound, makes no speeches, and tells no lies. Quite a rare state in this noble part of the world. At times a miserable state, I won't deny it, but absolutely pure. And purity, if I'm not mistaken, has always been of the greatest importance to Their Majesties. So, yes, for a few months, let's say I was pure, in my way. And during that time, most of it alone, I remembered something. I remembered that I'd had a childhood. And in that childhood I was a girl—no, don't contradict me, I'd never dare suggest I was the same sort of girl as you. I was just an ordinary girl, and my parents ordinary people. It doesn't amount to much in the big picture. But, all the same, I'd forgotten. Well, I've remembered now. And I intend to keep on remembering as long as I live. Please, do report this change to Her Majesty when you next see her, and assure her of my most humble respect."

It was soon afterward that our weekly family evenings were reinstated in the schedule.

HIS MAJESTY THE EMPEROR had a way of speaking at objects—vases, chairs, go sets, Louis XIV footrests, gold Kamakura screens, Tang horses—that, oddly enough, had a pacifying effect on those humans who were in the vicinity; one found it superfluous, in the end, to take anything personally. Treated vaguely, one became eminently vague, but so did everyone else. It was like watching the submersion of one's double in a pool of deep water: there was the vaguely familiar outline; then the ghost of an outline; and, finally, nothing much to speak of. By which time it was usually the hour to return home.

Her Majesty the Empress, on the other hand, retained her razor's edge all her life. She would keep it through more than sixty years of marriage, and well into her tenth decade. She would make history for her longevity. And when, nearing the millennium as Empress Dowager, her blade at last began to dull, it happened quite quickly. She was hardly aware of it. Indeed, she could not remember.

By then her assassin Oshima was long dead, and I was

Empress. On Sundays, I would visit my mother-in-law at the Fukiage Palace and she would smile at me as at a long-lost daughter. We would drink tea and discuss the weather.

Yes, we were old friends.

30

I HAVE A PHOTOGRAPH of my father, taken the summer before my engagement. He wears his gray yukata and stands, hands clasped behind his back in a pose of elegant rumination, dark hair smoothed with flaxseed oil, on the veranda of the house in Karuizawa. It is the same picture that my mother chose for the shrine at his funeral.

A stroke felled him in the spring of 1970, while he was out for a walk. When by dinner he hadn't returned, my mother went to look for him. She found him lying on his back in the road behind the house, his hands open as though, in darkest sleep, he were trying to catch the things being thrown at him.

He regained consciousness, but his mind was never the same. He lived only a few more months. Following his death, my mother passed on to me stories about the odd expressions of his surviving memory during his last weeks of decline, discrete time capsules that somehow his brain had preserved intact from the trauma. I believe she thought she was giving me something from him that I might be able to keep with me and cherish. But without his familiar voice to narrate events, and broken into fragments as they were, the stories had the opposite effect. They showed me that my father had been my only true witness. The only one who could say for certain that I had once been a child of life and laughter. And, now that he was gone, it began to seem to me that I had never been that child.

THE HOUSE IN KARUIZAWA WAS SOLD; alone now, my mother could not keep it up, and no longer had the desire to go there. I wanted very much to see it before it was gone. I tried to have the trip arranged but was repeatedly told that there was no time for any activity not already accounted for on my full schedule. On this matter, as on so many others, the Grand Steward would not relent. Desperate, I appealed to my husband to intercede on my behalf. He spoke privately to his parents, and the next week, to my surprise and relief, I was allowed to go. I took the children—Yasu was ten, and our daughter Kumiko, born in 1965, was five. Outside of published photographs, I could not forget, my father had never seen either of his grandchildren.

THE HOUSE WAS EMPTY. The furniture, pictures on the walls, old tennis rackets, tea bowls, bath brushes, everything I remembered from those happy summers, had been sold or disposed of. Now our footsteps—the children's lighter and quicker, for they were chasing each other from room to room—echoed. I emerged on the veranda at the back, and stood alone in the cool scented shade, smelling the pine trees and hearing the birds.

After a while I felt a tug on my arm, and found Yasu looking up at me.

"Mother, what did you *do* here?" he asked incredulously, for he thought the house boring, simple, and dull, and could not understand how I had ever been a happy child in such a place.

ON THE DRIVE BACK TO TOKYO, the children fell asleep. I sat between them, a head resting against each arm—a mother, simply, with swollen eyes. I was prepared, though never brave enough, to tell Okubo to drive on, past the palace, past Tokyo, to drive on as we were, my children and I, and never to stop.

31

"AREN'T YOU SOMETIMES LONELY, Shige?"

The end of that winter, early dusk, in the garden behind our residence. The few solitary pines more brown than green in the failing light, the birds gone, my husband's box-shaped houses for them holding nothing now but old feathers. Soon, a dinner to go to—or an awards ceremony, a concert; I could not remember. We were already late to get dressed, that much I knew, our lesser chamberlains waiting anxiously to shepherd us along; we could apprehend them there at the edge of the garden, hanging like bats. We hadn't seen each other all day, and when we ran into each other by accident outside our rooms my husband suggested a brief stroll in the garden.

"Lonely?" He picked up a small brown pinecone and studied it. We strolled the length of the garden in silence, the soft, decaying ground beneath our feet. At the far wall, as though by mutual consent, we stopped.

"Do you know," I said quietly, "I used to imagine returning home. But now, with my father gone, there is no destination, and no point of departure."

He nodded, but did not reply.

"I would like a friend, Shige. Someone to talk to."

He dropped the pinecone and turned to me, his eyes full of shadows. "We don't get to have friends, Haruko," he said. "We can't expect anyone else to understand what it's like."

ONE DAY THE PREVIOUS SUMMER, for the first time in almost thirty years, Dr. Watanabe had failed to appear for his duties. My husband had been concerned enough to place a call to the doctor's home, and was told by his daughter that her father was in the hospital, being treated for cancer of the pancreas. By then, the disease was already in its late stages.

I was in the Imperial Household Agency Building that morning, meeting with representatives from a women's group devoted to the preservation of Japan's domestic arts. I happened to glance toward an open door, and saw my husband waiting for me outside. With his bereaved hands and drawn face, he appeared small and young, more orphan than prince.

In the final days, as his old friend and counselor lay dying, my husband sat with him whenever his schedule permitted, and had to be dissuaded from sleeping on a folding bed in the hospital room. Around the shining, colorless areas of the doctor's wartime burns—those smooth scars which had never lost their aura of mysterious unknowability—the rest of him had finally surrendered and fallen.

When the life had departed, and the formal rites had

been performed, my husband retreated to his study. Late in the night I'd gone to bring him some tea and, pausing outside his closed door, heard a sound of such personal anguish that it checked my hand from knocking. I had turned away and returned to my own room, leaving him to grieve in private with his memories.

PART THREE

32

ON A FRIGID JANUARY DAY in 1989, before twenty-five hundred official guests from one hundred and sixty-four countries, my husband became the new Emperor of Japan.

He climbed his dead father's throne and sat upon it.

The *takamakura* is ten meters tall, fashioned out of gleaming black lacquer. Gazing down from the throne's highest point is a carved rendering of the phoenix—the ancient bird who, after wandering the desert for five hundred years, was believed to have consumed himself by fire, only to rise again from his own ashes with renewed strength.

In our language the phoenix, like the Emperor, is also a kind of paragon, a person or object of sublime beauty or excellence. And so, once in a lifetime, when a new emperor takes his rightful place high on the Chrysanthemum Throne and the phoenix peers over his shoulder at the awestruck world, one is granted a newfound sense of the complex mingling of man and myth which our nation has achieved with such distinction.

Strange that the phoenix, which long ago burned so hotly in the desert, should now be so cool to the touch.

But I have it on good authority that he is indeed rather cool.

And so the Emperor, with that bird's eye hunting his back, unexpectedly feels chilled to begin with, immortal yet like a newborn, lacking the warmth of the world. For that, he must wait another ten months, until November and the days of formal ceremonies and banquets known as *Sokui-no-Rei*. At the end of which, in the Great Food Offering of *Daijosai,* in the middle of the night, passing from one to the other of three wooden sanctums constructed for this purpose alone; beyond the prying eyes of every living soul; after taking a ritual cleansing bath in a wooden tub; after making an offering of rice and fish to Amaterasu Omikami; after uttering a prayer of gratitude for peace and an abundant rice harvest; after partaking of the plain, necessary foods of his people as a communion with the gods, he will at last present himself for the mythical embrace that will separate him from, and give him wisdom over, the earthly realm.

In the unwitnessed room to which he has made his solitary pilgrimage, there is a platform resembling a bed. This much is known. It is not for him but for Amaterasu Omikami, for when, deep in the night, She will come to bestow upon him the spirit of the gods. The new Emperor—my husband—wrapped himself in simple white garments, like a lover in his bedclothes, and humbly prepared himself for Her arrival.

I, TOO, BECAME SOMETHING ON THAT DAY: at the age of fifty-five, I became Empress of Japan.

And yet, though I was duly and publicly transformed, I did not ascend. No spiritual separation was asked for, or achieved. On the contrary: seated on my own high throne, I had never felt more earthbound.

33

OUR DAUGHTER, KUMIKO, was the first of our children to get married. By the evening of their wedding day, when she and her new husband—a civil servant named Seiji Ohno—returned to their two-bedroom apartment in an attractive though not extravagant neighborhood, and changed out of their dress clothes and sat down in their unremarkable sitting room with cups of freshly brewed tea to reminisce about the day's events, Kumi would no longer be a princess; she would already have been stricken from the imperial registry. By marrying a commoner, she would have become one. And this she would have done willingly, for love.

ONE EVENING, A WEEK BEFORE THE CEREMONY, I was passing her bedroom and saw a light under her door. I knocked and entered, and found her sitting on her bed, looking through an old album of family photographs. I sat down beside her; we were silent for a few moments, turning the pages of the album in her hands. We came to a photograph of her in a blue pinafore and round-toed shoes running on the beach in Hayama, perhaps three years old. The camera had a wide lens. Behind her,

her father was smiling proudly, and I was in the act of calling out—"Don't go too far!" I seemed to be saying, my mouth open (this was clearly not an official Court photograph)—and, off to the right, at the water's edge, was Yasu, staring moodily out into the bay, his back to us, hands stuffed into the pockets of his short pants.

With my finger, I traced one of her running feet in the photograph. "You will be leaving here, Kumi. But you will take your memories with you."

She searched my face with her eyes. "Was that your experience when you came here?"

"My situation was naturally different from yours," I said. "But yes, on the whole, that was my experience. My memory of my life before I came has only grown more precious to me."

"Perhaps that's not a healthy thing?"

"Perhaps," I agreed.

She closed the photo album, and replaced it in the drawer of her bedside table. "Mother, I'm afraid to leave. I'm frightened."

"I understand. I was afraid to arrive."

"Do you ever regret the choice you made?"

I met her eyes—feeling, suddenly, a sadness that I could not begin to explain to her, so different were our experiences. "I do not regret *you* for a moment," I said.

"And the rest?"

"The rest is too big to tell now. Someday, perhaps." I reached out and touched her cheek, willing a smile onto my face, and the tears from my eyes. "But by then, my dear, you will be a happy wife and mother, with your own pictures, your own stories to tell—stories of a much richer life than this one. I promise you. And, for that prospect, I will always rejoice."

IMPERIAL TRADITION DICTATED that her father and I not be present at the ceremony. But we decided that in this case tradition must give way. We would see Kumi take her vows.

It's the moment every mother waits for: to look at one's daughter during her wedding and see in her eyes that she has chosen according to her heart. An expression observed across a room—irrefutable evidence.

Then it's over, and one finds oneself again at a remove, isolated in a stately crowd, left to guess at the truth of things through the projection of one's own hopes and regrets, and stupidly fearing the consequences. An empress or a washerwoman, it makes no difference.

From that moment and place, my daughter walked out into the world that, long before, I had left. She went forward—happily, I prayed and believed—while, locked in my many-roomed palace, I seemed able only to endlessly return, following the unspooled thread of fading memories back to the loving nest of my childhood, which, more and more, felt like a dream.

AFTER THE RECEPTION, Shige and I said our goodbyes and rode with Yasu back to the palace. For my own peace of mind, for the fifth or tenth time I asked my son about the character of his old school friend, who was now my son-in-law.

"Seiji has always been the same, Mother," Yasu replied patiently. "I've said so before. He's one of the most decent and likable people I know."

"Then she's made a good marriage. She will be happy."

"Of course she has, and she will."

"Come now, Haruko," my husband said. "We are going to see her next weekend."

Painfully, I imagined how it would be: tea with my daughter once a month or so, the hour always too short by my reckoning, rigidly enforced by my schedulers. Whenever possible I would visit her at her home, where I might watch from a certain distance as she attempted to learn the ways of the world to which she was now officially joined: dry-cleaning bills, parking tickets, supermarket checkout lines, the price of ramen versus soba. The radical liberty to stay in bed if she felt like it, and the equally heady possibility of going out for a stroll on a moment's notice.

She would not miss our beautiful prison, the ritualized eccentricities of the inmates. It would be a relief to her to be less often in the news. She would be good at making her own tea, moving about her little kitchen with the brisk efficiency she had inherited from my mother.

Naturally, in this new life of hers, certain sacrifices of convenience and taste would be required. Every day filled with a host of tiny, deliciously mundane (or so I imagined) compromises, the possibility for a failure or a victory so small that no one but her might ever know of its existence. Imagine: the feeling of making one's own secret mark in one's own private place, outside the censure of those who would have things be as they have always been.

No, I didn't have to imagine it: I still remembered.

"We may see her, Shige, but we may not know her," I said. "That is what I'm afraid of. Kumi has moved to another country."

"This is what you wanted. You must try to be happy for her."

"I am happy for her—very happy. But that's not all I am. I won't have my feelings reduced for the sake of everyone's comfort."

My husband frowned but made no reply. The cavernous, soundproof limousine glided through the half-darkened streets. We didn't have far to go, yet it seemed a long way. The high yellow streetlights, through tinted bulletproof glass, appeared dreamlike, as though I were unconscious and a probing beam were shining against my closed eyelids to see if anyone was home.

"Yasu," began my husband rather officiously, broaching a topic that had long been on his mind, "the Grand Steward came to speak to me the other day. He was very put out. It seems the search committee for Crown Princess has come up against an unexpected obstacle."

In the gloom of the car, Yasu's expression was unreadable.

"Is it true you told the committee that you intend to

remain a bachelor for the rest of your life? Could you really have said such a thing?"

"I made a proposal once, Father," Yasu answered grimly. "Don't you remember? It was sincerely meant. And it was not accepted."

He turned away from us then, and would speak of the subject no more.

34

HE HAD TUMBLED INTO LOVE WITH HER, our sensible
son.

Her name was Keiko Mori. She had grown up in
other countries—was Japanese but, like him, different.
Spoke half a dozen languages. Was possessed of an inde-
pendent mind. Already was being called the most promising career woman of her generation—which was to say,
in our nation's history, since none had ventured there
before her. She was the daughter of a high-ranking
diplomat, and it had been speculated that she might one
day become the first female director of the Foreign Ministry. The family had a second home in Karuizawa. She
liked to ski and hike, swim and ride horses. Preferred
dogs to cats. Knew literature. Had, like Yasu, been to Oxford, where medieval barge traffic (his chosen field) was
considered a perfectly normal field of study.

We had her to the Togu Gosho for an evening of music. She was polite, she had an ear, but one could see immediately that she'd been groomed for more substantive
duties than the tinkling of keys or the bowing of strings.

Standing off to the side with her near evening's end,
I had said sincerely, "I envy you your career, Mori-san."

A look of genuine surprise: "Envy me, Your Highness?"

"Not your career, perhaps. Your sense of purpose. Your active engagement with the world."

"But, Your Highness, you must be more engaged with the world than any woman in Japan."

"No, Mori-san. I am merely busy."

IN REJECTING YASU'S PROPOSAL OF MARRIAGE, she had thanked him for the undeserved honor he did her, and assured him that there was nothing personal in her decision to remain a free citizen and continue the pursuit of her career in the Foreign Ministry. It had all been done with dignity and discretion.

I felt for him, of course. His raw sorrow echoed back to me other sorrows that everyone in our family shared. Life was, in the end, a matter of limits and laws. Love, too, if it was allowed to exist. I could not forget that I had married my husband out of love. At the time, to do so was considered an unprecedented act of freedom for us both. That it would turn out to be my last act of freedom became clear to me only in stages, as the hidden cost of love. My son, in his current sorrow, was paying another, more public cost, and paying it dearly.

In the months following his rejection, he swore to his father and me that he would settle for no one but her. If Keiko would not have him, then he would have nobody, and that would be that.

In the public arena, however, the mood was less romantic. It was much noted that the Crown Prince was not a mere man who might follow his heart's desires as he chose. He bore a responsibility to the people. With no brothers and only a single uncle—an aging and childless alcoholic playboy who was already showing the early signs of liver failure—Prince Tsuyo's refusal to take a bride was looked upon with alarm, even anger. If he didn't marry, he would have no male offspring; and, without male offspring, the future of something that was believed to have existed since the beginning of recorded history was thrown into doubt.

The country became obsessed with the prospect of this unprecedented calamity. A chorus of worry and complaint made a constant din in the less restrained elements of the press and on certain television talk shows. All sorts of measures were unofficially promoted, some sinister and others quite fantastical; some involving surgeons and scalpels, others apparently taking into account the rarely witnessed mating rituals of the alpaca and the emu. In bars and nightclubs in which my son had never set foot, it was loudly whispered that, because he had yet to marry and have a family of his own, he must therefore be homosexual. One "doctor," who insisted on wearing a white lab coat for every television appearance, put forth the theory that the repeated intermingling of related strains of the imperial bloodline for fifteen hundred years had resulted in a permanent condition of backward-swimming sperm: with his arms, into the camera, this man made the motions, clearly much practiced at home in front of a mirror, of a dying salmon spawning in reverse.

It was, of course, intended by those in the palace who wore the darkest suits and kept the longest hours that such slander should never reach Her Majesty's ears and stain my supposedly delicate sensibility. However, reports of various kinds did occasionally leak under the door of my private study. As the power and the faculties of the former Empress had waned over the years, and the old-guard chamberlains and ladies-in-waiting who'd been her most loyal soldiers—even the assassins like Oshima—one by one succumbed to retirement and illness, I had, with my husband's intervention, been able to quietly affect the Grand Steward and his government-appointed colleagues in the choosing of replacements. The gradual result was a small gain in my freedom, and perhaps in my influence at Court. Still, it was in the nature of the place that even such small steps forward as these soon reached their pre-scribed limits.

OUT WALKING IN THE EAST GARDEN before breakfast one morning, my husband and I were approached by Grand Steward Minamoto and two members of his staff, all brandishing umbrellas in sober defense of a light misting rain. Their appearance at such an early hour was most un-usual, and my husband, recognizing that whatever had brought them out must be of a serious nature, met with Minamoto apart from the others, so that they might con-fer in private.

I watched their two heads under the black spined shroud of the Grand Steward's umbrella. The mist made no sound falling on the tightly stretched canopy. Early in life, my husband had been taught that extraneous movement of one's physical person was disrespectful and weak, and his hands as he spoke with Minamoto were virtually still. As a rule, he ate with great economy and almost never stirred in his sleep.

The two men parted. The Grand Steward made a quick bow to me, and then he and his assistants walked off the way they'd come, their dark suits and umbrellas dissolving into the mist like specters. It was odd; after they were gone it was as though they had never been there. In their place, I became aware of a white heron standing with mirrored stillness in the shallows of the small pond to the east.

My husband rejoined me. His handsome face looked careworn, and his short hair, damp with mist, seemed more intense in its grayness and age, almost grizzled.

"We are right back where we started," he remarked unhappily. "The people are getting frustrated, and I can't say I blame them. I've just given Minamoto permission to make one last attempt on Yasu's behalf with Ambassador Mori. Mori's ambitious. If he wants something enough there's no telling the influence he can have over his daughter, however headstrong she might be."

"And if she doesn't love Yasu?"

"Didn't you have doubts when you accepted me, Haruko?"

"They were doubts about your world, Shige. About *this* world."

"Weren't you once called headstrong, too?"

"A very long time ago, and I don't believe it was a compliment." We had reached the bank of the pond. Imperceptibly, the heron shifted her position to watch us from the side of her head, her beady eye cutting through the white mist. "I'm afraid for Yasu," I said. "If he fails again, the people won't forgive him."

"And if he does nothing, and chooses to live out the rest of his days like a celibate priest, they won't forgive him, either." He sighed impatiently. "Look, the chance to fail again is the freedom he's demanding. So we are offering it to him with our full support. Or else I can promise you that we will be the last. We might as well keep walking now and cross the moat, walk all the way to Karuizawa, settle down, and open a teahouse."

"I wouldn't mind such a future."

"Well, I would. I believe it would kill me. And I can tell you that I'm made constantly uneasy by the thought that we're already too late—that history will surely remember us, but for all the wrong reasons. No, what Yasu needs is to fulfill his duty, marry and have children."

"Sons, you mean."

"Of course, sons," he said irritably. "The line must continue."

"Must it? Why?"

He stared at me in aggrieved shock. I stared back, shocking him further.

"You are the Empress."

"And am I not to be forgiven, Shige, for finally, after decades of silence, asking a simple question?"

In his anger, he said nothing and would not look at me.

"I am not sorry," I said.

Above our heads the mist fell in a whisper, and in the pond the heron took a slow, stick-legged step.

"It is wet," my husband said without a trace of affection. "You are shivering from the cold. Let us turn back."

"I am not cold," I replied, and walked on without him.

35

I WAS AT MY DESK late on an afternoon when the knock came. In the doorway, his head lowered, stood Yasu. On heavy legs he came forward and sat on the chair nearest me.

"It looked promising. I thought it was. We talked about politics, sports, books, life at Oxford. I didn't want it to end. And then I brought up the question again. She said no, and it ended."

I reached for his hand, held it a moment, and let it go. "What reason did she give?"

"Her reasons haven't changed. She wants to pursue her career. I admire that and told her so. She's afraid she would suffocate here."

"She said so?"

"She didn't have to. And tell me, who can honestly blame her? Who would ever choose this godforsaken place unless one had to?"

Our eyes met, and he realized what he had just said to me.

"Mother, I'm sorry . . ."

"No, it's all right. I don't disagree."

"I'm just . . ."

"Let's not talk about it, shall we?"

We were silent.

And then a light breeze, entering the open window by my desk, stirred the pile of letters to the Japan-American Society, the Japan Association of Nurses, the National Federation of Single Parents' and Children's Welfare Associations. . . . And something in the picture—the rote symbolism of official letters written by someone else and awaiting my signature, their very meaninglessness in the realm of feeling, resting starkly in the shadow of my son's loneliness—might have suggested, had I been properly receptive, a summing up of our lives; yet some survivalist instinct led me to overlook this truth for the moment.

I capped my fountain pen and placed it on the desk. The same heavy gold pen that Shige had rescued from the floor thirty years ago, when I could not speak, promising to keep it for me until I felt strong enough to ask for it back. At some point—I could not remember when—I had felt strong enough and he had returned it. We had gone on, many years passing in this place where the tide neither rose nor fell.

I looked at my son. Never had I seen him so lost and unhappy. "Do you think she loves you, Yasu?"

He seemed to struggle with the question before finally delivering his answer in a tone of defiant hope. "She's afraid. But I know in my heart she would eventually come to love me as I love her."

"What makes you certain?"

He shook his head; he could not explain it.

"I believe you," I said.

And so I did then, or wanted to.

36

AT SUNRISE ON THE DAY I was to meet Keiko Mori alone for the first time, I saw the morning star. It sat nestled in the clear dark blue high above the East Garden like a pearl in the inverted depths, waiting to be plucked if only it could be reached. I could not remember seeing it since I'd been a girl in Karuizawa.

I'd slept fitfully, waking before it was light outside. My husband did not stir as I slipped out of bed. The night guards looked alarmed to see me creeping about the residence in my robe; at first, they seemed to mistake me for an intruder. This was followed by an excess of bowing and apologizing; it took several attempts to get them to understand that I simply wanted some air. They tried to follow me, but I sent them back with the promise that I wouldn't wander far.

OUTSIDE, THE STAR WAS FLOATING by itself in the sky. For a brief while—or perhaps, who could say, it was simply me, on this particular morning—it seemed both ending and beginning.

37

"SHALL I WAIT HERE for Your Majesty?"

Okubo had parked the limousine in the narrow drive-way beside my parents' house. I was grateful that he'd thought to cover the imperial crests on the sides with black magnetized patches; though had the Grand Steward ever learned of this bit of harmless trickery, my driver would soon have found himself picking mushrooms for a living.

Yes, Okubo: still with me, and nearly as old as I was. Fond as I was of him, I'd done my best over the years to encourage his promotion within the Court hierarchy. But in his own quiet way he was stubborn, and each time the chance for advancement arose he would inform his superiors of his wish to remain in his present station. I trusted him completely, and would go nowhere of consequence without him.

"I think that under the circumstances, Koji, I would prefer total discretion," I said. "Is there some place you might go for an hour to pass the time?"

"I could wash the car again."

"The car looks perfectly clean as it is."

"Thank you, Your Majesty." He inclined his head, adding, "There's an excellent bookshop in Sendagaya."

Okubo and I shared an interest in well-written murder mysteries, and I often sent him on book-hunting errands for me.

"Yes, all right, buy me a copy of something interesting, and another for yourself. But, whatever you do, don't tell me who did it."

"Very good, Your Majesty."

"You look very serious today."

Gravely, Okubo considered my remark. "I'm sorry, Your Majesty. Today I just *feel* serious."

"Well," I agreed, "you're probably right."

He opened the door for me. We were early, free of imperial retinue and in relative disguise, and for a few moments it was possible to stand like a normal pedestrian outside the house in which I'd spent my childhood. A widowed house no longer large, and now in need of repair. A corner of tiled roof, visible above the sagging, lichen-covered rampart of garden wall, beset by cracks like broken pottery. The iron door leading to the garden scarred with rust and pigeon excrement.

"Thank you, Koji, but there is no need for you to wait."

He allowed his kind eyes to rest on me longer than usual, then he bowed.

"I'll return in an hour, then, Your Majesty."

THE GARDEN WAS A POEM in a broken frame.

Impoverished shrubs; flowers in need of watering; two weeping cherry trees, oddly stunted; gravel no longer white. Stones, too, must be tended to keep their spirits. In the center of the enclosure, a rusted metal chair faced south toward the only remaining sliver of view—an accident of daylight caused by neighboring roofs of unequal height.

The front door of the house was marred by scratches around the lock, as from a repeatedly errant key. Beneath the windows to either side, a damp, mossy stain was climbing the façade, showing what all things become with time.

Here we had stood on my wedding day: my mother on my right, my father behind me.

I went inside.

SHE CAME ALONE as arranged, by subway and on foot. One had to admire her courage. Her first words as I opened the door for her were that my directions had been excellent.

If not classically beautiful, she was certainly pretty, with a wide face, a steady chin, and intelligent, rather deep-set eyes. Her hair was cut short in a forthright style that suggested an interest in something more substantial than pure appearance; an impression supported by her choice of a navy suit (she had come directly from work, one had to assume), rather than anything more overtly feminine. She relied on little jewelry to make herself up.

Her smile of greeting, while correctly restrained, was in no way timid.

In the entrance hall, she removed her black low-heeled shoes and, at my urging, put on a pair of my mother's old house slippers, as I had done. We were an odd-looking sight now, with our tailored clothes and run-down footwear. If she thought it peculiar to be having a highly secret rendezvous with the Empress of Japan in a house cannibalized by its own neighborhood, she kept it to herself. She was cool, yet also surprisingly warm.

"This was my parents' house," I explained. "My mother died only last year, you may have heard. Will you come into the kitchen with me while I prepare tea?"

The kitchen was narrow and clean. The air had the faintly sour but inviting scent of miso paste, as if soup had been made on the premises only recently. I filled the electric kettle and switched it on.

"As you can imagine, Mori-san, it's not often that I get to wear slippers and meet young ladies for tea in the afternoon."

With a click and an expiring sigh, the kettle shut itself off. I poured the steaming water over the pale-green leaves. The bitter green scent rose up and made one respectful, as it always does. I carried the tray into the sitting room and served tea for us both.

My father's favorite part of the house. The shoji opening onto the garden had long ago been replaced by glass windows with venetian blinds, and the light spilling in now was slatted and oddly figured—hiragana drawn from shadows.

"My hope in coming here, Mori-san, is that we might speak to each other without constraint during a time of, let us say, certain complexities."

"Nothing would please me more, Your Majesty."

"I would like you to feel comfortable with me."

"I do already."

She spoke without hesitation or embarrassment, and I saw that she was telling the truth. Her years abroad had prepared her almost too well.

"There has been a great deal of pressure on you, and throughout it all you have handled yourself with grace, sincerity, and respect."

She inclined her head—neither modestly nor boastfully but with a matter-of-factness that to my generation of women was no more plausible than a flying horse. Her confidence was something that I hadn't fully perceived before—her sense, as a contemporary person, of being innately deserving of attention. She was used to feeling wanted and needed. And, were I to be honest with myself about this day, I would have to acknowledge that I was willing enough for her to feel wanted and needed—though at the expense, perhaps, of some of that abundant confidence.

"Please tell me truthfully, between us, were you not at all tempted by my son's proposal?"

"Of course I was tempted, Your Majesty."

"Do you have feelings for him?"

"His Highness is a good and admirable man."

"That is certainly a respectful answer. But do you think that it might be possible for you to love him as he so clearly loves you? I am sorry to be so direct, but we have reached a point where there is not much time."

"I don't know the answer to that question, Your Majesty."

"Then of what are you certain?"

"That there are things in the prospect of marrying His Highness which make me afraid."

"One can be frightened and still move forward," I said. "I did so myself."

"Then you must know what it is that I am afraid to give up."

"I do know. Your career."

"No, Your Majesty. My life."

In the silence that followed, I refilled our teacups. The sun had declined and no longer bathed the room. The tea was cold. In the shadows slowly encroaching upon us, the color in her cheeks revealed a new and womanly depth; I felt that I could see her as she would be when she was older.

"Mori-san," I said, "I hope that you will listen to me now with an open mind."

"Of course."

"I want to tell you that I understand your fear perhaps better than you know."

"I have heard about your suffering," she said respectfully.

"At the time of my marriage, I had no one but my husband to talk to—not a single friend inside."

"That must have been very difficult for you."

"I am not complaining. But I want you to know that if you marry my son I will do whatever is in my power to protect you and to be your friend and ally. I give you my word."

LIKE INFLUENCE, PERSUASION IS NOT A RECIPE, a series of prescriptive guides made up of three parts this and one part that. One will never really know how much one did. Whether it was too much, or too little, or just enough. Whether one was the catalyst for another person's actions or merely the excuse.

And yet one may know all the same. Riding home alone from our secret meeting late that afternoon, some gathering sense of responsibility for this young woman's future happiness clung to me; and it felt not like triumph, but already, somehow, like remorse.

38

BEFORE THE MONTH WAS OUT, she had accepted him. Who could honestly claim to know her true reasons, the contents of her heart? No matter, said the people. No matter, said the Court. No matter, said the Emperor and the Empress. For the good of the nation, the decision had been made. The future now was clear and brilliant.

Some commentators declared the coming of the new Princess a miracle, others our own velvet revolution, and still others a dream. Within weeks, Keiko dolls, hand-bags, scarves, teapots, sake sets, T-shirts, and "business-wear" were selling at such volume that shopkeepers around the country could not keep the items in stock.

She would have even less opportunity than her prede-cessor to learn what she was expected to learn. How to walk, bow, speak, not speak, recite, be silent, appear, dis-appear. The art and illusion of the imperial press confer-ence. The angle of general approach. Sixty hours of lessons, and then the window for lessons would be closed and locked.

It is said that one crosses the moat only once in a life-time.

SOON AFTER THE ENGAGEMENT WAS ANNOUNCED, a fertility test was conducted. Keiko passed without incident. The science of the thing may change, but the results are never permitted to vary—which would in no way exempt the new Crown Princess, in the weeks of ritualized ceremony following her marriage, from being subjected to a vigorous stomach-rubbing with sacks of bran by two Shinto virgins to increase her chances of producing male offspring. The sackcloth, I knew from experience, would be rough and irritating; after my own wedding, hives had broken out from my navel to my throat, lasting for weeks. No one had warned me of such a possibility. All I knew was that others had come before me; that others, presumably, had had their bellies rubbed like hens before laying, and had uncomplainingly broken out in rashes that had to be covered up. And then my skin had cleared, I conceived, and my first child was a boy. So who could say, in the end, that the ritual had not been effective? Who could say that what was written in the secret books was not the word of truth?

So Keiko had passed her test. But the test was by definition only the beginning, the first hurdle in an endless reproductive Olympics. The test, in short, said that one could; to be followed by the wedding, which declared that one must. For, apart from quietly and efficiently producing a male heir to the Chrysanthemum Throne, we wives have no special skills or attributes that might come close to satisfying the general expectations upon our person; indeed, there are no other expectations upon our person.

And our blood alone is of no particular value: it is water compared to the fine, noble wine of the ages, and not believed to improve with time.

And when the wedding is over, the processional completed, the carriage or car put away for another century, the tens of thousands of cheering subjects returned to work and pachinko and ironing, we are brought to our elaborate new home, given a cup of bitter tea, and duly expected to begin. But life, unfortunately, is not a nature show on television; and, even if it were, we are not the proper creatures for the task, being but heavy flightless birds who, once knocked down, are slow to rise again. Our ugly feet stick up in the air. Our eggs are few in number and famously fragile; not many are ever likely to hatch. That is our bird's sad biological story, and there is little or nothing she can do to change the plot.

39

8 May 1993
Hotel Okura
My Dear Empress Gazelle,

Greetings from your old friend who has never stopped thinking of you with great affection. Perhaps you have already guessed what brings me back to Tokyo on this rare visit. Has your future daughter-in-law ever mentioned her fairy godmother in New York? The eccentric Japanese lady of a certain age who took the girl under her wing during her high school years, accompanied her to Bergdorf's and her first R-rated movie (if you must know, it was Saturday Night Fever, *starring John Travolta, who later danced with Princess Di at the White House)? Years ago, I met Ambassador Mori and his wife at a dinner party, and we became friends. In time, I was introduced to their daughter Keiko. We got on well from the start—even then, she was a girl who spoke her mind. For the rest of her years in New York I saw her regularly, and now she has grown into a marvelous young woman. And if my bad influence is still occasionally apparent in her I can only apologize and ask that Your Majesty please consider her lively, forthright personality a gift sent to you with the greatest affection from your track team-*

mate of the past—a handoff like the ones we used to practice in the halls of Seishin.

I am taking foolish liberties with my familiar tone here, risking offending you and having myself banished before I've even arrived, but you must know better than anyone that I never learned any other way to communicate. It used to land me in hot water with Mother Clapp, and it still sometimes gets me into trouble with those higher up, of whom you, my dear, certainly would be the highest. Though my compulsively irreverent manner has seemed—notwithstanding my most recent marriage—to play better in New York all these years, I will understand if you no longer find me tolerable. But if for some reason you do, and you think of me with even a fraction of the warmth with which I think of you, then we might have much to talk about, and many conversations to finish.

On the guest list for your son's wedding, you will find me under my married name of Thomas. Quite reasonably, your eyes may have passed over the entry without recognition. My second husband's name was—or, I should say, is, for he is undeniably alive—Bertram Thomas. He has retired to the city of Naples, Florida, while I, fortunately, continue to reside in his large and handsome apartment on Park Avenue. He has his own airplane, which on occasion I use (with a brief stop in Hawaii, it brought me here quite comfortably).

Dear Haruko, I hope you are happy. Prince Tsuyo is a very lucky man. Keiko is a young woman of the kind that, running through the halls (or merely thinking of running), we once dreamed of becoming.

You must certainly be overwhelmed with your many obliga-

tions. Nonetheless, if you have a few minutes to spare and feel like seeing an old friend with gangly legs and a big mouth (it was not for nothing, you may recall, that I was called Squid on a Stick), I have taken rooms at the Okura and am already sick of shopping.

I am the first to admit that I have no idea what an empress really does. But if there were ever a poll for Most Valuable and I were asked, I would certainly vote for you.

Yours most affectionately,
Miko

40

I SENT OKUBO to fetch Miko at her hotel, with instructions not to mind anything bizarre she might say, for she was a longtime resident of New York City. Koji, though he had never been to New York, had read many murder mysteries set there, and he appeared eager to carry out the dangerous assignment I'd given him. I asked him to bring my friend directly to my private study because, this once, I wished to banish all thought of the great halls, endless approaches, and oppressively formal service that invariably marked any meeting in the imperial sphere. On this important day, all that I required was a simple lunch laid and waiting, and a quiet room in which to talk.

When the knock finally came, I was ready, and opened the door myself.

Miko smiled unselfconsciously while I studied her. After all the years, her figure had retained its charming awkwardness, the angular torso improbably balanced atop the long, coltish legs. And yet her gray hair gave the luster of her dark eyes and the warmly burnished hollows of her cheeks a new and arresting prominence, leading one to reflect that, though she had never been pretty, time had generously agreed to make her handsome.

"I am happy to report that you look much the same, though even better," I said.

"Still Squid on a Stick?"

"That would make me a very antiquated Gazelle."

"Funny," Miko said, "to me you look just like the Empress of Japan."

I noticed Okubo, standing stiffly behind my guest, making no effort to hide his disapproval at what he obviously considered the undignified tenor of our conversation.

"I warned you that she was odd, Koji," I said. "And she tends to make everyone around her odd as well."

"Not me," Okubo muttered.

"I *am* odd," Miko cheerfully agreed. "But your driver thinks I'm a spy, Your Majesty. Though if anyone's a spy, it's him. His discretion is inhuman, even for a Japanese."

"Your Majesty's friend asked me many demanding questions about Your Majesty, but I refused to answer each one," Okubo replied stoically.

"A brick wall," confirmed Miko.

"Thank you, Koji, you've done well."

With two bows of notably unequal depth, he left us.

"Just as I've always suspected—it's like the sixteenth century here," Miko said.

"I would say the tenth."

"I'll take your word for it. You were always better at history."

"You were faster."

"I make no comment—if I were to contradict you, they would put me behind bars and I'd never see Fifth Avenue again. What a lovely room. Is this your private office?"

"I've filled it with things from my previous study, but it stubbornly refuses to feel like mine."

"Whose, then?"

"Some woman in a book I haven't read."

"If you haven't read it, then I certainly haven't, either. Listen, my dear, you must come and see me in New York one of these years while we're both still breathing."

"Nothing would please me more," I said warmly.

"But of course you can't just visit someone whenever you feel like it."

"Not in the sense you mean."

"Is there any other sense that matters?" she asked seriously.

At the table, I poured glasses of lemon water from a sweating pitcher. A meal of cold poached salmon and steamed vegetables with ginger had been laid for us. Miko politely waited until I raised my chopsticks before beginning to eat, but it quickly became clear that neither of us had an appetite.

"I don't know about you," she said, pushing back her chair, finally, and glancing around the room, "but I think I would find all this rather oppressive." She spread her arms to take in my study, the windows, beyond the windows, the palace, the gardens, the woods, the moat: there was no end, it seemed, to what her arms contained.

"I suppose, at times."

"And at other times?"

"At other times, I don't find it anything at all," I said. "It is so much that it is not very much. It's a great nothing, a fantastic void, and I am nothing in it."

"You are philosophical today."

"No, Miko, I'm the opposite—I have no philosophy left. What I have instead is a very full schedule, day after day. The sad truth is I've become merely a pragmatic person."

"But that's how I remember you when we were young—at least compared to me."

"Yes, but with a few dreams still attached."

We were silent.

"Are we all two people?" I asked after a while.

"Oh, at least, I should think." Miko smiled. "I remember my husband once demanding that I stop trying to impress him with my fake Japanese humility and just find the courage to tell him the truth. I felt so relieved—finally, the truth!"

"Your second husband?"

"No, my second husband was a marriage of convenience, I'm sorry to say. He adores fake Japanese humility, and the truth isn't his friend. I meant my first husband, Simon. We were on our fifth date, and that was the moment I fell in love with him." She paused, and her gaze turned inward. "He died suddenly, a long time ago. Too soon for us to have children together."

"I am very sorry for you."

"Thank you. But you know, I've discovered something:

it is possible to recover from a catastrophic loss without ever getting over it. Sounds very American, doesn't it? While we were together we traveled a lot—we went to Antarctica once—and often now I think of those footprints we left all over the world. I see them in my dreams: two sets of linked tracks, like birds'."

"Cranes," I said.

She smiled at me. "Yes. Cranes."

"Your map is something to cherish, Miko."

She took a sip from the tall glass in front of her. She seemed to be studying me through the clear green imperfections, thinking about something. Then she told me that she had recently seen her brother, Kenji. "He's still a painter—a good one, I'm glad to say. And, like me, he's a little odd in looks and habit. After dinner the other night, do you know what he said? He told me that I'd become just like him!"

"Because you've lived abroad for so long?"

"Because, after a certain point, there is no coming back. For me, that point was Simon's death. For Kenji, it was the fire that destroyed his face. We have all lost something, those of us who are a little strange."

"And me?"

"You?"

"Aren't I strange?"

"Of course you are, Haruko, but in the way the gods are strange. Their powers make them forbidding to us."

"I have little real power, you must know. And I never want to seem forbidding to you."

"I was speaking generally."

"Please don't. You're the only one left who can confirm that I was once a girl like you."

"A girl, yes," said Miko. "But not like me. You were always magnificent."

"What have I lost, then?"

Before she could answer, we were interrupted by a knock on the door. We looked up from each other as from a trance.

"Who is it?" I called.

The door opened.

"Not yet, Koji," I said. "We need more time."

With a reproving glance at my guest, Okubo bowed and left, closing the door.

The room seemed suddenly starved—as if some act of nourishment and belief were needed to restore what had been disrupted. As if seeing Miko again, after such a long absence, were like the vast silvery web of childhood itself— never far away for being irrevocably lost.

It was she who broke the silence.

"Before I go, Haruko, there is something I want to say to you."

"Please"—as though I were telling her that she might, with my permission, go ahead of me through an open doorway.

I watched her hesitate, and then I watched her go through the doorway.

"A long time ago you entered a period of terrible private suffering," she said. "I remember seeing a magazine picture of you with your family on the beach somewhere—Hayama, I think it was—all of you dressed like perfect creatures, the children in adorable shoes. And I remember thinking that those children had the most beautiful mother in the world. You were so beautiful, Haruko, and so sad. You looked—how can I say this to you, of all people?—as if you were in that photograph all by yourself. And I remember thinking at the time, I must write to her and save her. Ridiculous, but that's what I remember thinking. Then nothing came to me—I had no wisdom of my own. My husband had died. And you were the Crown Princess. Months turned into years; I was a coward and sent nothing."

"No, Miko," I said. "I was the coward."

She shook her head. "Neither of us had anything to give the other when we needed it most. Then more years went by, and supposedly you weren't so sad anymore. That's what the newspapers in America said. You'd got your voice back. But to this day, my regret is the same."

"I never replied to your letter. And your husband . . ."

"We were out of touch. You couldn't have known."

"Yes, but over time here one gradually gets used to saying less and less. You see how it is. The soul is put on a hard diet. Talking with you now is like remembering how to eat again."

"Would you be surprised, Haruko, if I told you that, knowing what little I know about the road you've taken and how it's been for you, I worry very much about Keiko's future happiness?"

"That would not surprise me."

"Do you support the marriage?"

"She's the woman my son loves," I replied simply. "I support his happiness."

"And Keiko's happiness?"

"She must answer that for herself."

"I happen to know that her father pressured her extremely."

"That would not be uncommon. Fathers generally aren't shy when it comes to their daughters' welfare."

"Perhaps. But I believe that other people of influence made their wishes for the match known to her as well," Miko said in a firm voice. "In fact, I believe that you yourself made your feelings on the matter known to her. And she listened. Is that not so?"

I said nothing, my eyes on the rug between us: I could not contradict her, but neither would I apologize. The truth seemed too ambiguous to talk about, even to my dearest friend. In the long, hollowed silence, Miko got to her feet and went to the window, staring out at the garden.

"I love you like a sister, Haruko," she said finally. "But please understand that if one day Keiko is in desperate need, I will come for her myself. I will bring her home."

41

THE WORDS DO NOT CHANGE. Only the people.

The Crown Prince went first, preceded by the Chief Ritualist in his long white robe. Like the priests, His Highness wore a cap and headdress of black lacquered silk. In his right hand he held a *shaku* of polished wood, representing his authority over our worldly domain. His robes were the deep burnt orange of Amaterasu Omi-kami's first rising over the earth. Walking a few paces behind him was his head chamberlain, in violet trousers and a robe of deepest black, carrying the long white train that extended from His Highness's waist. Following was a second chamberlain bearing His Highness's sword, which for a thousand years had been passed from one Crown Prince to the next at the time of investiture.

The silence was not complete. Fine-grained white pebbles covered the floor of the courtyard, and their feet crunched softly.

Keiko Mori, in the last minutes of her freedom, held her gaze straight ahead. The twelve-layer costume weighed fifteen kilos, her hair perhaps three. Her feet, groping along beneath the silken shroud of the *naga-bakama*, were as tentative as the hands of the blind.

WE WERE IN OUR RESIDENCE, watching the wedding ceremony on television, our formal clothes and self-conscious
movements suggesting a backstage holding room some
hours before curtain time. My husband sat on a sofa, his
foot jiggling nervously. He took a handful of roasted peas
from a glass bowl, eating them one at a time with his fingertips.

"Is that what we looked like?" he mused aloud.

Watching Keiko walk with labored steps around the
graveled courtyard, I did not answer him.

She reached the shrine and bowed deeply. Then she entered. Once inside the sacred enclosure, she was no longer
visible onscreen. Yet I could still see her.

"THERE," SAID MY HUSBAND when it was finished. "Now
they just need to start having children, and the job will be
done."

"Boys," I said.

Missing my tone, he thought I was agreeing with him;
he turned and smiled at me. "Shall we have some lunch
while they're getting changed?"

"If you wish."

"What's the matter?"

"Nothing. I'm just remembering the smell of benzene
when they washed out my hair."

His expression turned bemused—he'd never in his life
had his hair washed out with benzene; he didn't know
what I was talking about.

"There is no smell like it in the world," I said.

"I suppose not."

He sounded bored, quite understandably. It was the future he wanted to talk about now, not the past.

AT A SIGNAL from the master of ceremonies, the Crown Prince and Princess approached. She was wearing a white strapless Hanae Mori gown, and the decoration of the First Order of the Sacred Crown, inlaid with pearls, was pinned over her breast. The tiara on her head—the same I'd put on after my own wedding—glittered with more diamonds than could ever be counted. She appeared transformed, and I could not take my eyes off her.

Yasu reported that the marriage had been affirmed before Amaterasu Omikami, and he thanked us for our guidance and wisdom throughout his life. We offered our blessings. And, as we exchanged the Cups of Parent and Child, I saw that my son had been born to be exactly as he was.

When it was her turn, my daughter-in-law's imitation of her husband's movements was correct, and her hands did not tremble. Her eyes rose to meet mine, and I smiled at her.

We stepped out onto the balcony, the four of us smiling and waving at the privileged guests. The sun shone down upon us all. One recognized many celebrated faces, and heard cries of homage and smatterings of applause.

"Keiko-sama!" a famous Kabuki actor called out, bowing to the waist.

Then others took up the cry, until it was general:

"Keiko-sama!"

"Keiko-sama!"

"Keiko-sama!"

At the back of the throng, dressed in exuberant colors, Miko was smiling and calling out like the rest.

Then it was time. We were led downstairs through long rooms and corridors, and once again Her Highness was cheered in loud and repetitive celebration. Waiting outside was an open-topped Rolls-Royce. At the front of a grand formation, policemen and palace guards sat astride magnificently groomed horses, with more gleaming automobiles and still more palace guards prepared to follow. She was handed into the back of the Rolls-Royce to sit beside her husband.

A sign of the hand, a clipped military order, the clopping of perfectly shod hooves on stone, the purring of a perfectly made engine: and the imperial procession began to move.

My husband and I remained behind—symbols, already, of the old order.

PART FOUR

42

BEYOND THE THICK WALLS circumscribing the twenty
hectares of land that we who call ourselves imperial do
not own, our country, after forty years of astonishing
prosperity, had by the middle of the 1990s entered a
state of decline.

Unmistakable signs of a severe and prolonged economic depression—published photographs of the president of one of the largest securities firms sobbing on
his knees on the floor of the Stock Exchange (his suicide
followed days later)—were soon followed by disasters of
other kinds. As though a plague had been cast upon us,
our television screens filled with images of vomiting,
coughing, sobbing commuters (more than forty-eight
thousand in all) streaming from subway cars poisoned
with sarin gas; of old women wrapped in blankets, their
hair covered with *hachimaki* headbands, sitting stunned
on sunken footpaths and half-destroyed park benches
throughout the burning, earthquake-leveled city of
Kobe; of pale, emaciated, terrified children who, physically and psychologically abused by their classmates and
teachers at school, refused to leave their bedrooms for
years at a time.

Younger generations, unfamiliar with the shameful feeling of defeat on their shoulders, the dirt-and-metal taste of hunger on their tongues, the permanent bitterness of ash in their noses, were suddenly faced with the prospect of an incomprehensible failure that was never meant to be a part of their inheritance. As though, ever since a war no one but the ancient few seemed to remember, the ghosts of our victims had been obscurely pursuing us—and now, all at once, had come out to walk boldly in the light, laughing and howling at our hubris and forgetfulness.

Such was the background against which other, more personal collapses must be viewed, I believe.

Strange resurrections, too.

FROM THE BEGINNING, Keiko's mistakes were well publicized, each one a debt she must already have realized she could never repay. Too many times she was caught walking ahead of her husband, and her grasp of the ceremonial language of the Court was often less than ceremonial—and, when she did speak, she sometimes used the first person, even going so far as to offer an opinion or two.

All of which was notable, though it paled beside the public's sudden, consuming interest in her physical condition. Within the Court, and occasionally outside of it, the new Princess's struggles to conceive—a miscarriage and numerous false reports of pregnancies during the first few years alone—were cruelly well documented. The men in dark suits knew what to do with such desperate anticipation, how to fan the flames of the people's demand for her new face while at the same time continuing, behind the palace walls, to build the same old monument of calcified despair. Yes, the young woman's belly must be seen to grow to full term, and soon; she must expand her dimensions to contain multitudes—or, at the very least, a single prince; nothing must stand in the way of her fulfilling her sacred duty. In the meantime, if she wished to walk she must walk behind, and if she wished to speak, it must be with borrowed words dressed in ancient robes.

She was not the first to run into harsh limits; I, of course, had been there before her. But she was the first to innocently believe—and who could blame her, having received my solemn promise—that she might somehow be protected from the implacable forces set against her.

FOR NEARLY AN HOUR at her first solo press conference, behind a low podium equipped with a microphone, she patiently responded to the prepared questions asked by the assembled members of the media—representatives of forty-seven newspapers, magazines, and newswire agencies—with the prepared answers she'd been given. Gradually, as her ventriloquist's performance marched steadily toward its expected non-conclusion, her voice grew raspy, and she could be seen reaching with increasing frequency for a glass of water hidden on an inner shelf of the podium. Unless one observed her closely—as

Shige and I did on the television in our living quarters—one might have failed to notice that, as the level in her glass dropped with each successive sip, she began to glance anxiously to her left, where her head chamberlain—a watchful, gray-haired man in a dark suit—stood before a folding table on which a full pitcher of drinking water freshened with thin slices of lemon had earlier been placed.

"There is time left for one more question," her head chamberlain announced at the end of the hour, to the relief of nearly everyone present. For nothing of consequence had been said that day; nothing of consequence would ever be said.

At the front of the room, a journalist from a major newspaper got to his feet. On his face, scarred from acne and thickened by years of cigarettes and drink, was a look of barely disguised boredom. It was his prescribed turn, his question was known in advance, and there was no general expectation of his receiving an answer in any definitive sense of the word. His question concerned the exceedingly small number of trips—two, to be exact, both domestic and both dull—that the Princess had made in the years since her marriage, and the regrettable infrequency, despite her years of extensive diplomatic training and known oratorical skills, of any direct public communication between her and her subjects.

The journalist sat down.

For several awkward moments, Princess Keiko remained silent. She reached for the glass of water, saw that it was empty, and set it down again. Against the podium it made a hollow sound, heard clearly at the back of the room.

Her head chamberlain, standing off to the side, shifted his feet uncomfortably.

"Before responding to your question, I would like to make certain that I have understood you correctly," she began. "Are you saying that, in my capacity as wife of the Crown Prince, I have essentially spent my time traveling nowhere of interest and saying nothing of interest? Is that what you are saying?"

There was a pause. The room waited for speech. The journalist who had asked the question reluctantly climbed to his feet again.

"Your Highness has understood my question accurately, thank you."

"Very well. Then may I say that I agree with your assessment? In almost four years, from the age of thirty-two to my age today of thirty-six, I have gone nowhere interesting and said nothing of interest. I could not have described the situation better myself. Respectfully, that is the very definition of how I have spent my time, right up to, and including, this hour of conversation."

The room was silent. Her head chamberlain briskly approached the podium and, drawing close, murmured a few urgent words in her ear, which was something of a moving target, for she could be seen shaking her head at him.

"Your Highness," he said firmly—loud enough for the

room to hear, a shocking occurrence in its own right. "I am sorry, but it appears that we are out of time."

"Thank you for the warning," she replied in a voice suddenly alive to the back row of seats. Her smile, like this new voice of hers, was desperately self-aware, and one saw that what had perhaps begun as a mere provocation—a dangling limb, tapped by a doctor's hammer, twitching instinctively to life—had somehow, before the eyes of the assembled group, become a near-rebellion, turning all present into witnesses. She held up her bare wrist for examination by the room. "Unfortunately, as you can see, I have in my current life lost the habit of wearing a watch. Who can say? Perhaps this may turn out to be one of those rare occasions in life when ignorance proves more persuasive than knowledge."

Suddenly there was to be heard a sound other than her solitary voice: the scratching of pens on paper as forty-seven journalists excitedly wrote down what had just been said. Standing beside the Princess, her head chamberlain stared with grim impotence at the podium, the microphone, the empty glass of water.

"In response to the question," she continued, "I would like to suggest that, in my opinion, there has been perhaps too much speculation concerning my activities and health. While, at the same time, perhaps there has been a general lack of understanding of the complexities of the situation. This has sometimes been confusing to me. I have experienced a certain degree of hardship which is not conducive to those goals that have been attributed to me. I believe in the old ways, but I am also from my own time. I did not choose my childhood, but, having lived it, it is what I know and remember. For that I can try harder, but I cannot apologize. And I sometimes wonder if it is not possible to reconcile such differences in some more forgiving manner, without blame or persecution."

She paused to gather her thoughts. But then she seemed to think better of continuing, or simply to lose the necessary resolve to fill an infinite silence with words of her own choosing.

"I will stop now. Our time is at an end. Thank you for your questions. Until today, the Prince has always been with me. Without his support, alone, I have had to speak in a new voice, and I find that my throat is parched from the effort."

"DOES SHE KNOW WHAT SHE'S DONE?" my husband said. He turned a switch and the small screen went dark. It had been a drama that only we of the Court were privileged to watch—a live feed, for our television sets alone—and now it had ended, leaving behind a profoundly divided audience of two. Shige began to pace around our sitting room, pausing to sniff loudly with irritation, to pick an invisible thread off his trousers, to aggressively adjust the window blinds, through which gray afternoon light was seeping like dirty dishwater. Finally, he stopped and looked at me. "Either she has no idea what she's done, or she knows perfectly well, and went ahead and did it anyway."

"And what is it that you think she's done," I said, "other than tell the truth?" My voice was calm—provocatively so, perhaps—but, inside my chest, my heart was rampant, as if I were still watching Keiko at the podium, her tongue dry as sand and her thoughts in revolt. Still seeing her holding up her bare wrist, deciding, as I'd never had the courage to do, in front of the world of men who would deny her a sip of water, to annul the clock and grant herself the freedom to speak her mind in public.

"The truth?" said my husband. "There is only one truth, Haruko, and that is her duty. The girl must do her duty, just like every one of us."

"She is suffering."

"Which is no excuse for a lack of respect."

I stared at him. "Hearing you talk like this, I am unhappily reminded of your mother."

He went still, his eyes cold. "And so you should be reminded," he said.

"Very well." I turned away from him. "If you will excuse me, I will go and finish some correspondence."

"My dear—wait." His gaze softened when I looked at him, and he sighed. "Please, let's not argue."

But I would not be so easily put down. "I promised to protect her, Shige. Before the marriage. You must understand what that means?"

"Of course I do," he said in what he assumed was a consoling voice, stepping closer and patting my arm as though I were an imperial pet. "And it was very like you to make that promise. But now *you* must understand, if you haven't already, that there is nothing you can do for her."

He went out then, passing close to me, yet untouched in his own space, inviolate, the Emperor of Japan.

43

ONE RECALLS ALL TOO WELL the effects of sunlight as it passes through the magnifying glass: the beetle, the grasshopper, under the relentless hand of its child tormentor, bursts into flame and is no more. Imagine, then, when one is but a human being.

One morning—after the first miscarriage and the false pregnancies—Keiko awoke in agony, and was rushed to the imperial hospital.

The diagnosis was shingles.

That evening, she and Yasu were to attend a dinner in honor of the president of France with my husband and me. And Keiko, with her lifelong affinity for Europe, adamantly refused to miss the event, insisting that she was well enough.

The formal kimono she wore was ivory, her obi crimson, darker than blood, with flowers sewn in white tulle. The obi had been drawn by her attendants as tight as possible around her slim waist, the area most affected by the shingles, and by the time she and Yasu arrived at our private quarters, from which we were to depart for the ambassador's residence together, I could see in her eyes the childlike terror that comes both before and after great physical pain. She walked with tiny eggshell steps, as though her back had been broken while she slept. The nerves under her skin—vessels of perfectly preserved trauma, one imagined, like poison darts in amber—were so inflamed that the merest contact with even the finest cloth was enough to shatter her composure.

The moment I saw her, I suggested that she return immediately to her residence to rest.

"Thank you, but I feel well enough to continue," she replied.

"But you must be in terrible pain."

"It could be worse. I could go back and submit to my ladies-in-waiting."

"Are they treating you badly?"

She stared at me without expression, each second of silence making the obviousness of my remark the more glaring and obscene. Unhappy with myself, I looked away, murmuring, "I wish I could help you somehow . . ."

"And sometimes, Your Majesty, I wish I lived in Paris." She paused then, seeming to regret her tone. "Please, there's nothing you can do. Don't pay any attention to me."

She was neither smiling nor frowning. She seemed— this is what I remember—in a state of such in-between agony that it was a kind of mortification, a shame belting her like her darker-than-blood obi. A shame of unknown origin, which she didn't feel she could admit to, and which was slowly killing her.

A few minutes later, as we were preparing to depart, my

husband inquired—a question of such hopeful ignorance and unintended cruelty that it made me want to hurt him somehow, to cause him some precise and wakeful pain— whether Keiko's condition did not, in fact, have some connection to the monthly calendar. Might she be pregnant?

A terrible silence. She turned her face to the side, took two broken steps as though to get away from the very ground on which we stood—yes, in her eyes at that moment, I was implicated, too—then stopped and quietly began to weep. Her tears were not abundant, but they were memorable.

When she was finished, she insisted on returning alone to her room to repair her makeup. Later, she joined us again, and one would never have known that anything was wrong.

At dinner, she was remarkable. She spoke fluent English to the American ambassador, impressive French to President Chirac, and was thought to be charming by all who saw her. The press was dazzled by her.

THE NEXT MORNING, she was summoned by Grand Steward Minamoto's first deputy. He complimented her on her obvious talent for languages, then informed her that it was not her role, then or indeed ever, to act on behalf of the Imperial Family in a diplomatic capacity. The sooner she forgot her English and French and concentrated her energies on getting pregnant, the better for herself and the nation.

SHE TOLD ME OF THE REPRIMAND HERSELF, when I called on her at the Togu Gosho the following afternoon to see how she was feeling. It was immediately clear that she was no better. She sat on the edge of a sofa in the receiving room, careful not to touch anything, her back perfectly straight, her jaw set against the pain. Still, she managed to find the energy to make a joke at her own expense.

"Really, it's my pride that's hurt," she said. "It seems that Minamoto-san doesn't think much of my English."

"On the contrary, he thinks too much of your English," I replied. "I thought you were brilliant last night. If you don't mind my saying so, I was proud of you."

"I don't mind your saying so." She attempted a smile, but a stab of pain twisted her mouth into a grimace. The sight was pitiful, and I reached out to touch her—but, at the sight of my approaching hand, she whispered, "Please don't."

I pulled back my hand. "I should let you rest," I said. "But, before I go, Keiko, is there something in particular that I might do for you? Something, I mean, to make your life less . . ." I paused, glancing through the open door into the passageway beyond—where a lady-in-waiting stood with eyes averted, as though she were not, in fact, listening to our conversation—and went on in a lower voice. "When I was your age, there were individuals who made my life difficult. The Empress was the most powerful, but there were others. Perhaps I could use what influence I have to effect the replacement of one of your ladies-in-waiting."

Keiko shook her head. "Thank you, Your Majesty. But there's no one enemy, or even a few. It's everyone. It's this place. It's my body—what it will and won't do. So, much as I appreciate your offer, I can't see what you could do to help me."

"I understand, and I'm very sorry for it."

It was the truth, though she shook her head at me again and did not reply. And then—hoping, without conviction, that she would somehow find the strength to help herself—I left her there.

44

IT WAS THE SECOND MISCARRIAGE that finally forced
their hand and exposed their suffering for all to see. The
news, in late 1999, that Keiko was pregnant was uncon-
tainable by even the most seasoned bureaucrats. Special
editions went to press; the television talked about nothing else; molds were made for pregnant Keiko dolls with
perfect little sweaters.

On the expectant mother's face during those few
weeks, after the initial flush of hope that preceded the
public's awareness of her condition, I thought I perceived a new kind of terror. She walked as though she
were bearing an inhuman weight.

And then, by the New Year, the weight was gone.

Had she been carrying a son? The question was too
morbid for words. And yet, for a while then it could be
heard making the rounds of gossip and innuendo, as
well as the more respectable circuits of public debate.
There is no true privacy in this private country, just
cruel reticence masquerading as discretion. They
stripped her clean.

Within these walls, inside the moat, panic finally set
in. Desperate measures were called for, and the young-

but-already-old couple, understandably desperate and helpless themselves, could not object. Secret actions were planned. Legions of expert doctors arrived in the dead of night or the quiet of early morning in cars with darkened windows. They dressed as businessmen, surveyors, language instructors, seismologists, Russians, Turks, albinos, snake charmers—anything but the medical men they were.

There was a hospital up north, in Fukushima, that was said to be the most advanced in the science of fertility. Within the hospital was a clinic, and within the clinic, one imagined, the specialists and their clean rooms and humming, spotless refrigerators. . . . Yasu performed the required functions somewhere in Tokyo, and the results of his labors were shipped fresh, by secret imperial courier, to the Fukushima clinic, where they were promptly introduced to Princess Keiko, who, under the guise of participation in a blood-donation program, had made the trip in person.

From there it was but a short journey to the imperial villa at Nasu. Yasu met her there, and they spent a week taking brief, slow walks along the seashore.

WITHIN THE YEAR, she was pregnant again. Oh yes, science is a mystery and a marvel. The Court was instantly rejuvenated, the experts called back in. Charts were drawn up of the frequency of the Crown Princess's morning sickness, even the dimensions of her swelling feet. Her blood and stool were analyzed at regular intervals, and the length of her walks restricted. She was nourished like a prize Kobe steer soon to be served to history. And not one of her many doctors or any of her chamberlains remarked on the fact that the woman under their charge—once the most accomplished and confident of citizens—was spending most of her days in tears. As if she already somehow knew the sex of the child and what it would mean for them both.

And all across Japan, meanwhile, the molds for pregnant Keiko dolls with perfect little sweaters were brought out of storage for the marketplace.

ONE MORNING IN THE SPRING, I paid a visit to the Togu Gosho to see her. She had complained of feelings of suffocation, being indoors so much, so we decided to take a stroll in the garden, where the ground was soft and wet but the air fresh, born in other parts of the world. Occasionally, as she walked beside me, her hands would come to rest gingerly on her stomach, like a pigeon's in-pointed feet.

Her minders were trailing us to ensure that she did not overexert herself. Still, we could speak privately, and around us in the garden the birds, renewed by the warmer weather, flitted here and there. The little wooden houses that my husband had built for them soon after our wedding had been renovated many times over the decades, and now looked almost new. An illusion, of course—yet, when I pointed them out to Keiko and told her their history, she thought it amusing that the Emperor had once had such a passion for starlings, taking time to observe their habits over months and finally choosing the colors that were most likely to entice them to return to their own nests.

"And me?" she said. Her smile had lost its humor, become the arid, thin-lipped border between dream and discontent; a place not unfamiliar to me. "What color in the world could ever entice me to come back to this prison once I escaped?"

We stopped walking, and stood looking at each other in silence.

"Do you know," she said abruptly, "sometimes I pray it's a girl—then they won't know what to do with us, and perhaps they'll throw us out."

IN THE SUMMER, her lonely prayer was answered.

His Majesty's messenger arrived at the imperial hospital with a thirty-centimeter-long sword embossed with the imperial seal. The sword was placed beside the infant's basket as a totem of divine protection. And for six days it remained there, all eyes drawn to it and all eyes blinded.

On the seventh morning, the unnamed girl was bathed in a cypress wood basin, while two courtiers plucked at the strings of longbows to scare away malevolent spirits. The Crown Princess watched from her bed, and the Crown Prince from nearby. And they prayed.

Later that afternoon, the naming took place. After the ceremony the girl's name and title, inscribed by the Emperor on handmade washi paper, were carried by imperial messenger to the Togu Palace and presented to the Crown Prince. From there, they were announced at the three shrines of the Kashikodokoro, and at the Imperial Household Agency. Finally, late in the day, the washi paper was delivered to the hospital.

I ARRIVED SOON after the messenger and his attendants had left. Keiko was in bed, wan and deflated-looking, her daughter—hardly bigger than a wet kitten—asleep in her arms.

The girl's name was Reiko.

"A pretty name," I said with a smile.

"Whatever may happen," murmured the mother to her sleeping infant, who made blind sucking motions with her lips.

"It will be easier once you're home," I assured her.

She looked at me with hopeless eyes. "Did you think of it as going home when you left here with Yasu?"

"I felt how you must feel."

"But you had a boy."

"I was still a mother like you."

She shook her head slowly, stroking the baby's red face with a finger. "Tell me, Your Majesty. What does one do for a little girl who will never be a prince?"

45

12 AUGUST 2003, TOKYO—In an act without precedent in the annals of modern imperial behavior, Crown Princess Keiko, 42, with her 2-year-old daughter, Princess Reiko, close by her side for comfort, last month sought protection from public scrutiny and the pressures of her position in her family's summer home in the wooded mountain resort of Karuizawa, where even her own official attendants have limited access to her.

Princess Keiko has been absent from all public events since early last year, showing the effects of pressure to produce a male heir to the Chrysanthemum Throne and the stress of adapting to the world's oldest monarchy.

It has been reliably confirmed that Crown Prince Tsuyo has visited her twice, but on both occasions he spent the majority of his time in a local hotel. This, too, is without precedent.

The hotel where the Prince has been staying on his visits to Karuizawa is the same on whose tennis courts his parents, Their Imperial Majesties, first met in 1957.

ON THE MORNING of her departure for karuizawa, she had sent word asking if she might say goodbye. Okubo delivered the message exactly as it had been relayed to him—"Please inform Empress Haruko that I would be most grateful if she would agree to receive me this morning before my departure"—adding of his own accord the suggestion that, as he had seen her car being packed with luggage, there was no time to waste. Fortunately, my schedule that morning was open, and I was able to go with him directly to her residence.

She was not expecting me; I was shown into a receiving room and asked to wait while she was called. Then I was alone in that large room with the grand fireplace and the Russian vase and the Provençal chest and the Tang horse and so many other objects. It was, like all of the rooms we would ever live in, a repository of artifacts from a remote world, at once our own and not our own. And it was full of despair.

On a side table were gilt-framed photographs of the family: Keiko and Yasu and Reiko; my husband and myself; Kumi and Seiji and their two daughters. The pictures were formal—the usual Court style, meant to form an impenetrable lacquer against the dust and cracks of time—and the smiles nothing if not resolute. And yet I felt as though I were seeing through our imperial armor to the vulnerable spirits underneath, intruding on lives that, however public, were never meant to be observed at close range and could not withstand the scrutiny of others. It was transfixing and appalling, and I shuddered to myself.

Just then she entered the receiving room. Not attempting a false smile for my benefit, already beyond pretense. Forty-two years old but today appearing closer to fifty, her eyes rimmed by dark circles.

I stood to greet her. "I came as soon as I received your message. Tell me, how is Reiko-chan?"

"Excited to see Karuizawa again," Keiko replied, though excitement was the opposite of what her voice suggested. She spoke slowly and with a visible effort at thought, the words emerging reluctantly, as if her mind were afraid of its own contents. "She believes we are going because of the heat here."

"And Yasu?"

"I told Reiko that her father is too important to go away for long."

"Where is he now?"

"I asked him not to be here this morning. It would have been too difficult."

"Would you like me to say anything to him for you?"

"We have talked already. He's worried about me— that's not a secret. He was the one, not the doctors, who recommended that I go to Karuizawa with Reiko to stay with my mother."

"He will miss you," I said.

"Yes . . ." Keiko's gaze came to rest on the photograph of her family, the three of them, and she seemed to sag then, to falter from unhappiness. "I feel terribly sorry for Yasu," she said quietly. "He has tried so hard."

"As have you."

She looked at me as if I'd touched her. The room was silent. In a moment, I saw that she was near tears, and I realized that we were still standing apart like strangers; we'd been standing all this time. I reached out and took her arm, murmuring, "Please, won't you sit down with me for a few minutes?" She did not resist, allowing herself to be guided to the sofa. The sofa was soft and deep, covered in the purest of fabrics, and we sank down into it as if falling onto a luxurious and necessary raft. And there we remained, quiet and together, slowly drifting, like survivors whose histories are known only to one another. Somewhere, in another room, a clock struck ten hollow chimes, sounding at once elegiac and like a children's toy. The notes took a long time to finish, and the silence afterward was mournful and seemed to startle Keiko—she made as if to get up, but I put a hand on her arm, and she sat back as though in surrender. And then, finally, years late, I turned to my daughter-in-law and offered her the only true thing I possessed: I began to speak to her honestly about my past.

I told her that when I lost my voice, it was my husband, like hers, who suggested that I go to see my parents in Karuizawa. And—hopeless and in pain—I had obeyed him. The hermetic silence of that drive, the sense of being in a cocoon and finally, if briefly, protected and yet moving; the sense of a journey not toward anything but, rather, back into what lay behind: the deep past and everything that had been. But what had been? Seeing my father, an old man suddenly, appear on the front steps of the house as though he were stumbling out of a temple where his prayers had gone unanswered. Hearing my parents speak to me, and about me, as though I were a cherished possession that had been stolen from their house and smashed to pieces by vandals and then returned to them, dropped from the sky, to see if they who had made me might be able to put me back together again. But they had not been able to put me back together again, at least not directly, because they themselves had been smashed to pieces by my leaving. And so there we all had been, a family unmade by history, and never had I loved them, and mourned them, more than at that time.

"I will miss you, Keiko," I said. "I hope you know that."

She stood up without replying, and I saw that she was staring at her daughter in the doorway.

Reiko seemed to have come flying from somewhere, wearing an emerald-green dress and white strap shoes, her shining black hair cut in straight bangs across her forehead. From across the room her eyes were mere slits, hardly visible yet vibrantly expressive, as though the face around them were all eyebrows—rising, falling, dipping, peaking, every manner of response but the literal. Just the sight of her caused her mother and me to smile back at her with love.

Which is how I remember us, on the morning when they left for Karuizawa.

46

THE OCCASION WAS A PRESS CONFERENCE on the eve of
Yasu's departure, alone, for a ten-day trip to Europe. His
itinerary was to include two royal weddings and numerous visits of state. The trip appeared to promise the sort
of highly visible international role that the people, and
Keiko herself, had once envisioned for the Crown Princess. She was to have been the new face of the oldest
family in the world. She was to have represented us at
our finest, not just to ourselves but to the world.

But by then she had been in Karuizawa with Reiko
for months. In hiding, seclusion, recuperation, repair—so
many definitions, none remotely adequate, all amount-
ing to the same thing: she was not pregnant. And not being pregnant, with a boy—and suffering from, the palace
insisted, an "adjustment disorder"—it was determined
that she was in no state to travel. That, indeed, travel
was in the best interest neither of herself nor her country.

Using all that remained of her strength, she had gone
away. But she had not made it very far.

My son appeared at the press conference alone, looking, one journalist reported, "uncharacteristically down-

hearted." There had been the usual vetting of questions beforehand. But, before a single reporter could be called upon, with a dip of his head and a raised hand Yasu indicated that he had something he wished to say. The hushed room grew still more hushed, and yet underneath the silence a buzz of anticipation could be felt: the Crown Prince was about to deliver spontaneous remarks on the subject of his wife's depression and their separation as a family. Would he, like his wife before him, go so far as to depart from the prepared script?

Yasu began to speak, without notes, to the assembled reporters. His voice was uncharacteristically heavy, his cadence slow and reluctant—as when, during a loved one's funeral, the air itself may seem congested with memories of the life just departed, the endless residue of loss.

"I would like to say that I am deeply saddened that Princess Keiko will not be joining me on this trip to Europe," he began. "It is difficult for me to leave her and Princess Reiko at such a time. Due to my wife's health and state of emotions, she has been told that she must not travel. This is the decision of those in charge of her health, and one must respect it. It is for her protection, I suppose. Yet I can only say that I am . . . It is difficult . . ."

Emotion forced him to pause. He stood and trembled. I, his mother, watching on television, saw him tremble, and I trembled with him. The reporters stared hungrily at him—his beleaguered visage the finally human face of defeated propriety, and so less than princely.

Somehow, he gathered himself and concluded:

"This is the sort of trip that she would have relished with her whole heart, and at which she would have excelled. But she is too tired to go. She is exhausted. I do not know what else to say. She is not well. My daughter is with her. I miss them both more than I can express. I tell you that I leave for this trip wishing only that I were already back home." He paused. "I have nothing more to say."

He answered no questions that day. He spoke from his heart, and then he took it with him.

47

"MUST YOU REALLY GO to Karuizawa tomorrow?"

"I want to see our granddaughter, Shige. I need to see her."

"How long will you be gone?"

"Okubo is picking me up at half past eight. I'll be back by evening."

We were walking back to our private quarters after dinner. Shige held out his arm for me to take, as though to assist me—but really it was so that I could assist him. A month had passed since his surgery for prostate cancer. A weakness had infected his legs, he'd confessed to me, making them feel hollow and ungainly. Privately, he had complained of chronic exhaustion.

With a stop along the way to rest, we made our way back to our rooms. As soon as the door was closed behind us and our servants out of view, he sank onto the bed and shut his eyes.

"Shall I help you get ready?"

He made no response, and I stood observing him without his awareness.

"At least let me get you out of your clothes."

"Can't you see I'm trying to sleep?" he muttered.

"Sitting up?"

He opened his eyes halfway. "You are a stubborn woman."

"Lift your arms."

He sighed but obeyed. I undressed him as if he were a child or a very old man, all the while trying to convince myself that he was neither. He was my husband. He was the Emperor. I helped him into his pajamas, then under the sheets. I smoothed his hair.

"There," I said.

His eyes opened again. "Haruko?"

"What is it now?"

"Have I told you how happy you've made me all these years?"

"Many times." I patted his thin legs through the bed-covers. "Well, perhaps once, when we were first married. Now go to sleep."

He closed his eyes, and soon was asleep.

For a while then I sat, fully clothed, before my dressing table, not even brushing my hair. I was looking not at myself but at my sleeping husband's reflection. I was saying to myself and to the mirror all the prayers that during the course of my long life I had forgotten to say. It is remarkable how the words come back.

The night before his surgery, I had demanded that a portable bed be brought into his hospital room so that I might stay with him throughout the nights, as well as the days, of his recovery. My request was met with resistance from many quarters, including from him. But I declined to listen to what the old goats were telling me. The extra bed was delivered, and I moved in with my husband. I was a terror and a force to be reckoned with; and, of course, it was all bluster and smoke. For ten days I had lived with him in those intimate quarters, witnessing the crude passing of his blood and waste, watching the life drain from him and then return. Sensing with every fiber of my being the snail-like pace of his uncertain recovery and of my own. For the truth was that I could not imagine going on in this strange, opaque world without him.

48

WE HAD BEEN RIDING in silence for nearly an hour when I asked Okubo a question that had been on my mind for some time.

"Do you remember, Koji, driving me along this same route forty years ago?"

"I will never forget it, Your Majesty."

"Anything in particular?"

"Mostly what I remember, Your Majesty, is how you never spoke a word. Not one word during the whole trip."

We drove on. The stretch of road climbed without respite. The morning was alpine blue, the clouds high. I sat in my roomy parlor in the back: the smell of leather, the knowledge of silence.

"Koji," I said eventually, "you have driven Princess Keiko before. Based on your observations, what do you make of her state of mind?"

"Her state of mind, Your Majesty?"

"Come now, you and I have known each other a long time. There's no need to be careful with me."

Okubo tugged uncomfortably on his earlobe. "Of course, Your Majesty. I have always been . . ."

He paused, and I remained inert, willing him to speak. "She seems to me . . ."

"Yes?"

"The saddest woman in the world," he said. With that, he fell silent.

"Yes," I agreed. I turned and studied my window. We'd reached the summit, where the road leveled off; soon we would cross the border into Nagano Prefecture, and then into Karuizawa.

REIKO WAS WAITING OUTSIDE the mori house when we drove through the gate. "Grandmother!" she cried, skipping toward the car. My heart leaped at the sight of her. I crouched down to receive her in my arms, and in the shimmering autumn air every last detail of her stood out as clearly as the clearest memory of my childhood: her high sweet laughter, her emerald-green dress, her hair smelling of plum blossoms, her socks speckled with tiny rust-colored leaves.

She fit into me like my own missing self.

Then, over her shoulder, I saw her mother watching us, a hand raised in a listless gesture of welcome. Too thin, with dull eyes and plain clothes. Nothing remaining of the aura of self-possession that had been the calling card of her youth. She moved toward the car not with the fluid strides of the athlete she'd once been but with small, mistrustful steps, as though afraid the ground might give way beneath her. I thought of those troubled teenage girls who will not eat save in little dogged bites, who have grown to fear the taste of life.

I looked down, smiling in spite of myself—for with a mischievous giggle Reiko had climbed atop my feet and was grabbing my hands to dance with me. I lifted her into the air and was rewarded with a squeal of delight.

"Reiko-chan, you're as light as a bird," I said.

"I'm bigger than Tok!"

"And who is Tok?"

"The dog who says hello."

"A talking dog?" Lifting her once more, I set her gently on the ground. "Run along now, little one. Your mother and I have important things to discuss."

"What things?"

"Boring things that wouldn't interest an intelligent girl like you."

She folded her arms across her spindly chest. "What things?"

Rather than try to answer, I called for Okubo. He was beside us at once, murmuring, "Come along with me, Princess Reiko."

"I want to ride," she declared.

"Eh?" said Okubo dubiously.

She pointed at his shoulders. Okubo sighed. He picked her up under her arms and placed her squarely on his shoulders.

"Say goodbye," he instructed.

"Goodbye." She waved.

He began to carry her toward the house, slowly at first.

"Go!" she cried, slapping him on his gray head.

And Okubo, wise man that he was, began to run.

KEIKO AND I WATCHED HER GO. All this time she had been silent. Finally, I turned and looked into her dark eyes.

She bowed her head. "You are good to have come all this way, Your Majesty."

"Please, after all that has passed between us, I wish you would stop being formal with me."

"If you wish."

I said that I did wish it, and I asked her to call me by my name. She agreed, but she would not say it. As though she had already gone beyond the naming of things, those vessels of the hope that she could not feel.

Then, by the house, came the sound of footsteps, and we turned from each other to look. Her mother was approaching. A handsome, immaculately dressed woman, Mrs. Mori welcomed me with a bow and urged me inside for refreshments.

We three women were a procession on the stone path leading to the house. Our steps were measured and our silence deafening. I glanced at Keiko, but she was lost in herself again, and I looked away into the trees and shrubbery around us, where birds in large numbers were singing. The birds of Karuizawa. Warblers and cuckoos, I remembered with a sudden stab of grief, and tiny black-and-white flycatchers with streaks of brilliant orange that darted through the pines and under the hanging eaves and now and then passed through an open shoji, becoming hopelessly trapped in the cool shadowy rooms of my father's house.

AT LUNCH, MRS. MORI AND I made polite conversation, to which Keiko contributed only when asked a direct question. Otherwise, she stared at her food without touching it, a shade of herself, eyes sunken and fingers picking absently at the tablecloth. No longer strong enough to do for herself what must be done, to eat, speak, stand up, leave. I wanted to shake her—and to embrace her. From the kitchen—where Reiko was eating with a nurse—we could hear snippets of the girl's constant questions and observations, a bath of vibrant sunlight casting us in still further shadow.

Later, Keiko and I retreated by ourselves to the viewing porch at the back of the house, which overlooked a small enclosed garden. The air was cooling, and our cups of hot tea breathed delicate tendrils of steam. Before us, a large striated rock was reflected in a pool of water; beneath a Japanese maple, a single crimson leaf rested on a hummock of moss like a fallen, burned-out star.

For a long time neither of us spoke. The air grew cooler while I finished my tea. Keiko had not touched hers. She stared at the garden without seeing it, and seemed unaware that I was with her.

In time, a second leaf fell. We watched it dive to earth.

Now two dead leaves lay on the ground. If we remained in our positions long enough, one understood, passive and doing nothing, soon there would be three. And three would be too many; three would be hateful, another unforgivable mistake to add to those already made. I thought of my granddaughter Reiko—so young, yet already sealed in for life. Who would never know any world but this one.

And, with a surge of bitter remorse, I thought, It is happening again. We are letting it happen. And it is not right or natural, but a crime against nature.

"Keiko." I called her by her name.

That was how it began. I said her name, and at first she was merely silent, staring dully at the maple tree as though waiting for the third leaf to fall. Then, after a long moment, she turned her head. The eyes I found looking back at me held no past and no future.

"You must take Reiko away from here and never come back," I told her. "Do you understand what I'm telling you?"

Suddenly then, behind those dead eyes—a light.

49

Reiko was squatting on the ground to the side of the house, the hem of her green dress dragging in the dirt and fallen leaves, carefully shaping a small mound of pebbles with her hands.

"Grandmother?" she said.

"Yes, Reiko-chan."

"Do you like it here?"

"In Karuizawa?" My old woman's voice suddenly thick with longing—for that name, simply, and for all that had happened here in my life, and for all that was going to happen. "I love Karuizawa with all my heart," I told her.

"But you sound sad."

Bending down with difficulty, I picked up a pebble and handed it to her. "Some day, Reiko-chan, you will understand how one can love something and be sad for it at the same time."

She was silent. She added the pebble I'd given her to her mound, causing a small avalanche. She would have to start over.

"I'm building my own palace," she said bravely.

"So I see."

"It takes a long time."

"Yes, little one, it does."

"When it's done, will you come and live with Mother and me?"

"If you'd like."

"Soon," she insisted.

She picked up a fresh handful of pebbles. She knew so little, and so much. The air had turned cooler, and I wondered if I should take her inside.

"Grandmother?"

High in the tree above our heads a crow was watching us. "Yes, Reiko-chan."

"Can we stay here always?"

Winter was not far off: a bare sun, dead leaves on the ground. My granddaughter building a palace out of pebbles, looking at me as though I were a person of answers and consequence.

I squatted down beside her and tucked her hair behind her ears. And then my hands lingered, touching her, because I could not bear to let her go.

50

I STOOD BY THE WINDOW in my study, watching the black car slowly approaching along the drive. The night before, Okubo had said to me, "Your Majesty, some of the things that will happen, you must not know about." And I had agreed; there would be details that I would not know about. But for now the car was drawing nearer, and through the bare tree branches reflected on the opalescent windshield Okubo's head and shoulders became visible—a spirit in a floating forest. Then the car came farther, nearer, my heart beginning to sound in my ears, and the picture rearranged itself, and the forest disappeared. He was just a man, my driver and confidant, the only one we could trust, coming from a small, little-known airport one hundred and eighty kilometers southwest of Karuizawa, where, outside the reach of anyone's knowledge or interest, under her husband's unrecognized name, like an anonymous ship of salvation, that morning Miko's private plane had landed from Hawaii.

51

THE SKY THAT MORNING was the gray of smokestacks, pressing down upon the manicured grounds over which my husband and I, following our banal routine, were walking.

"I have been thinking," he said to me.

I turned to look at that face which I knew better than any other; better even than my father's face, which time had slowly begun to steal from me. We had been married for forty-six years. And for all that, safely ensconced within his rings of water and stone, he was yet guided by a blindness that, any moment now, would be stripped from his eyes.

He stopped walking and stood with his hands resting on his hips, his chest rising and falling. His face was free of physical strain, but I was aware, having recently discovered at his bedside a fitness magazine for older citizens, that the open positioning of his arms represented a conscious effort to pull more oxygen into his lungs.

"I have decided that when Keiko and Reiko-chan return from the country we will all go to Hayama for a few days," he said. "I will speak to Yasu about it. I'm prepared to insist on the matter. We call ourselves a family, but if you ask me that hardly seems the case anymore." Slowly, he bent down and picked up a twig from the gravel path, slipping it into the pocket of his exercise suit. "We've come apart at the seams, Haruko, and it's high time we put ourselves back together." He sighed wearily, letting his hands drop to his sides. "Shall we continue or turn back?"

"Let's turn back."

It was then, as we doubled back past the hovering scrutiny of our small security retinue, that we noticed the approaching pack of dark-suited men. Nearing my husband, Grand Steward Minamoto pulled a folded handkerchief from his pocket and patted his perspiring face. His hand appeared to be trembling, and his bow of honorific greeting, though perfectly pitched as ever, had about it an air of vibrating urgency.

"Minamoto-san. Is something the matter?"

"Your Majesty, may we speak in private?"

"You may speak freely as we are."

Minamoto gathered himself. "Your Majesty, it would appear that the Princesses Keiko and Reiko have disappeared."

My husband stared at him. Several seconds elapsed before he was able to speak.

"Disappeared? What are you saying? Explain yourself."

"Neither Princess is anywhere to be found, Your Majesty."

"I don't understand—where have they gone? How long have they been missing?"

"Princess Reiko was last seen asleep in her bedroom in Karuizawa at approximately eight-twenty yesterday evening. Princess Keiko went to her own room at approximately ten past nine. Early this morning, the nurse went to check on Princess Reiko and found her gone. A minute later, the discovery of her mother's absence was made."

"No one saw them leave the premises?"

"No, Your Majesty."

"But what you're telling me simply isn't possible!"

"We are interviewing everyone in the vicinity. We are searching for them with all of our resources."

"The airports and train stations?"

"Our people are making inquiries."

"Did they have access to a car?"

"No, Your Majesty. And no unaccounted-for vehicles were seen entering the property during the period in question, and none of the vehicles attached to the property are missing."

"They could have been kidnapped," my husband said gravely.

Minamoto hesitated. "I am afraid that the Karuizawa police might already have got wind of the situation. If the news were somehow to leak to the press, we could have a catastrophe on our hands."

My husband's rebuke lay in his gaze, a lacquered black. "And tell me, Minamoto-san, what do you call what has already occurred, if not a catastrophe?"

The Grand Steward was silent, and my husband turned

to me, the full realization of the news appearing to land on his suddenly stooped shoulders.

I said nothing. I took his arm and, far more actively than we'd left it, we returned to the residence. There, stoically pacing outside our rooms like a prisoner resigned to his fate, was Yasu.

52

ACCORDING TO IMPERIAL INVESTIGATORS, Princess Keiko had left behind what few trinkets and keepsakes she'd brought with her to Karuizawa months earlier: a small plain box in which floated rice kernels painted to look like dancing spirits; a tortoise figurine carved out of soapstone; an ivory hair comb; a bonsai whose ancient dwarf limbs, bent as though broken, seemed to reflect a pose of eternal grief. Apart from a single set of clothes, only one object was known to be missing from her room: a photograph of her daughter riding a pony. It had been removed from its lacquered frame, which, emptied of purpose, still stood upright on her bedside table.

Princess Reiko's bedroom, too, was missing but a single set of the girl's clothes and a sole object: in her case, a small stuffed dog given her by me.

Throughout the entire house no luggage was missing, no food, undergarments, overcoats, jewelry, hats, hairbrushes, lipsticks, eyeliners, hair irons, items of personal feminine hygiene, books, magazines, letters (there were twelve—nine from Yasu, two from Ambassador Mori, one from me, none with any information that might shed light on their fates), money, credit cards

(Mrs. Mori's—for, like me, upon her marriage to the Crown Prince, Keiko had given up the conceit of credit and debt), prescriptive medications for depression, anxiety, insomnia; mementos, flowers, children's toys, baskets woven of reeds, stones from the mountains, birds from the trees, history from the vaults. It was as if a great hand had descended from the sky and plucked this broken woman from the place in which she could find no rest, and carried her and her daughter off without so much as grazing any surface of the cell in which they had been living. To where or in what state of life or death they had been delivered, there was no way of knowing. They were simply gone.

53

IN KARUIZAWA, EVENING FELL SWIFTLY. The Mori house, and the town, too, continued to swirl with frantic activity, men in uniform arriving and departing.

It was a war, though a war without an enemy. The enemy had been the victims, and now the victims were gone. And yet the war was just beginning. Perhaps it will never end.

The search was comprehensive. It would be safe to say that the world had never before seen its like. With impressive speed, Grand Steward Minamoto closed down the avenues of gossip and dissemination. The police and the press were contained in the usual manner, if with a sense of bureaucratic ferocity never previously displayed. The future of the imperial institution—the future of the nation, it was said—was under attack. A message conceived as the least damaging to Court interests was quickly sent forth. It was announced that the doctors attending the Crown Princess—experts all, from the very best hospitals far and wide, the people were assured— had determined that, for the sake of Princess Keiko's fragile mental health, her absence from all public events should be "extended indefinitely." One could not say when either she or Princess Reiko would be seen in public again.

As for Prince Tsuyo, alone again in his private life as he'd once expected to be, it was noted at his next press conference that, though he seemed sad, he did not seem paralyzed or helpless—nor did he feel it necessary to deviate from the prepared script of his remarks. At the end of the hour, his father and I, urged on by the Grand Steward, took the occasion to join our son at the podium, a show of familial unity that, according to many in the press, reassured the people that the Imperial Family was still very much intact.

Meanwhile, in the silent shadows of our nation, the hunt for the missing went on. Secretly, invisibly, the country was scoured to its very boundaries, every conceivable line of inquiry pursued to its empty conclusion. The lack of evidence was so astounding, and so complete, that over time it had the effect of a powerful narcotic on those who participated in the search, separating them from their honest perceptions and absorbing all curiosity. Strong men grew tired, and began to think of rest.

54

"YOUR MAJESTY?"

We were driving into the city, leaving the palace behind. An afternoon's journey, a ride to nowhere. Okubo's gaze shifted from the road ahead to purposefully meet mine in the driver's mirror—taking, in that fractional step, a bold stride through a doorway that, however long-standing and satisfying our acquaintance, had never before been open between us. In the tiny polished glass that was his conscience and mine, we looked steadily at each other without disguise.

He had just passed me an envelope bearing neither stamp nor postage mark, on whose face was written, in Miko's familiar hand, a single thrilling word: "Gazelle."

My fingers trembled as I unfolded the square of handmade paper, its corners shivering as though in a breeze. But the windows of the car were closed.

"Your Majesty?" Okubo was still watching me in the little mirror.

Momentarily overcome by what my old friend had drawn on the paper she'd sent me from America, I could not answer him.

Two cranes. Two cranes in flight.

"Our friends, Koji?" I managed, finally.

"I have it on good authority that our friends are safe and well, Your Majesty," Okubo replied. "Especially the youngest. Though everything is new for her in America, and she misses Your Majesty very much."

"I miss her, too."

I was crying quietly. We drove on, Okubo making gentle detours. I remembered my childhood, and it felt like my life. And, while I was still alive to tell it, I wanted to tell my granddaughter about that life. Yes, I wanted to tell you, to help you understand.

THE LIGHT HAD BEGUN TO FADE. At the edge of a large park, Okubo stopped the car.

"It's getting late, Your Majesty. Should I turn back to the palace now?"

Wiping my eyes, I smiled at him. "Not yet, Koji."

I opened my window then, and felt the real, forgotten breeze touch my skin, in the city where I was born.

ACKNOWLEDGMENTS

My particular thanks to Binky Urban, my wonderful agent of twenty years. I don't know what I would do without her.

In addition, for help—at different times, and in different ways, large and small—with the research and editing of this book, I would like to thank the following people: Antoine Audouard; Rachel Cohen; Vincent Crapanzano; Courtney Hodell; Eri Hotta; Kikuko Imamura; Donald Keene; Jane Kramer; Susanna Lea; Sidney Mackenzie; Paula Merwin; William Merwin; Nader Mousavizadeh; Mimi Oka; Alan Schwartz; Jennifer Smith; Nan Talese; and—always and in every way—my wife, Aleksandra Crapanzano.

ALSO BY JOHN BURNHAM SCHWARTZ

BICYCLE DAYS

When Alec Stern arrives in Japan, he discovers a land of opportunity, where an impressionable young man fresh out of college can find, in one stroke, a new job, a new family, and a society that lavishes attention on Japanese-speaking gaijin. Yet, even as he claims a place in this new world, Alec is haunted by memories of the one he left behind—a world which disintegrated with the breakup of his parents' marriage.

Fiction/Literature/978-0-375-70275-4

CLAIRE MARVEL

In the middle of a rainstorm Julian Rose, a self-effacing Harvard graduate student, takes refuge beneath a girl's yellow umbrella. The girl is Claire Marvel, lovely, mercurial, mired in family tragedy. She is the last person someone like Julian should fall in love with. But he does. What ensues is a great and difficult passion strewn with obstacles—not least those arising from Claire and Julian's disparate characters. And as these young people find and lose each other, then seek each other anew, Schwartz places romantic love within an entire continuum of attachments that require the full reserves of our openness and courage.

Fiction/Literature/978-0-375-71915-8

RESERVATION ROAD

Two haunted men and their families are engulfed by the emotions surrounding an unexpected and horrendous death. Ethan, a professor of literature at a small New England college, is wracked by an obsession with revenge that threatens to tear his family apart. Dwight, fleeing his crime yet hoping to get caught, wrestles with overwhelming guilt and his sense of obligation to his son. As these two men's lives unravel, *Reservation Road* moves to its startling conclusion.

Fiction/Literature/978-0-375-70273-0

VINTAGE CONTEMPORARIES
Available at your local bookstore, or visit
www.randomhouse.com